make love!*
*the bruce campbell way

Also by Bruce Campbell

If Chins Could Kill: Confessions of a B Movie Actor

STARRING

BRUCE CAMPBELL

PIXEL WRANGLING & GRAPHIC SARCASM BY

CRAIG "KIF" SANBORN

AND FEATURING THE PHOTOGRAPHY OF

MIKE DITZ

THOMAS DUNNE BOOKS

ST. MARTIN'S PRESS NEW YORK

THOMAS DUNNE BOOKS.
An Imprint of St. Martin's Press.

www.stmartins.com

ISBN 0-312-31260-1
EAN 978-0-312-31260-2

First Edition: June 2005

10 9 8 7 6 5 4 3 2 1

For Chook

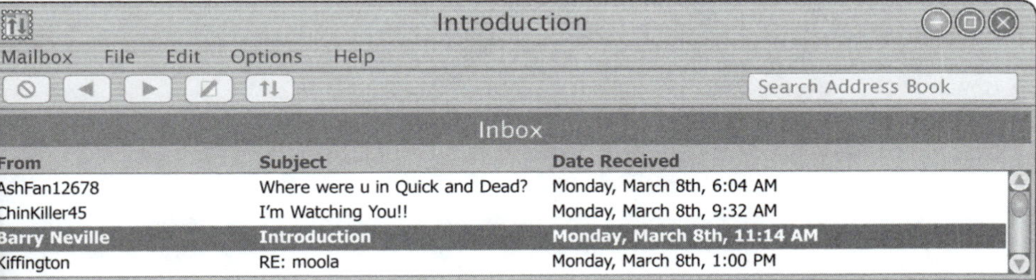

From: Barry Neville
Subject: Introduction
Date: Monday, March 8th, 11:14 AM
To: Bruce Campbell

Dear Bruce,

Hello. Hope you are well. Sorry for the delay in responding to your book, *Walk This Way*. At St. Martin's Press, we're very thorough, and we wanted to get feedback from a wide variety of people within the company before we made our decision.

You know, travel books are tricky. If there isn't a special twist, we find that they tend to rot on shelves. While we all got a kick out of the graphics, particularly the shots of your feet walking on different surfaces, we don't feel that there is any room for another book of this type in our release schedule.

As always, we wish you the very best on this project, and any writings with other publishers. You'll always get a look here.

Yours truly,

Barry Neville

p.s. But please call me, I have another idea.

1

Let's Make Love!

I read the e-mail out loud and wrinkled my nose when I got to the "another book of this type" part. "What kind of horseshit is that?" I wondered aloud.

I dialed Barry's office in New York, stabbing at the numbers on my phone.

Pat, Barry's loyal secretary, answered: "Barry Neville's office."

"Pat, how the heck are you? This is Bruce Campbell."

"Oh, hello, Bruce, I'll see if Barry is in."

That's one of my favorite phrases in the "get past the secretary" game: "I'll see if he's in." Pat knew whether Barry was in or not — he was only twelve feet away in his ten-by-ten cubicle. I was expecting to hear "he just slipped out," or maybe "he's tied up in a conference call," but suddenly, she jumped back on the line.

"I'll put you right through, Bruce."

Getting an editor on the line first try made me instantly suspicious —

that meant Barry had either good news…or the opposite.

"Hello, Bruce," Barry said, sounding reasonably happy to hear from me.

I decided to get right into it. "Okay, so you don't want to do the book."

"Well, no," Barry replied. "We kicked it around, but we couldn't make it work."

"I understand that, but what's with 'another book of this type'? You told me that travel books were hot stuff."

"That's true, but I said they *could* be — if they were done right."

"And what's so wrong with *Walk This Way*?"

"Honestly?"

"I guess, yeah."

"This book made me feel like I was walking."

"Good. You felt in the moment — what's wrong with that?"

"I'm referring to the pace," Barry clarified. "It made me tired."

"Oh."

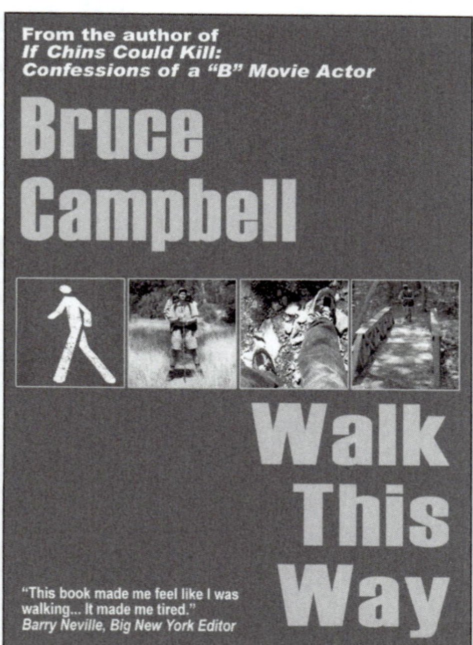

"And how many suburban walks can a person take? I know you were filming on location a lot, but I'm not so sure a book about the routes you took to keep from being bored would be a big seller. Call me crazy."

"Okay, you're crazy."

"Look, Bruce, I hope I am. As your friend, I hope you go and sell a million copies. We've been wrong before. But look, this doesn't have to end here. I want to pitch a book to *you*. I think you're a great match for the material."

"What is it?"

"A relationship book."

The intensity of my laugh startled Barry, but he pressed on.

"I'm serious. I can get that book approved," he assured me.

"Well, yeah, but, wow, that's a whole new deal."

"Relationship books are huge. If you win with one of these, you win big."

"I dunno," I hemmed. "I'd have to think about that and call you back — I'd have to see if I could get my head around it."

"Okay, sure, I understand. Take your time. The offer stands."

As I hung up, I pitied Barry. *Poor bastard.* My editor still remembered me from the TV show *The Adventures of Brisco County Jr.,* where I successfully managed a new girlfriend almost every week. He couldn't shake the images of my character Ash from the film *Army of Darkness*, where I coolly manhandle my leading lady with lines like, "Gimme some sugar, baby."

He'd seen me up close and personal with some damn sexy women, the likes of Vanessa Angel, Alyssa Milano, and Elizabeth Hurley, so in the world according to Barry, I was the living embodiment of a chick magnet — the perfect choice to write a relationship book. Barry is a nice guy, but he's also a fool. What he fails to realize is that the Bruce Campbell who romanced his way through a succession of beautiful leading women bears no resemblance to the Bruce Campbell who forgets anniversaries and hoards Victoria's Secret catalogs. In the real world, none of what he sees on the silver screen relates to me, the actor — or any actor, for that matter.

Let me walk you through a few of the key differences. For starters, love scenes are never the result of an actor's romantic prowess, or insistence. These are obligatory elements of any cinematic romance story, and actors in leading roles are often confronted with them. In reality, shooting a love scene is about as exciting as groping my sister – and thankfully, I don't have one.

Actors don't make up all that clever dialogue. I'll throw in a quip or two, sure, but I'm mainly hired to say words that are written for me. And when it comes to scenes about relationships, I'm happy to have the help of a clever writer who is, at the end of the day, manipulating a given situation into how it *could* play out, not necessarily how it *would*.

As an actor, I don't have any say in how the relationship will go, or even who my romantic partner will be. The writer has determined my on-screen fate far in advance — and that's a really scary thought, because the only people who have *worse* relationships than actors are writers, because they spend most of their time alone, never talking to anyone, staring at a computer screen.

Hollywood is successful at portraying relationships because it manages to bring our fantasies to life; it presents a "what if" world in which we can lose ourselves for a few hours. In movies, when it comes to men and women, everything happens at the speed of light. Couples fall in love at first glance. Later, during sex (which happens on the first date), men get instant erections and can make love for hours. Women achieve orgasm in record time, some going for three in a row. The sex will always be good, and it must always be in some imaginative place, like a freight elevator or a nuclear submarine. Poor Barry, I can see why he was so confused — like all of us, he had been brainwashed for years.

Aside from all that, what the hell does a guy who lost his virginity at age twenty-three know about the opposite sex? Jack shit, that's what. When it comes to women, I don't know my ass from a hole in the ground. I learned about sex through the mass marketing of the early

1960s, when Fred Flintstone was doing cigarette ads and products like Space Food sticks, Tang, and leaded gasoline were the order of the day. Sex back then meant sleeping in separate beds, closed mouth kissing, wearing PJs to bed (even adults), and no sex before marriage. No wonder I had such a bogus view of the world.

As my "female awareness" sprang to life in the late sixties, the sexy babes on television at that time were Anita Bryant, a conservative singer selling orange juice; Julie Newmar, who played Cat Woman in the TV show *Batman*; and Marta Kristen, the teenage daughter on *Lost in Space*. I didn't know right from left, but I can tell you this: it wasn't the intricate plots, or the acting that held my attention, it was the way these foxy women filled out their skin-tight costumes week after week.

Women didn't seem like people who had sex; they just wore lots of makeup and smelled funny. Sears catalogues, and later my dad's *Playboys*, helped straighten a few things out, but there were more questions than answers.

Barry's inflated image of my machismo.

Motion pictures often wind up being an early, vital source of insight into the sexual dynamics between men and women. The problem was, I couldn't get into any movie that might have been of use to me (the cursed M rating, for Mature Audiences Only) so my model for intergender relationships

"Lower and to the left, missy."

came primarily from John Wayne westerns between 1962 and 1973. My mother was a huge western fan, and since my father couldn't have cared less, she'd drag me along instead.

Given my prolonged exposure to the bizarre, archetypal behavior of cowboys, I shouldn't have been surprised by an incident on the playground when I was nine. I "rescued" a girl who was being harassed by a bully (a cattle rustler, as I saw it) by socking him once in the jaw (that's all Duke ever needed) and down he went. I grabbed the girl (the feed store owner's daughter, Sue), whipped her around, and kissed her but good — closed mouthed, because we did such things proper then. To my shock and horror, Sally Sue Jenkins slapped me across the face.

"Get out of here, you weirdo. My brother was just trying to give me lunch money...."

"Sorry, ma'am," I said, nodding. "Didn't mean to cause no fuss."

Dating? I was too busy making amateur films in high school to take advantage of those prime years. Relationships? That's a good one. The "relationships" in my civilian life can be counted on one hand, minus the use of my thumb. Don't come knocking here, brother, I married the first woman who ever came on to me. The weight of hypocrisy would be too much to bear if I wrote a book about a subject on which I was essentially retarded.

The phone rang.

"Hello."

"Hi, it's Barry."

"Dude, c'mon, I don't have an answer for you yet."

"What are you talking about? I haven't called you in a month."

"Who is this?" I asked.

"This is the *other* Barry. Your *acting* agent."

"Oh, *that* Barry. Hi, what's up?"

"I have a possible gig for you."

"Let me guess — something for the Sci-Fi Channel?"

"No."

"A convention in Butt Crack, Kansas?"

"Nope," Barry said with a smile in his voice. "A romantic comedy."

"Get out of town."

"It's a green-lit, A-list romantic comedy starring Richard Gere, Renée Zellweger, produced by Robert Evans, directed by Mike Nichols — shooting in New York in the fall."

"Don't mess with me, Barry. I'm going through some shit right now."

"Bruce, I'm not that kind of a guy," he assured me.

"So, I would play the what, chauffeur? Bus boy?"

"The wise-cracking doorman — he's like the comic muse to Gere. It's the best role in the film. He tells jokes, he gives advice on relationships. You get the idea."

"What's it called?"

"*Let's Make Love!*"

It sounded good — *too* good, as they say. "Do I have to audition?"

"Well, yes, unfortunately. I sent them your demo reel, but they still need you to read in New York. But as a little FYI, Mike asked for you specifically."

"Bullshit," I shot back immediately. "Mike Nichols doesn't even know

I exist, and his casting people sure as hell don't."

"Hey, don't shoot the messenger, Bruce. I'm just passing the information along so you can make an informed decision."

I sighed loudly. "Barry, you know how much I hate auditions. In twenty-five years I've gotten exactly *three* acting jobs from auditioning, and I must have had, what, a hundred of them?"

"Two hundred and nine," Barry corrected.

"You keep track of things like that?" I asked, incredulous.

"Yeah, the head of the agency likes charts and graphs."

"What a dismal record."

"That aside, this is a great opportunity, Bruce. Movies don't get any bigger, or *better* than this."

I glanced in my Frequent Flyer file — America West was looking good for a free ticket. "What the hell...set it up."

I hung up and stared at the phone. This would be a worthless cause, but at least it was a chance to meet Mike Nichols, a truly big shot director.

New York City in May was beautiful — trees were starting to bloom, the sky was a freshly laundered blue, and aside from the stench of decomposing trash, I felt positively invigorated. I walked with a spring in my step all the way up West 26th Street, to an old brownstone where Mike Nichols keeps his office.

The first thing an actor does at an audition is sign in. I always take my time with the sign-in sheet, because it's a chance to see the competition. The list tells me who else is or was there, what time, for what role, and who represents them.

The sign-in list for *Let's Make Love!* made my jaw drop: *Bill* Campbell, for starters, a namesake nemesis if there ever was one, Ben

Affleck, Adam Sandler, John Turturro, Liam Neeson, Chevy Chase, and on, and on.

Everyone on the goddamn planet is auditioning for this role. What am I doing here?

I scanned the room and my hopes were further dashed: Gary Sinise was sitting next to John Malkovich, who was telling a bawdy joke to John Cusack, who was trying to study his lines.

SIGN-IN SHEET

PROJECT: LET'S MAKE LOVE

NAME	REPRESENTATION	TIME	ROLE	AUTOGRAPH*
Bill Campbell	A.I.A. Ltd	9AM	Foyl the Doorman	
Ben Affleck	M. Damon	9:15A	Fowl	
Adam Sandler	RHTS	9:30	door guy	
John Turturro	Fink/Coen	9:45am	Foyl	
LIAM NEESON	"OSCAR"	10:00	~~DANLAU~~ DOORMAN	
CHevy CHase	N/A	10:15	anything, please	
Sir Antony Hopkins	HRH	10:30 a.m.	Mr. Foyl	
Gary Sinise	CSI NY	10:45	Foyl	
Carrot Top	Satan	11	Ghost of Xmas Past	
Robert Patrick	AFPA	11:15	Foyl	
J. Malkovich	FUJ Agency	11:30	Foyl	
Edward Norton	Joe	11:45	Foy	
Robin Williams	My agent	noon	door guy	

The "competition."

I was seriously considering feigning a strange illness and making an early departure, when I became drawn into what I feared most at auditions: a conversation.

"So, we meet again."

The husky voice belonged to tough-guy actor Robert Patrick, who stiffed me out of an *X-Files* role.

"Yeah, I guess so," I said. "You won the last round."

Robert smiled confidently. "I did, didn't I? Good gig, that *X-Files*."

"Yeah, but long hours, I'm sure," I managed, trying to make it sound like I didn't want the part anyway.

"The pain goes away on payday," he said, smiling. "Hey, you been working much?"

The issue of employment is always an Achilles heel for an actor who hasn't worked in a long time, and Robert wasted no time in going for it.

"Well, not really," I admitted.

Robert raised his eyebrows and whistled silently to himself — the "Oh, I see" expression.

A moment from my audition.

"I was writing for a while," I tried to clarify. "So, then I did a couple conventions, and then...." I stopped myself before it got embarrassing. There wasn't anything to brag about in the conventional sense. I knew it, and now he knew it too.

"Hell, I wish I had your problem sometimes," Robert said, possibly trying to make me feel better. "I can barely get back to my Montana ranch, I work so much. I may have to sell it and move to the Palisades."

I smiled and excused myself, feeling a sudden need to use the bathroom. During tense audition situations, the only sanctuary is the men's toilet. Under the right conditions, I can kill an hour or more, reading stall graffiti and making sure my hair is just right. It's a great place to gather yourself, get centered, and have one last frantic look at your lines.

Once inside the tile-and-porcelain sanctuary, I gave myself a pep talk. *Okay, chump, you're here, get over it. Do your thing and move on. Enjoy the moment.*

As I stepped back into the waiting room full of famous actors, my name was being called.

Go time.

I followed the secretary down a long hallway and wiped the sweat from the palm of my clammy right hand one last time.

I entered the room and couldn't help but gasp. Richard Gere was there, smiling and shaking hands with an exiting Johnny Depp. As Johnny passed, he winked. "Hey man, have fun."

Have a coronary, that's what I'll have.

The secretary introduced me to Mike Nichols, a very serene man with a wicked handshake.

"Damn nice to meet you, Bruce. Been a big fan for a long time. Hey, nice turn in *Icebreaker* — convincing stuff."

He didn't actually see that piece of shit, did he? "Well, there's one folks don't usually mention," I said, incredulous.

"Oh, the indies are my favorite," he said, nodding. "That's all I watch, really. It's where the new ideas are."

"From your lips to God's ears, Mike."

Mike gestured to a lit area across the room. "Why don't you go on over there, Bruce, and we'll have a go at this."

"Okay, sure."

"Have you met Richard?" Mike asked, nonchalant.

I turned to see Richard Gere offering his hand, and smiling.

"Hi, Bruce, loved your stuff on *Xena*."

I stammered a response, losing my train of thought.

"Any questions?" Mike asked.

"Yeah, actually. How 'Southern' should the guy be?"

Mike shrugged. "Why don't we just have a look at one?"

I shrugged too, having only asked the question so I wouldn't appear as terrified as I was. My Southern accent was merely passable anyway, so it was an irrelevant exchange.

"Let's do the first scene," Mike said, nodding to the video technician who began taping.

I had prepared two scenes for the audition. This first one was snappy, back-and-forth patter between the lead character, Harry Grayson and the doorman, Foyl Whipple. The second scene — only done i asked — was an eloquent speech from Foyl, to Harry, about true love

The first scene began like this:

```
Foyl holds the door open.

                    FOYL
               (with a smile)
      How are you tonight, Mr. Grayson?

Harry stops on his way out.

                    HARRY
      Foyl, how is it that every day,
      you manage to have a smile on
      your face?

                    FOYL
               (holding his grin)
      Just another day in paradise, Mr.
      Grayson.

                    HARRY
               (starting to walk)
      If you only knew about the real
      world, Foyl.

                    FOYL
      I know a little something about
                  (CONT'D)
```

FOYL (CONT'D)
the real world, Mr. Grayson. I'm holding a door in the dead of winter for a man who doesn't know how to treat a woman.

Harry stops in his tracks and turns back to Foyl.

HARRY
I beg your pardon?

FOYL
Personally, I treat women like royalty.

HARRY
I don't treat anyone like anything, Foyl. I'm just me. I just am. And how is it, a doorman has all the answers?

FOYL
A doorman takes the pulse of humanity. Every day, he hears the talk, he watches behavior, he knows what there is to know about people.

HARRY
Tell me one thing about me that I don't know.

FOYL
You're in love more than you'll ever let yourself be.

HARRY
(pegged)
That's what I like about you, Foyl. You always give it to me straight.

FOYL
(with a wry smile)
It's the only way, Mr. Grayson. Well, you have a great day.
(then, after Harry leaves)
You should be holding the door for *me*....

The group around Mike Nichols chuckled politely, and the scene was over. There is always an awkward moment between reading the first scene and the second scene. But before I could even get anxious about it, Mike stood up.

"Thanks, Bruce. Thanks for coming in. I think we've seen all we need to."

The words were: "Thanks for coming in. I think we've seen all we need to." The meaning was: "Thanks for wasting our time, Bruce, I think that's all we can stand."

Richard Gere offered his hand again. "That was fun, Bruce."

"That was fun": actor-speak for "that sucked ass."

Symbolism was everywhere. Richard's sincere handshake was the kind you give to someone after a death in the family. Something was dead all right — my ability to audition. Barry can now raise the "failed auditions" tally to 210. Knowing not to linger after a mediocre offering, thanked my way out of the room and grabbed the elevator straight down.

Outside, I walked aimlessly down the street, repeating the words of the first scene verbatim, nailing the delivery each time. Actors are always at their very best on the way home.

Oh, well, I thought. *At least I tried.*

During the multiple flights home, I was comforted by thoughts of the long fun summer ahead — river rafting, hiking, and all-around fun in the Oregon sun. The previous winter had been a wet one, and that usually resulted in a kick-ass summer.

But when I arrived home, three new phone messages waited on my machine. I only get multiple messages when someone either dies or needs money, both of which were cause for dread. The first message, while somewhat cryptic, changed my mood immediately:

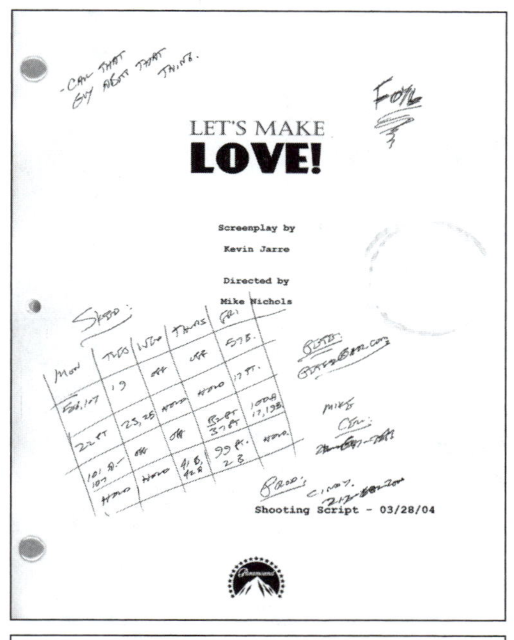

LET'S MAKE

LOVE!

Screenplay by

Kevin Jarre

Directed by

Mike Nichols

Shooting Script - 03/28/04

My copy of the unrevised shooting script.

Beep — "Hey, Bruce, it's Barry — call me!"

The second was from my manager, Robert. He's always more subdued, but I could tell he was giddy:

Beep — "Bruce, Robert here. Something good...."

The third message was strictly business, but the most definitive of all:

Beep — "This is Dale, your lawyer."

When Dale calls, it means I'm either going to spend money defending myself in a lawsuit, or I'm going to spend money negotiating a film deal, but either way, I'm going to spend money.

I didn't check any more messages because I was too busy dancing a victory jig around my office.

But before I could say, *Holy shit, I got the part*, the phone rang.

"Hello?"

"Bruce? Mike...."

"Mike Nichols?"

"Yeah. Listen, welcome aboard. I'm really pleased," he said with genuine warmth.

"This is insane. I feel like you're Ed McMahon and I just won that Publishers Clearinghouse thing."

"We both won on this one."

"Mike, I don't want this to sound weird, but why?"

"Why what?"

"Why was I cast instead of every name actor in Hollywood? Was my audition that good?"

"Actually, I cast you *despite* the audition," Mike clarified. "I wanted you in *Let's Make Love!* because you're ready for the next step. You've paid your dues, Bruce. Those other actors who auditioned — and Sean Penn was astounding — have all gotten their shot in the A leagues. I've always wanted to put you in a role that can feature the depth you showed in *Tornado!* I have to tell you, the scene in the field with that guy's daughter blew me away."

Is Mike messing with me? I wondered.

"And while *McHale's Navy* sank like an anchor, the pathos you brought to an average navy guy was heartbreaking."

I never thought I would live long enough to hear the words "heart-breaking" and "*McHale's Navy*" in the same sentence, but it was heart-ening nonetheless, especially from an icon like Mike Nichols.

"You've been playing below your game," Mike said politely, "and it's time to change all that. I'm happy to be in a position to finally make it happen."

"Jesus, Mike, what can I say? Thanks...."

"But you can't let me down," he warned. "I fought for you over the objections of the Paramount guys. Your character is the emotional linchpin of this movie. If he doesn't work, the movie doesn't work — simple as that. Kid, this is the kind of role the Best Supporting Actor award was created for, but you'll have to work your ass off."

Before responding, I took a moment to catch my breath. "I'm...I'm up for it, Mike — and thanks for the —"

But Mike had hung up already.

As I ran both hands through my sweaty hair, I noticed that they were trembling. As an actor, it was a sensation that happens once every five years — the sensation of elation and panic at the same time — other-wise known as The Butterflies. Every time I got butterflies in my stom-ach previously, the acting experience had been a good one.

Mike was right. This role was going to be special.

2

Doorman for a Day

got the part — now all I had to do was pull it off. It was one thing to vork on a cheeseball, straight-to-DVD horror film for two weeks in /ancouver, where the only challenge is finding new ways to express ear or pain. But to act in a Mike Nichols film is to exist on another plane, with no "B" anything in sight. Working with the likes of Mike Nichols and Richard Gere, my input would not only be welcomed, it vould be *expected*.

Prior to *Let's Make Love!,* my method of preparing for a role was naking sure I had enough razor blades and a fresh container of dental loss. But this time I would need more than just a close shave and iealthy gums. To meet the challenge, I had to prepare with a new level of intensity. If I was going to make a favorable impression in a legitimate Iollywood production, I couldn't drag my feet. This time, I had to invest and go the distance. If I was going to *play* a wisecracking doorman relationship expert, then by God I was going to *become* one!

I rifled through the shelves in my office, digging out every acting book I had either ignored or derided over the years, and began to read them anew for the next forty-eight hours. I hadn't read as much or as intensively since my six months of college, but it was a liberating experience. In recent years, my sense of acting had devolved to hitting marks, catnaps in my trailer, and free haircuts. But after tearing through books like *An Actor Is* and *The Id of Acting*, I began to see my craft in a new light. Acting is more than tailored clothing, it's an expression of truth, a liberating exploration of the soul, a deeply personal journey that is shared with the entire world.

The books were a marvelous inspiration. While serving up a hodgepodge of theories, each one left me with the desire to take my craft to new heights. I realized that to prepare, an actor must seek, ask, study, ponder, and most importantly: learn.

One of the tricks I learned in *Acting for Dummies* was to write a "back story," or biography, of the character I was portraying. They're helpful because nine times out of ten, even the writer hasn't gone to this length to create a character and it's up to the actor to fill in the blanks. I decided to take a whack at it:

The Back Story of Foyl Whipple

by

Foyl Whipple

I was born outside of Savannah, Georgia, in 1958. My daddy, Dwight, was a pea farmer, but mostly he made ends meet by selling "shine" off the back porch. Mother Beulah was a housewife, but there was always extra money to be made by disappearing into the back room with strange men during Friday night poker games.

My two older sisters, Joyce and Eunice, took off when I was three. There was a lot of shouting when it happened. Growing up as the youngest of three poor children, I didn't have nothin' to call my own.

I landed a job as a dishwasher at the Savannah Gentlemen's Club, but because of my family background, I couldn't get beyond bus boy. I knew if I was going to make something of myself, I had to go to a place where it didn't matter who I was, or where I came from. I decided to try New York City, mainly because it was too busy runnin' itself to give a hoot about me. The thought terrified me so, but I never looked back.

After bein' a bricklayer, cab driver, and dishwasher, I got me a job as doorman at the Park Avenue Arms. Not long after that, I met my future wife, Trudy, waitin' tables at a local deli. After chasin' her down for two years, we tied the knot in nineteen eighty-three, and kicked out a couple of cute kids, Rhett and his older sister Lottie, named after my gramma. We live in Brooklyn, just a spit away from Prospect Park, where most week-ends we're out there playing ball, or hunting coon in the restricted areas with my bird dog, Yeller.

I'm happy at the Park Avenue Arms. I been there for twenty years, and worked my way up to head doorman. I know everyone by name, their apartment number, how long they've been there, their extended families, and the name of their damn pets. I even know who's doin' who, but I don't gossip about it. I love collard greens, Budweiser, and sleepin' in on Sundays.

One of the joys of being an actor is occasionally doing what is know as a “tagalong.” Journalists do it all the time — they ride with an under cover crime unit, or “embed” themselves in a military operation to ge the inside scoop. Actors do the same thing — they shadow FBI agents observe operating room procedures, or interview real-life characters s they can faithfully portray a given role. I’d played working stiffs befor — a mechanic, a custodian, a cab driver — but never a doorman.

Hoping to receive a crash course in this ancient art, I offered to joi the curbside staff of the prestigious Waldorf-Astoria Hotel in New Yor City, and was fairly shocked when they took me up on it. To be hones I already had my eye on a sweet gig at the Garden City Marriott, an was simply using the Waldorf as a test run. Later, I found out that some one in upper management had given the go-ahead as long as I signe an *Army of Darkness* poster for her son.

Actors get to learn a new craft with almost each role. Some skills ar fun to pick up, like sword fighting or horse riding, yet others, like lin dancing, aren’t worth the pay. In this case, I was about to get a cras course in baggage handling, cab calling, door holding, hat tipping, an generally intuitive, cheery behavior.

My day started Monday, June 2nd, at exactly six o’clock in the morr ing. The first challenge was to find the employee locker room, dee within the bowels of this 1893 behemoth. It wasn’t hard — I just kep heading down.

Eventually, I arrived at the main locker room. Tiled and elegant, bu well worn from the hundred years of Waldorf employee use, it coul easily double as a bomb shelter. The lockers were large and had plen ty of hooks. Inside one of them hung my uniform, neatly pressed an ready to wear.

Personally, I have always loved wearing uniforms. Nothing motivate me more as an actor than a crisp, well-tailored outfit. The Waldorf doormen looked particularly nice, I thought, with their brown pants starched stiff, and a golden stripe down the outer seam. The jacket was a well-molded, padded-shoulder affair with epaulets. White gloves, a snappy hat, and a referee's whistle rounded out the look. I felt like a cross between a dictator and a band leader.

Shortly after I finished dressing, at 6:15 A.M. sharp, the Door Chief, an imposing fellow named Eldridge, called us together.

As seen on TV: The landmark Waldorf-Astoria hotel.

"Listen up, door people: This is the start of a new week. We're going to face today's challenges with the enthusiasm, grace, and dignity that the Waldorf establishment demands. We're going to service our clients. As door persons, you provide the first impression of this hotel, and often the last — make it a good one. Okay, be smart, be safe — lift with your legs."

With that, the doormen and doorwomen clapped enthusiastically, and poured up the numerous flights of stairs to our posts outside the Waldorf.

I took my place as "curb monkey." Initially, the job description included opening car doors and helping folks with their luggage. From my acting perspective, however, this was a chance to hear stories, and more importantly, ad-lib some sage advice about relationships.

Before you could say "Bellman!" a black Lincoln town car rolled up.

I opened the rear door and escorted a very elegant older woman to the curb. Her tiny dog was stuffed under one arm. She looked back in disgust at her wealthy but disheveled husband doddering along.

Don't I look a-door-able?

"Hurry up, Wallace," she hissed. "We'll miss the buffet."

"Then go ahead, go," he grumbled, stepping up on the curb. "I'll be there in good goddamn time enough."

His wife did exactly that — she left him alone, next to me, searching for tip money.

"A word of advice, son," Wallace offered.

"Sir?"

"Never get married. I've done it four times now, and each one is worse than the last."

"Do you have poor choice in women, sir, or are you just a poor husband?"

"Ha! I'm the best husband she ever had. I give that dried-up old prune everything she wants," he said, still fishing in his pockets.

"But do you give her what she *needs*?" I pressed.

"You're an impudent little prick, aren't you?" the old geezer said, not finding any tip money. "I'll have to catch you on the way out."

"Sure, sir. You have yourself a great day."

I watched him waddle after his long-gone wife, and felt sad that they had basically given up on each other. They were beyond even the formality and polite deference of a relationship in decline — their marriage had devolved into guerrilla warfare.

Before I could ask "How does that happen?" a cab pulled up to the corner. The door opened and a burly man about my age got out.

"I got it, pal, thanks," he said, in a way that told me not to expect any tip.

I could tell he was one of those self-described "players" who hated staying at a fancy hotel — or at least hated *paying* for it.

Stepping out of the cab after him was a much younger woman, who was clearly impressed to be at the Waldorf.

"Do you have any luggage, Mr…?"

"Peterson. John Peterson. Uh, no, I —"

The cab driver popped the trunk to reveal two overnight bags.

I reached for the luggage, getting a good look at the I.D. tags, none of which said Peterson. But before I could grab a handle, my tightwad friend waved me off again. "I've got those bags, pal. Don't worry about it."

As "John" grabbed the bags, I could see the exposed skin on his ring finger — the circle of pasty skin caused by the prolonged wearing of a wedding ring (now missing). Sensing that he was up to no good, I stepped back and let him carry his own goddamn bags.

Mr. "Peterson" paid off his cab driver as if he had lost a bet, slowly and agonizingly. I was able to make eye contact with the young vamp participating in this fling. Maybe twenty-three, the woman was certainly insecure, but mostly just naïve.

As Money Bags walked past me, I couldn't help but chime in — I was, after all, doing research.

"A word of advice, Mr. Peterson," I said, deftly blocking his path. "Or should I say, *Mr. Walter*?"

"Is there something you want from me, buddy?" the cheating man demanded.

"No. I want to give you some advice: there is still time to save your marriage."

"What the fuck are you trying to say?" he asked, becoming very agitated.

"I'm referring to the, ahem, *affair* you're having. The highs aren't worth the —"

Whack!

"You little punk," the mug added, shaking out the pain in his right hand.

I had been knocked semi-unconscious only once before, and that was courtesy of a nine-iron to the bridge of my nose when I was a kid. I awoke to the fuzzy image of Eldridge, the Door Chief.

"Hey, Bruce, you with me? Come on, man, talk to me."

I rallied myself enough to sit up on the sidewalk, on one elbow at least. "I'm here, chief, I'm just not *here,* here."

"Do you want me to call a paramedic?"

"No, I'm good," I said, trying to stand.

"You want me to call the cops?"

"No. I just need to walk it off."

"What the hell happened, man?" Eldridge asked. "Rodriguez said some guy really clocked you."

"Rodriguez was right," I assured him. "Sorry, chief, I was trying to help a guy out, and he just blew up."

"You didn't give him advice, did you?"

I looked at Eldridge and tried to focus. He was a hard guy to lie to. "Well, yeah, sorta."

Eldridge shook his head, like I was his wayward son. "No, man, you don't ever do that. You take their bags, you hail a cab, you hold the door, but more than anything, you hold your tongue. Be *pro*-fessional, not *con*-fessional."

"Okay, chief," I nodded. "Will do."

Eldridge fished out a handkerchief. "You might want to wipe your nose. Now, be careful, Bruce. Don't be gettin' killed on your first and last damn day."

As I paced around the plaza, breathing deeply and nursing my near-broken nose, a cab full of upscale women were making their last stop of a very late evening — the *Sex and the City* express.

As I held the door for each of the three women, I tried to access the uncanny, soul-penetrating X-ray vision that my character, Foyl, possessed. I knew that somehow he'd connect with each of them and divine their personalities and problems with alarming accuracy.

"Goob bordig, ladies," I offered, through a damaged nasal passage. "Welcome to the Waldordh."

The first woman, a stunning blonde, completely ignored me. I surmised that she was used to having doors held open. She looked like a Karen to me.

"Karen, right?" I guessed, snapping a finger as she passed.

The woman spun back to me, alarmed at the question. "No," she barked, and turned away.

Behind "Karen" was a hot African-American woman with an ultra-fitted business suit. She at least made eye contact.

"Thank you," she said with a smile that also said "not in your wildest dreams, Jack."

Foyl would know what she did for a living, just by the way she dressed.

"You're welcome...*secretary* lady."

The woman shot me a dagger-in-the-eye look, and flipped her business card my way. It read: GINA CARREY, VICE-PRESIDENT, NEW YORK BANK & TRUST.

"Have a good day...*doorman*," Gina whispered.

As I reached for the hand of the last woman, I couldn't help but notice how cold it was. I decided not to overthink my guess — this time I went on gut instinct. "Okay, you're a corporate lawyer, and you're here for the signing of a very hush-hush merger."

The cold lawyer lost all remaining color in her face. "How did you know?"

"Oh, lucky guess, I suppose."

"I have nothing more to say," she said curtly, and bolted toward the hotel.

One for four was a sucky average, but the exercise in human nature made me focus an otherwise wandering mind to laser-beam intensity. Through Foyl's eyes, I began to notice details of everyday life that would have eluded me otherwise, like fresh pigeon crap on a gargoyle's face, the color of the gum stuck to the bottom of my shoe, or the number of horn honks during a rush-hour minute. I knew that this new way of looking at the world would not only help me grow as an actor, but as a human being.

During my union break, I grabbed a ham-and-egg sandwich from the employee commissary and took my place among the army of Waldorf employees.

One out of four, I recounted. *Not bad for the first try.* I was also starting to get an attitude, and I liked it. In *Let's Make Love!,* my character, Foyl, was very assertive. I could do assertive.

As I hunched over to eat my sandwich, Eldridge passed by and put his hand on my back.

"How you doin', rookie? How's that actor's nose doing?"

"I'm okay, sir, it's just a little tender."

"That's good. You know, I like you Bruce, but if you worked here full time, I'd have to fire your ass."

"Really? Why?"

"I've already gotten three complaints about you, not including the guy who said your pushy behavior forced him to whoop your ass."

"I understand. I'm sorry, Eldridge, I let my character get the best of me."

"Just keep a lid on it. You only got two damn hours to go. Try not to make a scene."

"Aye, skipper," I saluted, wiping the excess mayonnaise from the corner of my mouth.

As I pushed through the opulent doors to the outside, I saw a brigade of dark sedans glide to a stop near the main entrance. On the sidewalks, men in plain suits scanned the area and escorted pedestrians away from the area beneath the distinctive gray-and-gold awning.

Before I could figure out what was going on, I was approached by a clean-cut man with a receiver in his ear.

"May I see your I.D., please?" he asked, hand out.

"You first," I replied. "I work here, you don't."

Somewhat impatiently, the man showed me a U.S. Government–issue I.D., so I pulled out my laminated employee I.D. He studied it only slightly more closely than an ADD-afflicted airport screener. His furrowed brow should have tipped me off. "This is issued for only one day."

"Today, right, but it's still valid."

"That doesn't make any sense. Why would you have an I.D. badge that's good for just one day?"

"I have a reason, but it's none of your business, really," I replied.

The agent slammed me against the brick wall. "Do you know who I am?"

"Agent No Name?"

"Correction. I'm Agent Samuel Grunow with the U.S. Secret Service, so what you do is *all* about my business. Try again."

"I'm an actor, for God's sake," I croaked out of a partially crushed windpipe. "We hang around weird places to get the feel for a role. How do I know you're not an actor, studying for some new Fox reality show called *Asshole Federal Agents*?"

Grunow didn't respond — not to me anyway. "Uh, we've got a possible zero, three, niner, here, repeat, zero-three-niner, over?"

Is that good or bad? I wondered.

"Copy that," Grunow said, not looking at me. Then, "I'm going to have to ask you to remain in my immediate custody."

"But, if you're *asking* me, I have choice."

"You must remain in my immediate custody."

"I *must.* That sounds like you're telling me. And I'm a little fuzzy on the 'immediate' thing. Does that constitute a proximity?"

"Approximately."

"An approximate proximity. And, now this 'custody' thing — is that sole custody, or joint custody?"

"My immediate custody."

"Can I get a restraining order to cancel your immediate, approximate, proximity custody?"

"You have the right to remain silent."

"Whoa, cowboy, are you arresting me?"

"You are a Person of Interest," he said, showing a remarkable lack of emotion.

"A person of — hey, I'm a doorman, and I'm just here doing my job — on *private* property."

Just then, Colin Powell, who at the time was still Secretary of State, emerged from a black town car and headed toward the grand Waldorf entrance.

"Holy moly, that's the Secretary of State," I gawked. "You may have a job to do, buster, but so do I...."

I made my way quickly toward the front doors, appalled that nobody was there to open them. Colin was walking at a fast clip, and to beat him I had to

If only our first encounter had been this civil....

break into a slow jog. Agent Grunow whipped around and began to transmit a heightened "alert code," and all of a sudden the plaza got real busy.

In case you've ever wondered, a "person of interest" shouldn't make fast moves toward the same person that a massive security detail is trained to protect. No less than seven agents descended upon me, barking hushed orders into hidden headsets, and I was tackled left, right, and center before I could reach the front doors. Within three seconds — the time it took to whisk Colin Powell to safety and dislocate my shoulder — I had blacked out.

Two hours later, I awoke in an "undisclosed location." Seconds after stirring, a door opened, revealing the same young, clean-cut agent.

"Mr. Campbell, I'm Agent Grunow."

"We met, yeah."

The winner got to go up against Martin Lawrence's entourage at the Hotel Niko in Atlanta.

"Can I ask you a few questions?"

"Knock yourself out."

"What business did you have at the Waldorf hotel earlier today?"

"I was preparing for a role in an upcoming Mike Nichols film — you may have heard of him?"

"And why were you approaching the front door of the Waldorf?"

"Well, as a doorman, one tends to have a natural gravitation toward them."

"But with all due respect, Mr. Campbell, you're not a real doorman, you're an actor. So, according to the United States government, what you were doing at the Waldorf was technically unnecessary."

"That's a little presumptuous, Mr. Grunow," I said, with my nose just a little in the air. "Art is subjective, and what I was doing was very necessary. I was rehearsing."

"Isn't acting just make-believe?" Agent Grunow countered. "Why do you have to go somewhere and pretend, before you go somewhere and pretend?"

I knew that the common man had no appreciation for what actors do to prepare, and James Lipton wasn't there to explain it, so I let it go. "Look, what exactly did I do wrong?"

"You refused to remain in my custody — an agent of the United States Secret Service."

"Sorry, but you don't sign my checks. And FYI, you were feeding me a lot of fuzzy law. What is a Person of Interest, anyway? Are they considered more like a suspect, or an Unlawful Combatant?"

Agent Grunow didn't respond. Behind him, the door opened, and another clean-cut agent handed him a dossier. After studying the enclosed material, with an occasional glance toward me, he closed the folder and pursed his lips. "You're free to go."

"That was a fast turn of events," I said, rising to my feet. "Am I now a person of 'dis-interest'?"

"With the exception of numerous calls to 900 numbers, your background check was clean."

"That's good to know, in case I run for Attorney General," I said, heading toward the door.

"But I should inform you, Mr. Campbell," Agent Grunow warned. "We are adding you to an ISL."

"Let me guess: International Shit List."

"Internal Security List," he explained. "It's a database, shared globally with cooperating law enforcement agencies. Our friends around the world will ask a few more questions next time you travel, check your luggage a little more closely — that sort of thing."

"Thank you, Agent Grunow," I said, shaking his hand firmly. "Thank you for making America more secure."

At my hotel, I did the only logical thing a marked man could do: soak my aching feet in Epsom salts and surf the Internet. My Web guy, Kiffer, had recently posted a notice about getting the role, and I knew I would get a response, but I hadn't anticipated the tenor.

The first e-mail posted on the message board, from "XDethX," summed up the general sentiment rather well, with a subject line that read: "NOOOOOOOOOOOOO! Say it ain't sooooooooooooooooo!"

Needless to say, this was from a hardcore *Evil Dead* fan. Admittedly, it was probably a mistake to announce that I wouldn't make the Cherry Hill, New Jersey, Spook-a-boo Horrorthon because I was working on a Mike Nichols film, but what was I going to do, lie?

Unfortunately, 99 percent of the e-mails were negative. To the average genre fan, working on an A-list Hollywood film meant that I had turned my back on the very people who shouldered me through years of struggle, only to walk away when the going got good.

I could feel their pain, but as an actor, as a purist, my first responsibility was to the character. In addition, I couldn't walk away from a story that would likely touch more hearts than a midnight showing of *Evil Dead II* in Gary, Indiana. When done right, movies are the best kind of goodwill ambassador — they uplift, inform, enlighten. I had a prime opportunity to enrich the lives of people all across the globe, not to mention myself through some serious residuals, and I wasn't about to let that slip away.

As I tucked my pruned, puffy feet under the covers, I ruminated about the e-mails, taking them to heart. Even though I was in an A movie, it didn't mean I had to let go of my B-movie sensibilities. Actors of my ilk had plenty of tricks in our low-budget bags, and I shouldn't be shy about using them.

3

Sometimes a Great Notion

I walked into the first read thru of Mike Nichols's *Let's Make Love!* an emboldened, professional actor. I was early, had already learned my lines, and was bubbling with notes, ideas, and questions.

The routine is pretty much the same at all Hollywood table readings, particularly the high-end ones. Nobody gets up that early, so readings rarely begin before eleven o'clock. Coffee, tea, and a Best Western–style assortment of danishes are the standard layout. Most first reads are in hotel conference rooms or a production office, and the cast sits around a large table, usually in assigned seats, where they introduce themselves one by one, and read the script, page by page. This is followed by a question-and-answer session, then everyone glad-hands for a while, and splits.

Mike Nichols was different. He hosted the read thru at his brownstone/office, and there was a spread like you'd see in a magazine: omelets by Mike's personal chef (Rolfe), cappuccinos, pastries, chocolate-covered strawberries – enough sugar and caffeine to freak out a long-haul truck driver.

The reading itself took place in Mike's massive library, where the cast relaxed in overstuffed chairs around an imposing stone hearth. *A guy could get used to this,* I thought, dunking my second bear claw into a steaming cup of chai. *I hope I don't fall asleep.*

Renée Zellweger was seated next to me. I didn't recognize her out of makeup. She was very tiny, with curly lips and a calm disposition. Fortunately, I had the perfect icebreaker:

"Hello, Renée?" I asked casually, like a fellow actor would, even though I was oddly nervous about meeting this now-famous actress. "I'm Bruce Campbell. I play Foyl, the doorman."

"Oh, right," she said, smiling. "Nice to meet you."

"A good buddy of mine worked with you a few years back."

"Really? Who was that?"

"John Cameron. He was an assistant director on, what's that film? You were just an extra in it? It wasn't *Mall Rats*...."

"*Dazed and Confused*?" Renée prompted, not wowed with my recollection.

"That's the one. My buddy said he kept picking you out of the crowd and bringing you up front. He thought you were really gonna be something. Now look at you, with your award and everything."

Renée wasn't sure whether to be embarrassed or flattered. "Well, thanks...uh, this should be a lot of fun," she said, turning back to her script.

"This should be fun" is another phrase actors use, meaning: "I don't have any scenes with you, I don't really know you, and I don't have anything else to say to you."

I was about to hide behind my script when I noticed legendary producer Robert Evans across the room. He didn't seem overly occupied at the moment, and I knew him enough to break the ice.

"Mr. Evans," I said, extending my hand to this dapper man wearing a black suit and a cream-colored turtleneck.

Before she was famous, Renée was dazed, confused, and squirting ketchup.

Robert Evans looked at me through graduated, owl-eyed shades. "Hello?"

"Let me reintroduce myself. I'm Bruce Campbell. I'm playing Foyl, the doorman."

Robert's look remained blank until recognition dawned. "Of course. How nice for you."

"You know we almost worked together."

"Did we?"

"Yeah, back around ninety-five, you were doing *The Phantom* and I almost got the part that Billy Zane got."

As soon as the words had spilled out, I realized the zero interest a producer would have in discussing his bomb movie with an actor who didn't even get the lead role.

Robert didn't respond and was suddenly a thousand yards away. I pretty much froze in position as he walked away, not knowing what else to say that would make any difference. But before I could lament my lameness, a familiar catch phrase caught my attention.

Rob Stern
Meathead

Paramound Studios
Suite 1540
Los Angeles, California

(323) 555.9565, ext. 42
FAX: (323) 555-9566
e-mail: whipping_boy@paramound.con

"Groovy."

I turned to see what looked like a kid in his early twenties, wiping his hands together. He sported a beard, but it was a young beard, almost pubic.

"Hey, Ash," He said.

"I'm *Bruce*," I corrected, offering a hand. "Who are you?"

"Rob Stern — Paramount."

"Oh, one of the suits. What do you do there?"

"This is my project," Rob said, nodding. "I mean, I'm overseeing it."

"So, this one's on your watch, as they say. Big responsibility."

Rob laughed uncomfortably, pausing only to smell his fingers. "I guess you could say that."

"Do you like the script?" I asked, making conversation.

"Do you? What do *you* think of it?" Rob wondered, suddenly insecure.

"Well, it's very middle-of-the-road, but that was the idea, right? I'm assuming it's PG-13, and you'll release it next spring before the blockbusters kick in, blah, blah, blah — I get it."

Rob looked around as if what he was about to tell me was secret. "Well, we're in the middle of a *major* rewrite."

"I hope you're not going to cut me out before we even shoot, heh-heh."

"I wouldn't say that too loudly. Mike and I don't exactly agree about Foyl's role in the film."

"Meaning what?" I asked, mildly horrified that I wasn't entirely wrong.

"I'll give it to you straight, because I have a rep for that — Paramount never even wanted you in the first place. Do you have any idea how many A-list actors wanted that role? At one point, I had Costner, Cruise, and Crowe all on hold — all waiting for a yes. Luckily for you, Mike made it happen because he's, well, Mike Nichols."

"So, what, you're waiting for me to fall on my face so you can replace me with Danny Bonaduce?"

"I wouldn't put it like that exactly, but he did do a hell of a read," Rob said, spotting someone more important across the room. "Well, gotta go."

Eventually, the socializing ended, and the read thru began. Actors took turns introducing themselves and when it got to me, I was as excited as I was nervous.

"I hope you don't mind, Mr. Nichols."

The director — *my* director — broke in. "Please, call me Mike." Then, to the cast, "Everybody, it's just Mike."

"Okay, sure," I said. "I hope you don't mind, I gave Foyl a last name."

"Oh, that's fine, we could use it on a name tag or something. June will make a note of it."

"It's Whipple."

"That sounds very…southern," Mike said, nodding. "A little obscure, but salt-of-the-earth." Mike looked to screenwriter, Kevin Jarre, his collaborator on the romantic comedy hit *Working Girl*.

"I think it's good," Kevin said, smiling.

"I also wrote his back story," I said, eagerly.

"Did you now?" Mike asked, with less enthusiasm. "Well, that's, uh, that's..."

"I made a copy for everyone. I hope there are enough to go around."

The room became silent as I walked around, handing them out. "It's three-hole punched so you can keep it in your script. The paper is reinforced, so it won't rip out. Those New York autumns can be wind-eee."

I handed one to Mike, who immediately handed it to June, his secretary.

"Wow, even a few left," I said, finishing my loop around the room.

I was about to sit down, when I realized I hadn't made the most important point. "Oh, uh, I'd also like everyone to refer to me from this point forward by my character name, Foyl."

"Thanks for that, uh, *Foyl*," Mike said, pointing to the back story in front of June, who was looking at it with feigned interest. "All right, let's keep moving along here, we've got a lot of ground to cover."

To facilitate the actual reading of a rather clunky writing format, Mike and his team used a customized screenplay which removed the minutiae, and deftly summarized the action that took place between the dialogue. We moved at a rapid clip, and arrived at page seven, scene nine — my debut — in no time.

"Mike, if I may?" I asked, raising my hand.

"Yes, Foyl."

"I'd like to try a little something with this. Just to fool around, you know?"

"Give it a whirl, Foyl. No time like the present."

Based on my character research, Foyl would have had a very pronounced Southern accent, so my line "Good evenin', Mr. Grayson, how are you tonight?" sounded a lot like, "Guuud eeeyvnin', mistuh Graiiison, haaaaur uuu t'naight?"

Richard Gere paused for a moment, adjusting to my approach, then recited: "Not so good, Foyl, not so good."

"Why not, Mr. Grayson?" Foyl asked, sounding like "Whaaa naught, mistuh Graiiison?"

Our director tried to hide his heavy sigh, but he couldn't. "Excuse me, Foyl?"

I didn't like being interrupted, but what can you do, that's the rehearsal process. "Yes, Mike?"

"Where are you thinking Foyl is from?"

"Outside of Savannah, Georgia — like it says in the back story."

Richard started laughing. "I'm sorry, but for a minute there, I thought I was acting across from Gomer Pyle."

The other cast members couldn't suppress their laughter. I could feel my face flush red from the negative vibes. *I may have to file a grievance with the Screen Actors Guild,* I noted to myself.

"But this is a romantic comedy, Mike," I objected. "Can't it be a little broad?"

"Foyl, as you can see, the Southern accent is funny," Mike explained, "but for the wrong reasons. Personally, I'd vote for an elegant Southerner, a gentleman, not a shit kicker. It's too on-the-nose."

Certain directors, particularly those of the caliber of Mike Nichols, have a way of making statements that are both explanations and decisions at the same time. Whatever the case, without a peep, I toned it down for the rest of the read thru, and

SCREEN ACTORS GUILT
5757 Wilshire Blvd.
Los Angeles, CA 90036

SCREEN ACTORS GUILT

GRIEVANCE FORM

Name BRUCE LORNE CAMPBELL Fake Phone Number (818) 555-6980

Website Address WWW.BRUCECAMPBELL dot COM

Last Speaking Role in a Film to Gross More than $100,000,000 Domestic Box Office SNOOTY USHER

Date of Occurrence 04-12-04

What is the nature of the grievance? HUMILIATION, SHAME, AND IGNOMINY

What effect, specifically, did said action have on you? I WAS SCARED AND WANTED TO HIDE

How exactly has your finely-honed craft suffered? SEE REVERSE SIDE

Additional Information (Give particulars and try not to adlib):
RICHARD GERE, RENEE ZELWEGGER, AND SOME OTHER JERKS LAUGHED AT MY SOUTHERN ACCENT. ONE OF THE OTHERS (LINDA LAVIN) SAID KEANU REEVES DID BETTER ACCENTS THAN ME.

Settlement requested ALL FOREIGN DVD SALES FOR SPIDER-MAN 3.

I hereby state that the information is correct and I am in accordance with California Laws in respect to the restrictions and/or privileges of vehicle licensing and transportation. I have read the Student Handbook in regards to driving regulations administered on this particular campus and agree to abide by them.

Member's Autograph

Date 04-14-04

Bureaucrat's Signature (Associate Producer credit pending)

Date

FOR OFFICIAL USE ONLY

Date

Setup ______ Confrontation ______ Resolution ______

avoided any further reprimands.

Afterward, the cast members mingled as expected, exchanging e-mail addresses, or discussing a particular scene. I worked my way past Renée, who gave me that same semi-forced smile of recognition to Richard, who was just saying good-bye to Christopher Plummer, the great actor who plays his father, the evil businessman.

Richard nodded when he saw me and walked over. "Hey, Foyl, I had an idea. What do you say, before we get into rehearsals with Mike, that you and I get together at my place here in town and we'll run the lines — massage the scenes. This is a relationship film; apart from the relationship that Renée and I have, my relationship with you has to be unique as well."

"I totally agree, Dick."

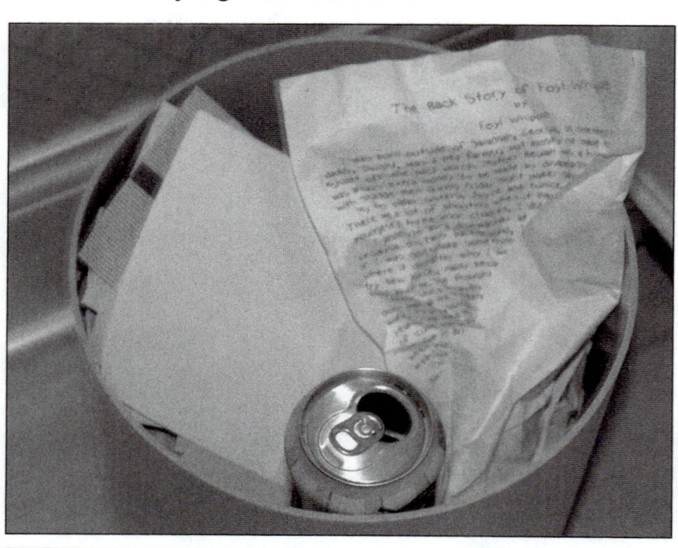

Sadly, Foyl's biography received similar response to my own.

"Richard," he said, politely correcting.

"Right, Richard."

"You don't smoke, do you?"

"Not officially, no," I assured him.

"Okay, uh, well, it was great to hear a first pass at this. I'll have my assistant track you down."

With that, Richard bolted before I could respond.

The crowd around Mike thinned, so I thought I'd take a shot at talking to him. I got within his peripheral vision, and he looked over right away.

"There he is," Mike said, as genially as he could for being a little pissed off.

"Hey, Mike, I don't want to take up any of your time, but as you can see, I've been researching this role."

"Yes, yes, that was very obvious," he said, nodding. "Just don't give yourself a hernia in the process. Today was a little rough, Bruce, I'm not going to lie to you."

"I'm sorry, Mike, I was pretty nervous."

"That's understandable, but don't get too lost trying to do a performance. Foyl never forces anything, he lets it happen naturally."

"Yeah, that's been a problem for me," I confided.

Mike shifted his weight uneasily. "If I might make a suggestion, Bruce, as an actor, you need to listen more. Half of communication is listening to what the other person has to say. I sensed that while the other character was talking, you were more or less just waiting to say your lines. Acting when you're *not* talking is even more important than when you are. Anyway, that's my take on it."

I found myself nodding with everything Mike said, but the word *communication* stuck. As an actor in search of a character, this single, simple word, understood and applied, could make the difference between a lousy performance and a memorable one. With renewed vigor, I marched past unread, crumpled bios, randomly abandoned in every direction, and out to the world at large.

I hear you, Mike — I hear you loud and clear.

4

Mind the Gap

Communication is the glue that binds civilization together. For instance, my wife, Ida, and I don't share information all at once over a quiet supper; rather, we tend to spout things as we think of them during the course of a day. It doesn't matter whether we're on different floors or behind locked doors — we insist on doing it, knowing full well that it always causes two things: a breakdown in communication, and irritation.

Here's a typical conversation:

"Hey, Bruce, I'm going to the store," Ida would yell from upstairs. "Can I get you something?"

"Bye," I would call back, reaching for the remote control to mute the TV. "Hey, are you going to the store?" I would then ask.

"I just said that," she would say, growing increasingly annoyed.

"Great — can you get me something?"

You can see how even the smallest bit of missed or repeated

information can quickly turn what would ordinarily be a civil conversation into one that's twice as long, and half as civil.

I asked myself, what if relationship problems all boiled down to gaps in information? Finding the answer to this one would require wisdom, persistence, and the keen ears of Lester Shankwater.

With four days before Richard Gere and I planned to rehearse, I had plenty of time to meet Lester outside Sign of the Beefcarver in Sandusky, Ohio. When I was a kid in Detroit, it used to be called Sign of the Beefeater, but the makers of Beefeater's Gin threw a hairy fit and forced them to change the name.

On this balmy summer evening, Lester and I weren't there to sample the prime rib, which isn't bad, aside from slightly watery au jus. No, tonight we were sitting in his sky blue Astro minivan preparing to eavesdrop on a couple experiencing relationship problems. Lester's business card proclaims him to be a RELATIONSHIP CONSULTANT.

"At the behest of various clients, I record couples and analyze their communication skills. I also provide what I call the Cyrano Technique, that's what I'm doing tonight. I guide clients through rough spots in communication, in real time."

"Like 'love' coaching?"

"I like to refer to it as Unity Reinforcement."

"How does someone end up doing this for a living?"

"Well, it just sort of fell into place," Lester explained. "I used to sit in the Food Court at the Sandusky Plaza Mall — I worked at the Radio Shack there for ten years — and I would hear the most infuriating conversations between couples, and I thought to myself, I can help these people."

"What gives you special skills in this field? Do you have a degree? A Ph.D.?"

"Those are just words on a piece of paper. I have a great ear. I can fill in the blanks in most conversations, and I'm very intuitive. The service I provide is goal-oriented. I don't want repeat clients, you know what I mean? I can only listen to idiots for so long."

"How does it work?"

"The deal is this: I discuss the desired effect he or she wants for a date, a party, a phone conversation, etc. Do they want to be funny? Do they want to sound more intelligent? More professional? I don't like to toot my own horn, but who do you think feeds Anthony Robbins all of his ideas — live, in real time?"

"That's damned impressive, Lester."

"Anyway, once you and the client agree on a strategy, I wire him with a very high-tech, low-profile, two-way communication rig. I can hear him talk, he can hear me. In special cases, like tonight, I've got a bug on her too. My client planted it on her purse. That's in case we need 'inside information,' know what I mean?

"This seems slightly insidious."

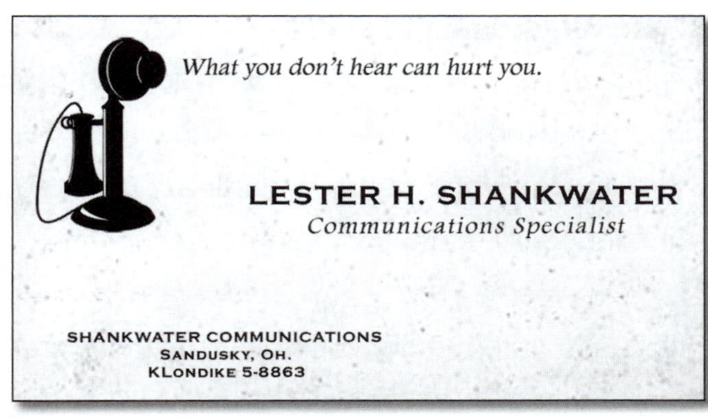

"*Discreet* is the word we like to use. Depending on the situation, I can also use my parabolic microphone. It can isolate specific sounds far away. They use them at football games. Let me show you."

Lester stooped over and made his way to the back of the van.

"So if you don't mind my asking, what's with the sky blue Astro minivan?"

"For starters, blue is not a threatening or evil color," he said, moving a large case. "It's a heroic color, a good-guy color."

"And the minivan?"

"Answer your own question, fella," Lester urged, assembling a long, thin Senheiser microphone with a miniature satellite dish around it. "Say the word: *minivan*. Not very threatening, is it? Nobody's going to hassle a minivan. Besides, it's got plenty of cargo room, and the mileage is better than you might think."

Lester crawled back into the driver's seat with his parabolic microphone and rolled down the window. "Who shall we capture?"

I spotted a couple walking, or *trying* to walk, from the bar to their car. "How about those two?"

"Easy as a turkey shoot," Lester said, pointing the unusual microphone toward them. He fiddled with a few knobs and hit a speaker button. A man's voice came in startlingly clear, sounding very close:

"For your information, I can drive just fine, okay?" he slurred.

"That's amazing," I marveled, not really caring about the conversation. "It's creepy how you can hear them breathing, and the rustle of their clothes."

"It's fun stuff," Lester said with a smile. "Shit, I can tell what kind of slacks a man has on, just by the sound."

"How long have you been doing this?"

"Three weeks — full time, that is."

"But, you know, the average person doesn't have audio-visual aids when they're communicating," I protested. "People have to learn how to do that by themselves, don't they?

"Not if I can help it," Lester said, unapologetically. "I provide something better than probability — I provide *possibility.* Take this fellow tonight: his name is Darryl, he's got a hot babe, Mandy, but he lacks the confidence and sense of humor to make advances."

"So you're going to, what, feed him some one-liners?"

Lester looked at me like I was a fool. "This is serious stuff, Bruce. Darryl has problems communicating his thoughts and feelings. There is so much he wants to say to Mandy, but she'd never know it. I'm going to help Darryl break his cycle of self-defeat with positive, assertive, and sometimes daring prompts."

Lester pointed across the Beefcarver parking lot. Darryl was just arriving with Mandy in his Ford Focus. Lester jumped into action, flipping switches and adjusting dials. "This should be fun. Darryl's a very willing subject. It's always better during these live events when you don't have to argue with the client you're trying to help."

Darryl was a tall, thin thirty-something, with sandy blond hair that hadn't seen a style change in fifteen years. Or maybe I was just a little out of step with Sandusky, Ohio. He was sporting what I believed to be a leisure suit, and the plaid design was threatening to scar my retinas. Mandy, on the other hand, was petite and cute, though in a too-put-together sort of way. She had so much makeup on it was impossible to tell what she really looked like.

"Man, what a babe," Lester said, scoping her out with binoculars.

I looked slightly askance, but Lester shrugged. "Hey, it's Sandusky. Okay, Darryl, we're recording. Give me a nod if you can hear me."

Across the lot, Darryl nodded in compliance.

"Okay, tonight you're going to be a good listener, you're going to be more assertive, and you're going to try some humor. Here we go. Tell Mandy that she looks really pretty tonight."

Darryl tensed up as he escorted Mandy toward the restaurant. "Boy, Mandy, you look pretty...*tonight*."

"Don't improvise," Lester scolded. "And don't change the inflections either. This is about specific communication. She looks *very* pretty."

"You mean tonight I'm pretty, as opposed to every other night we've been together?" Mandy asked, teasing him.

Darryl got a confused look on his face. He wasn't sure whom to respond to first. "Very pretty," he said finally.

"So tonight I'm very pretty, but every other night, I'm just pretty?" Mandy asked, baiting him.

Darryl got the same confused look again, and Lester stepped in to bail him out.

"Absolutely not," he said, prompting. "You're always pretty, usually beautiful, but tonight you're stunning."

"Absolutely," Darryl said, repeating incorrectly. "You're always pretty, usual, but tonight you're sunning."

Lester's jaw hardened audibly while his eyes narrowed. "Maybe he's impaired in some way...."

"Uh…thank you, I think?" Mandy said, not knowing whether it was a compliment or a psychotic break.

"You may have to dumb it down," I suggested, watching Darryl fumble for the front door of the restaurant. "What's he going to do when he doesn't have you around to feed him everything he says?"

"This is just a crash course," Lester said, defensively. "He'll eventually start using his own vocabulary."

"That could be scary."

"Be sure to help Mandy with her chair," Lester cautioned. "You're ıssertive, but you're also a gentleman."

Suddenly, a loud impact almost blew the speaker in Lester's van. It ᴊas followed by a few grunts, and a flurry of generally violent noises.

"Ow!" Mandy shouted.

"Whoa, sorry, Mandy, what happened?"

"What do you mean what happened? You kicked the goddamn chair ight out from under me, and I fell on my ass."

"I didn't kick the chair on purpose, Mandy, but I think I may have tripped n it. Sorry."

Lester and I could hear Darryl helping Mandy up and into a new chair.

"That was smooth," I said.

Lester raised his eyebrows. "Okay ow, Darryl, once you order drinks, 's time to make some magic."

We heard a new voice chime in. Good evening, folks. My name is Carol, I'll be your server. Can I get ou anything to drink right off the at?"

"Let her order first, Darryl," .ester coached.

"Uh, she can go," Darryl said.

"Okay, well, to recover from my ᴊounds, I'd like a vodka tonic."

"Complement her choice," .ester insisted.

Communications "specialist" Lester Shankwater.

"Hey, I love vodka too. Excellent."

Lester looked at me with increasing frustration. "Do we have a bad onnection?"

I shrugged. "I'd be more worried about *Darryl's* connection."

"Okay, Darryl, order something different. Wing it."

"I'd like a…Long Island ice tea," he said, grinning. "With a flaming Jell-o shot chaser."

"Allll-right," Carol said, sensing what she was getting into. "I'll put those orders right in."

Lester referred to a few notes he jotted down. "Okay, Darryl, it's time to shine. Take her hand."

"Wooh!" we heard Mandy exclaim. "You scared me."

"Sorry," Darryl said. "Just wanted to hold your hand."

Lester winked at me. "We've got to kick it up." Then, to his guinea pig: "Okay, Darryl, I want you to look in her eyes — right in them."

"Why are you staring at me?" Mandy asked, sounding disturbed.

"Because I can't take my eyes off you," Lester suggested.

"Because I can't stop keeping my eyes off you," Darryl tried to repeat.

"Okay, that's nice," Mandy said. "Thanks. But don't grip my hand that tight."

"Mandy. I have to ask you something," Lester said.

"Mandy. I have you something to ask," Darryl repeated.

"He's either Russian or dyslexic," I said.

"What is it, Darryl?" Mandy asked.

"Do you know how much I think of you?" Lester offered.

Lester and I both winced, because we knew that Darryl was bound to disappoint.

"Do you know how often I think of you?" Darryl asked.

Lester looked at me, deadpan. "Close enough."

"No, how often?" Mandy inquired.

"Day and night," Lester said.

"Twenty-four seven," Darryl translated. "Non-stop."

"I hate when they embellish my simple and elegant statements," Lester lamented.

"So, like are you obsessed or what?" Mandy asked, not even close to being won over.

Lester let out a sigh, and continued. "No, Mandy, but I have a hard time expressing myself, and I just wanted you to know it."

"That was a pretty long sentence," I cautioned.

Lester shrugged. "What can you do? My course is one size fits all."

Darryl answered with, "No way, Mandy. I just have a time with hard expressions. And I just wanted you…to know it."

Lester and I weren't privy to Mandy's perplexed expression, but I'm sure it was worthy of *I Love Lucy*. "Hard expressions? What does that mean?" Mandy asked, really wanting to know.

"I can't get hard expressions across," Lester suggested, trying to salvage his failing operation.

"I can't get hard things across," Darryl tried.

"Okay, I'm trying to follow you," Mandy said. "You can't express hard expressions?"

"No!" Darryl said, uncharacteristically forceful. "I can't hardly express how much I…I like you."

There was a long silence. Lester looked at me with a glimmer of hope in his eyes. "See? Darryl is learning to swim on his own."

"I need to use the bathroom," Mandy said, not responding to Darryl's awkward declaration.

"Okay, I'm gonna have a smoke," Darryl said, quickly jumping from the table.

Seconds later, he emerged outside the restaurant and pulled a pack of Lucky Strikes from his jacket.

"Darryl, can you hear me?" Lester asked.

"Yo," Darryl said, nodding his head toward the van. "Going pretty well, don't you think?"

"Like gangbusters," Lester said, trying to stay positive. "Hey, hang on for a sec, we're doing some random monitoring."

Lester turned to me. "I'll bet you twenty bucks that Mandy's gonna make a cell call while she's in the little girl's room. And if she does, we'll get the inside story on how well he's doing."

Lester gestured behind him at a bank of high-tech gear. "Radio Shack don't lie. If Mandy dials out or gets a call, the sensor Darryl put on her phone will activate. From here, I punch in, match the frequency and we hit pay dirt."

In about three seconds, a loud beeping filled the minivan. Lester smiled and activated the speakerphone.

"We get rid of everything we don't need," he said, as garbled signals and overlapping transmissions dropped away one by one. Eventually we could hear the slightly nasal voice of Mandy, clear as a bell.

"Oh, not so good, Jackie," she said.

I glanced at Lester. "Is that Mandy?"

"Yep," he said. "The sensor on her phone syncs up with my unit out here. I'd explain, but it's pretty complicated."

The secret conversation continued:

"What's wrong?" Mandy's girlfriend asked.

"Well, this guy Darryl has been creeping me out all night. He's talking in weird sentences, his eyes bug out, and, oh my God, he almost crushed my hand."

"Is he at least rich?"

"Are you kidding me?" Mandy said, through derisive laughter. "He's wearing a *leisure suit*."

As the girls gossiped, I couldn't help but watch Darryl. The poor sap didn't have a care in the world. He confidently hiked up his polyester pants and swiped a finger across his thin moustache, straightening any stray hairs.

"Oh my God! You gotta bail, girl," Jackie insisted.

"Please, Lord, let some man one day just take me away," Mandy pleaded.

Lester raised an eyebrow.

"Screw this guy," Jackie proclaimed. "Come on over. I got some cheap red wine. We'll get drunk and laugh at how useless men are!"

"Great! Sounds like a plan," Mandy said. "Well, I gotta go. I gotta pee real bad."

"Okay, love you, girl."

"You too. Bye."

"Trouble in paradise," I said to Lester, who was running his fingers through his hair and flipping switches off. "You

In addition to all this equipment, the van also comes with passenger-side airbags and six beverage holders.

The horribly misdirected Darryl.

don't seem terribly upset."

"Hey, I can't stop fate. If the guy is an idiot, he's an idiot. I'm gonna drain the lizard, and do a little, uh sound check with Darryl. Do you need anything?"

"No, I'm good," I said, jotting a few notes in my actor's log.

From inside the now-silent van, I watched Lester approach Darryl and give him a big pat on the shoulder. They had a brief, "educational" conversation, and Lester made his way inside the Beefcarver for a "drain."

What the hell is wrong with people? I wondered. *What's so hard about telling it like it is? Are we such freaks that we can't just deal with this shit ourselves? And why do we have to hire "experts" to explain and counsel us on every single detail of our waking lives? Most of the time, I'm pretty happy being a slob who doesn't know shit about anything.*

My wandering eyes fell on a bank of newspaper dispensers across the parking lot, lined up beneath the restaurant's large picture window. I checked my supply of quarters and hustled across the lot to see what local flavor I could find.

Clink-clink. I dropped in thirty-five cents and got myself a *Sandusky Bugle,* "The Word of Truth for a Hundred and Fifty Years." But before could glance at the headline, I spotted Lester inside the restaurant — and he wasn't going to the bathroom, he was headed directly toward a corner table. I shuffled closer to the restaurant for a better look, pretending to read the newspaper. From the closer vantage point, I saw Lester drop a folded piece of paper on a table without even slowing down. He deftly swung back around and slipped into the men's room.

Tricky boy, I thought. *What are you up to?*

Lester's timing was marvelous, because as soon as he slipped out of sight, Mandy exited the women's room and made her way back to the table. She couldn't help notice the paper, and she unfolded it for a look. Mandy looked around the room, but nobody responded. She glanced at her cell phone.

The door to the men's room opened, so I hustled back to the van, obscured by the local paper. Lester bounced out the front door and joined Darryl, who was just crushing out his cigarette.

Inside the van, I fished out Lester's parabolic microphone and aimed it toward the two guys. A few minor adjustments later, I was getting a fabric-rustling audio close-up of their conversation.

"Darryl, I'm proud of you," Lester said, grinning. "You've done really well."

"You think so?"

"So well, in fact, that I'm going to allow you to fly solo for the rest of the evening."

Darryl squinted at Lester. "Meaning?"

"You've graduated, you idiot — you're free!"

Darryl gasped. "Wow, really?"

"You can now pursue relationships on your own two feet," Lester assured him. "Repeat after me — I am a communicator!"

"Gosh, okay, uh, I am a —"

Riiiiing — the sound of Lester's cell phone interrupted Darryl's climax.

"Excuse me for a second," he said, turning away the slightest bit to answer. "Hello? Oh, *helloooo*." Lester turned to Darryl with a wink. " have to take this, sport. Good luck and Godspeed."

"Okay, thanks for everything," Darryl said, and he marched inside the restaurant with new bravura.

I nodded, knowingly. *That little stinker*.

Beeeep! A red light flashed on the control panel. It sounded just like the one I heard when Lester tapped Mandy's phone. Looking at the dials, I located the two-button combination — the power to the receiver and the channel designator. Within thirty seconds, I had Mandy dialed in. She was giggling like a schoolgirl. A familiar, if faint, voice joined in

"I'm a communications specialist," Lester Shankwater cooed.

I swung the parabolic mic toward Lester across the lot, and got perfectly clear reception. I couldn't help but notice a Panasonic CD recorder and a stack of seemingly empty CDs. I popped a CD in the sleek machine and hit Record. For a brief second, I felt like I was starring in a poorly reviewed, dumped-to-Saturday-night, syndicated action show, *Brick Brackman: Audio Detective*.

"I'd love to teach you some new ways to share information," Lester flirted.

"Yeah, I'd love that," Mandy agreed. "The guy I just ditched couldn't put a sentence together if his life depended on it."

"Well, I'd love to hear your story. I'm out in the lot."

"Okay, I ditched out the back. Want to meet at the Dumpsters?"

"Sure," Lester said. "Give me five minutes to do some ditching of my own, and I'll meet you there."

"Okay, I'll see you."

"Ciao."

Unless they're fifth-generation Italian, guys who say "ciao" are losers. This guy was a first-class chump. I recorded a few more seconds of Lester's happy whistling and self-affirmations, then hit Eject and stuffed the CD in my pocket. I placed the parabolic back where it was, returned the knobs to their original settings (more or less), and switched off the power.

Lester smiled as he approached the van, but I was already getting out the other side. "Hey, Bruce, listen, something's come up."

"Yeah, I know what's come up, and her name is Mandy."

Lester knew that for me to have such information I must either be possessed — or I must have used his stuff! "Yeah, well, you better keep my card, actor boy. You may not like what I do, but one day you may *need* what I do."

Larry's van squealed away, toward the Dumpsters in the back, where a lot more than love hung in the air.

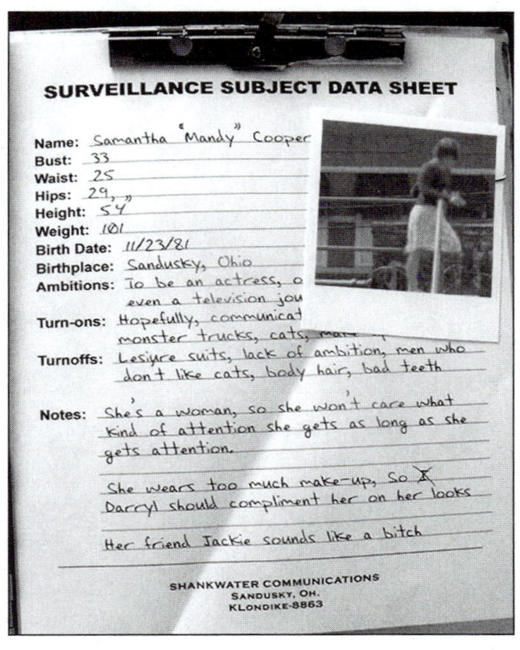

SURVEILLANCE SUBJECT DATA SHEET

Name: Samantha "Mandy" Cooper
Bust: 33
Waist: 25
Hips: 29
Height: 5'4"
Weight: 101
Birth Date: 11/23/81
Birthplace: Sandusky, Ohio
Ambitions: To be an actress, o
even a television jou
Turn-ons: Hopefully, communicat
monster trucks, cats,
Turnoffs: Lesiure suits, lack of ambition, men who don't like cats, body hair, bad teeth

Notes: She's a woman, so she won't care what kind of attention she gets as long as she gets attention.

She wears too much make-up, so Darryl should compliment her on her looks

Her friend Jackie sounds like a bitch

SHANKWATER COMMUNICATIONS
SANDUSKY, OH.
KLONDIKE-8863

As I walked toward the Beefcarver, Darryl came back outside and lit another smoke. His stooped shoulders told the whole story. Even though we had never met, I felt I knew him well enough to approach.

"Excuse me — Darryl?"

"Yeah?" he said, warily.

"You and I have the same acquaintance — Lester Shankwater."

"Yeah, well, I hope he isn't a close friend of yours, because I'd punch his damn lights out right now. He gave me bad advice."

"He did more than that, I'm afraid," I said, producing the telltale CD. "You and the Better Business Bureau might find this pretty interesting."

"Darryl, this could be the beginning of a weird, heterosexual, male relationship."

Darryl hesitated, as was his nature, but then he took the CD. "Thanks, mister."

"So. You hungry?" I asked.

"Well, I was, but I'm not sure anymore," Darryl replied.

"I'll buy dinner if you give me a ride to the Best Western afterward."

Darryl managed a weak smile. "I think I can handle that."

I put a hand on Darryl's slouching shoulder and we turned to head inside. "You know, Darryl, this could be the beginning of a beautiful friendship."

Small airports are sometimes more security conscious than large ones, simply because they don't have the big-ass machines to see inside all the luggage they transport, and it results in a lot more hand searches. I know this for a fact, traveling in and out of my small Oregon airport, and the Sandusky County Regional Airport was no exception.

As I stepped up to the head of the security line, impatient to leave this dreary part of the Midwest, Transportation Security Administration agent Bill Beasley put a palm up toward my face. "Boarding pass and I.D., please...."

I handed over the documents, and Agent Beasley gave them the once-over. He looked from my driver's license up to me and squinted.

"Why do you look so familiar?"

"I have that kind of face, I guess," I said, responding the same way I do to people who partially recognize me.

Bill looked me up and down to see if I was ready to walk through the metal detector. "Please make sure your belt and shoes are off."

"But my belt never beeps — even in L.A."

"Take it off, please."

"Same with the shoes. They don't go off in any airport."

"That's nice," Bill said, unimpressed. "Take them off, please."

"Oh, for crying out loud," I grumbled, tossing my shoes into a gray bin and shoving it on the conveyor belt. "In all the years of traveling, I have never *once* set off one of these —"

Beep! The metal detector sounded sharply as I passed through it.

"Oh, what now?" I said, tossing my hands in the air with a sigh.

TSA agent Ellen Heche was ready with a black, hand-held wand. "Please step over here and stand on the peanuts for additional screening."

"Why?" I asked belligerently, "Because I have a gum wrapper in my pants?"

"It could be as simple as that," Ellen said with a muted smile, waving the wand down and around my body. "Arms out. Let's hope it's —"

Ellen's wand started to make strange noises as it passed over a lower, cargo pocket on the front of my pants.

I reached down and pulled out a promotional pen from Lester Shankwater. "Typical. Heh-heh. Sorry about that."

"We're gonna have to put that through the machine," Ellen instructed. "Please put it in one of the bins."

I was set to launch into a lengthy tirade about pens and aircraft safety, but given the current security climate, I thought better, and dropped it into a small, blue tray.

Waiting for the stupid pen to roll out the other side, I put my shoes and belt back on. But as I approached the machine again, I saw no pen just three agents huddled around the X-ray monitor, looking at the fifty-cent object with great interest and concern. Their attention turned to me, and the grim look on their faces said it all. A deputy from the sheriff's department stepped forward and gestured to a room with bluish reflective windows.

"Mr. Campbell, would you please come with us?"

You never want to hear those eight words from a sheriff's deputy, but what choice did I have?

In the small, bare room, TSA agents Ellen and Bill sat nearby, while Deputy Willard Fitz paced menacingly in front of me. This was surely the most exciting thing to happen during Fitz's two-and-a-half-year career with the Oshgosh County Sheriff's Department, and he was going to make something of it.

"Are you aware that recording of any kind within one hundred yards of a TSA facility is against the law?" he asked.

"Not really, but okay, I'll go with you...."

"Particularly for a person on the ISL."

The ISL? I wondered. Then the connection hit me — the International Security List. I grabbed Lester's pen from the small desk in front of me and had a closer look. Sure enough, it wasn't just a pen with an advertisement on it; it was also a tiny recording device, capable of storing four hours of crystal-clear digital audio.

In a security environment where connecting the dots is a new priority, I could see how a rural airport, a recording device, and a previous brush with the Secret Service might set off a few alarms.

Officer Fitz got a stern look on his face and produced a small, laminated card from his back pocket. "Mr. Bruce Campbell, are you now associated with, or have you ever been associated with, the terrorist organization Al-Qaeda, or any of its affiliates in the known world?"

"Officer, for God's sake, I'm not a terrorist, I'm an actor. I mean, I almost *played* a terrorist once — in *Collateral Damage* — but I lost out to Cliff Curtis."

Without responding, the deputy proceeded to the next of his appointed questions: "Do you harbor any ill will toward the United States of America?"

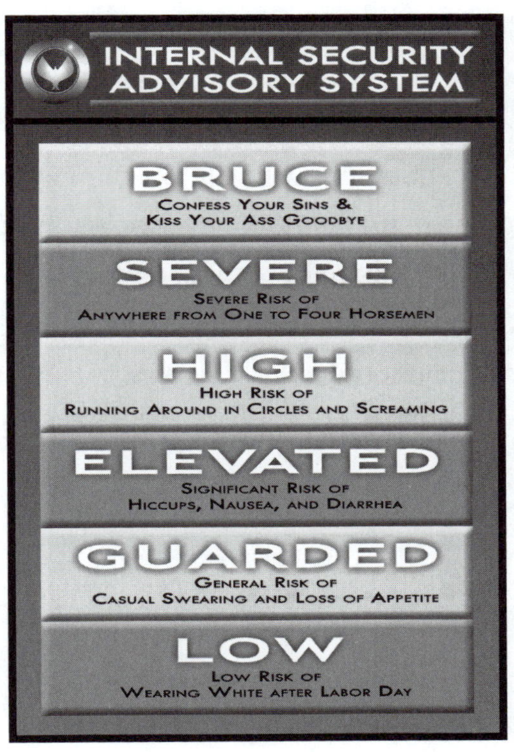

I slapped a hand on my forehead — it was going to be a long day. "Look, let's be reasonable. Why don't you just play what's on the device, which will be nothing, and I can go about missing my next seven connections. How does that sound?"

Federal law enforcement types are always suspicious of suggestions made by potential felons, but the three in this room exchanged shrugs and Deputy Fitz pressed Play for all to hear.

The initial sounds weren't very distinct, and had a muffled quality. Mostly, we heard the sound of fabric scraping across the microphone, like the device had been inadvertently turned on in my pocket. Then, the audio quality grew more hollow, as if the recorder were now in a large, bare room.

Sounds like a bathroom, I thought to myself. *Oh, dear God, not that*

Before my brain could reconstruct an unfortunate bathroom incident a barrage of visceral sounds too horrible to repeat in print boomed out of the pen. Earlier in the day, in a rush to get out of Sandusky, I grabbed fast food from a chain I hadn't seen since I was a kid, and it went down all wrong. Fortunately for the security of our country, Lester's mighty pen had captured the sounds of my gastrointestinal concert in excruciating detail.

Deputy Fitz managed to halt the noise coming from the damning pen, and we sat in silence, avoiding eye contact. The key word for the next few minutes was embarrassment, but the "evidence" convinced the agents that I was not the man they were looking for.

"Uh, I'd say you're pretty much free to go, Mr. Campbell," Deputy Fitz said, gathering up the papers in front of him. "Sorry for the hassle."

Civil liberty intrusions aside, and apart from the fact that my own government no longer trusted me, what disturbed me most about the incident was the fact that I wasted precious time away from my craft, particularly at a time when I was already apprehensive about my next appointment.

5

An Idiot and a Gentleman

Richard Gere's pad was not hard to find. In fact, it was right where he said it would be, off Central Park West and across from Strawberry Fields, sitting on some of the most expensive real estate in the world. The exterior looked like it was rubbed down with fistfuls of money every morning. Decorations in the lobby were low-key and sleek. I checked out the doorman, who was, of course, nicely put together. As I passed him, we nodded in working-class solidarity.

The elevator ride up to the fortieth floor was fast and quiet. I found Richard's apartment and knocked on the door. It wasn't like we were dating, but I figured I should bring something as a courtesy for our work session. I knew he was a Buddhist, so I skipped the bottle of Chivas Regal and got him something better.

Richard opened the door, looking relaxed and happy in a comfortable, monklike outfit. I had no idea how old Richard Gere was, but he looked great. He had skin that actors die for, smooth and blemish free.

His salt-and-pepper gray hair was very distinguished. "Hello, Foyl," he said, smiling. "Come on in."

Richard's penthouse was very different from others I had seen. With most of them you get the sense that the owner no longer has the slightest clue who they are or what their taste happens to be, and their living quarters invariably devolve into quasi–hotel suite extravagance — the hallmark of professional decorations. Richard's, on the other hand, far from being overdecorated, was subdued, almost serene.

"Hey, uh, we can skip the Foyl thing for tonight if you want," I suggested. "I don't want to get too crazy about that."

"Okay, Bruce, whatever you'd like. What have you got there?" Richard asked, referring to my gift.

"Oh, that. It's a little 'great to work with you' thing."

"Wow, that's really cool," he said. "Come in and make yourself comfortable."

I handed him the wrapped package, and he led us toward a sunken living room. "Would you like some white tea?"

"I don't even know what that is."

"It's the purest tea. You've heard of black tea, green tea, and so forth?"

"Yeah, I get it. So, Lipton would be considered a brown tea then, wouldn't it?"

"No," he said politely, "but I think you'll like the white."

"I'll take milk and sugar."

Richard looked back as he headed into the kitchen. "You don't put anything in white tea. It just is what it is."

"Okay," I said. "Sounds...*great*."

Richard came out with a tray and joined me, cross-legged, on the floor. He poured us each a tiny cup of the herbal tea. "To this film," he said, raising his cup.

"To this film," I echoed, as we clinked. "May this film live long and prosper."

Richard and I sipped the brew and settled back. "How do you like it?"

I tried to think of something nice to say about his tasteless tea, which smelled like day-old hiking socks. "It's very different. Very savory."

If you think this is bad, you should see what he put in the soup.

"You don't like it, do you?"

"It's not a matter of *like,* really...."

"So let's see what you brought me," Richard said excitedly, as he grabbed at my hastily wrapped gift.

He tore at the newsprint and tape and eventually revealed a twenty-inch-high Buddha, happy, bald, and pot-bellied.

"If you rub his belly, he'll talk to you," I suggested.

Richard threw me a sideways glance, but rubbed Buddha's little belly nonetheless. A small, tinny voice emanated from a cheap speaker, deep inside: "If one speaks or acts with an impure thought, suffering follows one, like the wheel of the cart follows the foot of the ox."

"Wow, Bruce," Richard said, shaking his head. "It's... it's..."

At a loss for words, Richard carried the Buddha into another room like a stinky diaper, then sat back down, gathered himself, and got down to business. "So, Bruce, I thought we would start by talking about our relationship."

"Well, so far it's not *bad*. I mean, I just met you, but —"

"The *characters*," he corrected. "The way Foyl and Harry interact."

"Right, gotcha," I said, taking a sip of the fetid, lukewarm tea.

"I think our characters should be night and day, hot and cold, high and low. Know what I mean?"

"Sure," I said, playing along. "I'm the salt to your pepper, the Yin to your Yang, the cream in your coffee."

The surest way to never achieve Enlightenment is to use a photograph of Buddha in a cheap gag.

"Well...something like that," Richard acknowledged. "But you're the calm and cool one, I'm the hothead. We have to be very different is what I'm trying to say."

"I agree, Rich."

"*Richard*."

"Uh, right. Can I pitch something to you along those lines?"

"Sure, Bruce," Richard said, calmly. "It's part of scene study. You and I will fool around with the material until it feels right, then we'll present it to Mike."

"Great," I said, feeling relieved, "because I'd say that our relationship isn't anywhere near what it needs to be."

"How do you mean?" Richard asked, intrigued.

"Well, it's pretty staid, isn't it? We're supposed to be these great friends by the end and all, but after what? The stuff that we go through should all be amped up to have more meaning."

Richard got a little worried. "Look, Bruce, I'm not a writer. If you're suggesting some rewrites..."

"No, no, not at all, just the way some of it's staged, and how we might react. Like, for example," I said, jumping to my feet, "the scene where you get mugged outside The Arms. Right now, there's just a tussle, and I come in to help."

"Right. I thought it works pretty well," Richard said. "Do you have a problem with that?"

"No, not if you want the audience to fall asleep."

"Well, I wouldn't add more violence if that's what you mean. I'm not a violence guy."

"I understand that, but it doesn't mean we couldn't dispatch this mugger with a little flair. Could we give something a try?"

Richard got to his feet, if hesitantly. "Sure."

"Okay, the script says that the guy comes at you from behind. You be you and I'll be the guy. He gets you in a bear hug, so what do you do?"

"I'd go limp and not resist."

"That might be what *Richard Gere* would do, but what about your character? He'd do what?"

Richard stepped in front of me, and I grabbed him from behind.

"I play Harry Grayson," he said, eyes squinting a little bit, "a tightly wound ad executive."

"That's right," I agreed, tightening my grip around his surprisingly good physique. "He wouldn't roll over for anybody."

Having uttered that, Richard heaved his arms up and arched his back. The strong, unexpected force sent me backpedaling across his shiny floor and directly into a Ming vase — CRASH! I dropped to the floor amid a hail of expensive pottery shards. All I could do was look up in horror.

Richard stood across the room with a wide grin. "That was fantastic!"

"Holy schmoly," I said, getting up from the shattered ring of crockery. "I am *so* sorry, man."

"Forget it, forget it, stay in character," Richard urged. "What next?"

"Well, as the guy was about to get up, Foyl would run in and give him the old one, two."

Richard, getting excited, ran over. "I'll be the guy now. Show me what you would do." He assumed the dazed position on the floor, and I ran in as Foyl, hoisting him to his feet.

"That's when I'd rear back and give him a haymaker."

"What's that?"

"It's a punch that has a real big wind-back, and a big follow-through. Okay, ready? I'm gonna go. You react how you think the guy would."

I reeled back and pretended to hit Richard. His timing was excellent, and it spun him sharply around — face first into his trophy case. Golden Globes, Oscars, and *People* magazine's Hottest Man of the Year awards tumbled to the floor, breaking and twisting.

Richard spun out of the debris and instinctively braced himself to receive another attack. "Damn, that was cool. You know I always turned down these kinds of films, but this is really a gas. I feel like this guy would charge you back, but then Harry could come back in and stop him somehow."

"Exactly," I said, snapping my finger. "You take him out with a roundhouse kick."

"A roadhouse kick?" Richard asked, as if struggling with the very concept.

"*Round*house kick. I'll show you. I had to do this once in a Sci-Fi Channel film called *Terminal Invasion*. First you start the turn, kicking the leg out."

Richard turned and kicked out. It was awkward at first, but he became more comfortable the more he tried it.

"FYI, it's the force of the extension that actually brings you back around," I suggested. "You know you've done it correctly when you land right back where you started."

"Right," Richard said, getting the hang of it. "Cool, let's try it. You play the mugger again."

"Okay, now since you're hitting my chest, go ahead and make a little contact. Sometimes, I can't react correctly if I don't feel it."

For all of you who thought the video game *Evil Dead: Hail to the King* sucked.

"Are you sure?" Richard asked, looking flushed.

"You bet," I said, wondering if I was pushing him too hard. "I'll pick it up from where I'm standing back up in the corner."

I assumed the position of the mugger and slowly rose to my feet, preparing to charge forward. As I picked up speed, Richard let out a fierce yell, the kind that comes from someplace primal. He spun around quickly, and his right leg fully extended itself into my chest.

Stuntmen hate it when actors do their own fight scenes, and this is why: as if I had been pulled by a wire, the impact from Richard's kick sent me back in the opposite direction. The only obstacle between me and the floor was a thick glass table, which my bony back smashed into a thousand pieces.

I wasn't sure which to react to first, my impacted vertebrae, or the second-degree burns over 50 percent of my body from the overturned white tea kettle. Richard raced up to survey the damage, but the look in his eyes wasn't fear, shock, or anger — it was elation. "Hot damn," he said, trembling from the exertion. "Now *that* would be a scene."

I responded by coughing. A simple rehearsal had turned into a donnybrook. As I looked around the room, I realized that I hadn't seen such carnage since *Evil Dead II* — during what we called the "Zoom-Boom" sequence, where an entire cabin gets destroyed by possessed trees — and Richard Gere's New York penthouse was the last place on earth I ever expected to witness it again.

I began to worry that my background in rough-and-tumble films made me ill-suited for the subtleties of a romantic comedy geared toward adults, but Richard felt otherwise.

"I want to show this to Mike," he said, with fire in his dark eyes. "Foyl and Harry now have a new relationship, and I *like* it! Let me get you some arnica for your bruises, and we'll work the next scene."

6

Mike Mounts His Movie

Bumps and bruises notwithstanding, at exactly ten o'clock the following morning, Richard Gere and I presented the new "mugging" scene for Mike Nichols and the screenwriter, Kevin Jarre, during rehearsal at Mike's brownstone.

Mike and Kevin had collaborated before on *Working Girl*, and were at a comfortable place in their professional relationship. I had been fortunate enough to work with Kevin on a TV pilot called *Missing Links,* and although it failed to mature into a full-blown series, we had enjoyed the experience.

The sound of Richard and me getting our breath back masked the quiet consultation Mike was having with Kevin. My sternum hurt like hell, but I managed to get through it. After a minute, Mike spoke.

"Hey, fellas, wow," he said, not necessarily happy. "Let me just say that I'm glad that nothing is broken and I hope you're both okay. But I have to ask you, what led you to take it in this direction?"

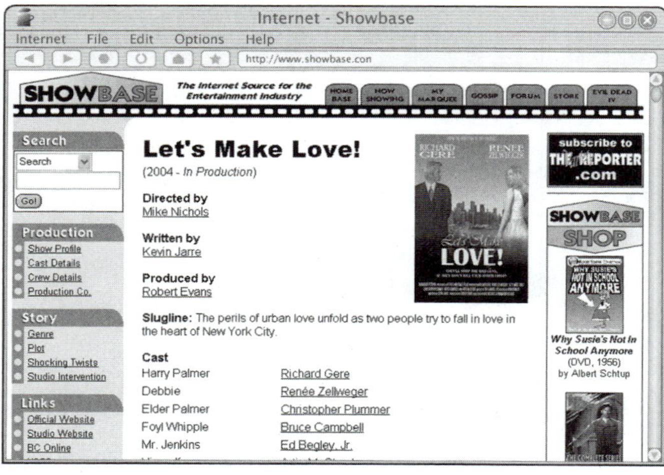

Of course, nothing is official until it's on the internet.

I looked to Richard.

"Well, Mike, we just wanted to get the most out of the scene," he said.

"It was just a mugging, Richard." Then, looking at me, "you guys made it into a scene from *Walking Tall*."

"But, now Mike," Richard interjected, "let's not forget that Harry Grayson has a military background — Desert Storm, Desert Shield."

Mike walked over to the coffee machine, thinking. "Yeah, okay, I guess I could see that, but Jesus, I dunno."

"And he's a New Yorker, through and through, Mike," Richard pressed. "He's got coffee in his veins."

Mike put Cremora in his cup of coffee, swirling it around with a plastic stirrer, then stopped and looked at me. "And what was in Foyl's past that might make us believe that he can do what you just did? I didn't read 'has the ability to perform numerous karate moves' in your back story."

I couldn't expect Richard to bail me out on this one. "Well, Mike, Foyl had a brief stint in the National Guard, and he had a very domineering father, which led to numerous violent altercations."

Mike stared at me, unblinking. It's like that during rehearsals sometimes, where lots of long silences hang in the air simply because things have to be sorted out.

"Think of it, Mike," I urged. "This is a romantic comedy, but there's nothing that says you can't have some zingers, some mush-mush to give the flick a little kick in the ass."

"Mush-mush?" Mike asked.

"Yeah, that's my pal Sam Raimi's term. It's when he uses every available means to jazz up a scene, to goose it. You add *mush-mush*."

"Is this a story about mush-mush, Bruce?" Mike asked, with a lack of expression that was intimidating.

"Well, no, but it's like the seasoning of a meal, like the —"

"Mike," Richard offered, "could Bruce and I show you another scene that we worked on? It might give you a clearer idea of where we're coming from."

"All right, gentlemen, have at it," Mike said, walking slowly back to the worktable he shared with his secretary, June.

Richard and I had a quick confab.

"Look, let's tone this next one down a little," he said. "Mike doesn't seem to be a fan of the broad stuff."

"Okay, yeah," I said, agreeing. "He was about to eat me."

"But let's keep the intensity," Richard reminded. "In this scene, it's your job not to let me through that door, no matter what."

Richard was referring to a sequence near the end of the movie where Foyl must stop Harry from entering the building to see Renée's character, Debbie. It's a contest of wills, and Richard's character wins. We took our positions in the open floor, facing each other and began.

```
                    FOYL
             (trying out a more
             genteel Southern
             accent)
        Sorry, Harry, I cannot let you do
        this.
```

"Better, Bruce," Mike said, "I like that much better."

"I do too," Richard said, looking at me apologetically.

"Okay, fine," I said, mildly annoyed.

"Let's continue," Mike instructed.

```
                HARRY
          (determined)
    I have to get in there, Foyl. I
    have to see Debbie.

                FOYL
    Well unfortunately, sir, she
    doesn't want to see you.
```

That was Richard's cue to advance. Mike scooted his chair forward in anticipation. Kevin was paying close attention, not only to the words, but to our actions.

As Richard advanced, I retreated.

```
                HARRY
          (warning)
    We'll just see about that.

                FOYL
    Don't push me, sir.
```

Richard forced me up against a side door, which we were playing as the entrance to the apartment building, and he put his hands on my collar.

Mike stood up. "Knock his hands off, Bruce."

I did, and it felt right. Richard is a very intuitive actor, and he reacted by putting his hands right back up, only this time more firmly in place.

```
                    HARRY
          You know what she means to me,
          Foyl.

                    FOYL
                (through gritted
                teeth)
          Yes, I do. And that's the
          problem, sir – she means nothing
          to you.
```

"That's an action line, Bruce, move during it," Mike instructed. "Move away from the door. Richard, are you okay with Bruce forcing you back?"

"Sure, yeah, let's try it," he said, fully in the moment.

With a nod, I pushed Richard back from the wall. He resisted with his toned body, but I made some headway. "That yoga shit really works for you, doesn't it?" I said under my breath.

Mike took a step away from the table. June followed to take notes, because she knew he was prone to throw directions over his shoulder in the heat of a scene. "Now, Richard, you've got to get in that building," he reminded in a fatherly tone.

Richard and I looked at each other, getting set.

"You want to do the next bit?" I asked.

"Sure, why not?" he said, smiling.

With that, Richard swung an arm over my head and got me in a headlock. I quickly elbowed him, and his grip released enough to get free, but he was already working his way to the door. I tackled him from behind and we rolled around on the floor slamming into one of Mike's custom cabinets.

"*That's* the intensity," Mike said, becoming more animated. "Kevin, you onboard?"

Kevin shrugged, but he was chuckling just the same.

"June, you got those moves?" Mike asked.

"Pace, collar, push back, headlock, elbow, tackle, roll — got it," she said, writing furiously with a No. 2 pencil.

Richard had since rolled on top of me, and I worked my leg under to push him off. Mike saw what I was about to do.

"Make sure it's away from the building, Foyl. You want to keep him away. Let me see it!"

I let Mike see it, all right — and Richard too, because I pushed him back harder than I had intended. Richard backpedaled right past June and into the coffee station. Spoons, napkins, Nutri-Sweet packets, and freshly roasted, shade-grown Hawaiian blend coffee went everywhere.

"Oh, man, I'm sorry, Richard," I said, worried that I had broken the star's back.

"Don't you apologize to him, Foyl," Mike scolded. "Stay in character! You just did what you needed to do, and now Harry Grayson will do what he needs to do."

Richard took that as his cue and ran toward me. I got ready to perform the next bit of rehearsed action, but Richard was coming too fast. What happened next wasn't anyone's fault — in fact, it's a problem that often occurs when two actors are allowed to "fight" together in a scene. Actors and fighting is a little bit like wildfire — if it isn't watched closely, it can get away from you.

The move we rehearsed was this: Richard would charge, but I would step aside and whack him in the back, sending him to the ground — simple.

But Richard was going too fast for that, and his lunging shoulder impacted my thigh, sending me out of control.

Richard was also knocked off course, but inertia kept him going until he belly-flopped into a table of pastries, sweeping it clean — tablecloth and all. I was too busy spinning like a top to notice. In fact, the only thing I knew for sure was that the stairwell of the brownstone was getting closer.

When I hit the raised lip of the concrete stairway backward, I knew that what lay ahead was not going to be good. Any stuntman will tell you, falling backward down the stairs is "a broken neck waiting to happen."

As I tumbled backward, the expansion of time caused by impending trauma allowed my mind to free-associate. I thought about the time I was acting in a Super-8 movie in Michigan, around 1976. Sam Raimi, boy wonder at that time, was directing a film called *The Great Bogus Monkey Pig Nut Swindle*. My role, a bad guy, required me to take a punch over a concrete wall and fall into a "river" below. The camera rolled, action was called, and as I hurled myself over the wall, the same bubble of expanded time enveloped me. Below, images flashed in slow-motion detail: ripples moving across the dingy water, the twist of a leaf in the wind, the *concrete slab*, hidden two feet beneath the surface.

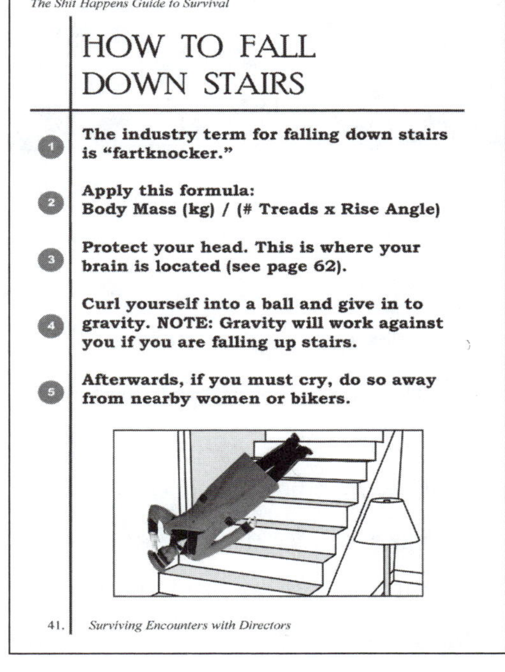
The Shit Happens Guide to Survival

HOW TO FALL DOWN STAIRS

1. **The industry term for falling down stairs is "fartknocker."**
2. **Apply this formula: Body Mass (kg) / (# Treads x Rise Angle)**
3. **Protect your head. This is where your brain is located (see page 62).**
4. **Curl yourself into a ball and give in to gravity. NOTE: Gravity will work against you if you are falling up stairs.**
5. **Afterwards, if you must cry, do so away from nearby women or bikers.**

41. *Surviving Encounters with Directors*

I hit the first set of stairs, and a loud snap from a damaged bone rang out as a harbinger of things to come. The sound of the fall was as spectacular as the visuals: *Whack*

– bam – "Ooof!" – clump – scrape – "Ow!" – duff – snap – wham!

I finally got to the bottom of the steps, but momentum carried my cartwheeling body through a locked, metal fire door that will forever retain a torso-shaped dent. I tumbled into the adjacent alley, finally stopped by a row of metal garbage cans.

Mike ran to the top of the stairs. He could see all the way down to where I was sprawled among the wreckage in the alley. "Oh, my God," he yelled, sounding horrified. Then: "That was beautiful! June, did you get it all?"

"Let me see," she said, checking her notes. "Leg push, coffee crash, charge, hit, spin, table clear, stairs, including whack – bam – "Ooof!" – clump – scrape – "Ow!" – duff – snap – wham! Then, door and alley — got it."

"Excellent," Mike said, working his way down to me. "Now *that's* the way to mount a scene!"

I tried to roll over, but my back wouldn't allow it. Oblivious to my trauma, Mike knelt next to me.

"Bruce, I have to admit, I was pretty resistant to this new direction," he said. "I'm a character guy, you know? I don't really do the flashy stuff. But I think I'm starting to get it now, and to be honest, I love it."

Mike grabbed my wrenched arm and hoisted me up. "Let's not forget, in this scene Foyl loses the fight, but he's still a gentleman. That's the core of his being, it's what motivates him."

Mike gave me a healthy pat on the back and jogged back up the stairs, whistling a happy show tune.

Ready for a hot bath, a massage, and a nap, I stumbled through the lobby of my SoHo hotel looking like the loser of a bar fight — at 11:00 A.M. I approached the slightly disturbed desk clerk and smiled cordially.

"Good morning — any packages for Bruce Campbell?"

The clerk, an intern type, looked behind the desk. "All I have is a FedEx for *Let's Make Love!*"

"That's me."

"Could I see some I.D.?"

"They don't ask for that in Oregon, you know," I grumbled, rummaging through my bloody jeans.

"Well, you're not in Oregon anymore, are you?" she said, with obvious disdain.

I found my license and waved it in the clerk's face. Reluctantly, she handed over the package.

Every delivery from the outside world is like Christmas to the gypsy actor, so I can get excited by a gas bill. Back in my room, I ripped the box open immediately. Expecting the usual stuff from the home front, I instead found a strange amalgamation of used B-movie DVDs, VHS audition tapes (one marked Danny Bonaduce), news clippings, and a rambling note from Rob Stern, the Paramount punk I recently met.

The package was clearly not meant for me, but you know what they say about possession and the law. The attached note was addressed to Mike Nichols, and outlined Rob's agenda:

ROB STERN

Mike-o,

Stern here. As we strive to transform Let's Make Love! from something you'd sleep through on an airplane to something parents will hand down from generation to generation, the road may be a little bumpy.

To help pave the way, I've enclosed some additional doorman auditions that rock (hey, until we actually shoot, the "door" should stay open), and some great B movies of the past - check out the groovy shooting styles. Let me know if any of this helps.

Fighting for you from the coast,

Rob

I was surprised how quickly I could tear a piece of paper into a thousand pieces, flush it down the toilet, and cram an entire FedEx box into my undersized hotel kitchenette garbage can. For the record, it took exactly nine seconds.

"Doorman auditions my ass," I hissed, stomping on the parcel one last time. "Track that, motherscratcher...."

The little pissant really *was* looking for other actors, and had the audacity to flaunt it, knowing full well that Mike had already made his decision. My first reaction was to shove the audition tapes up Rob's generous ass, but the calm, resonant voice of Mike Nichols echoed in my head: "*Being a gentleman is what motivates Foyl…the core of his being*...."

If Mike wanted a gentleman, then by God he was going to get one. I was going to become the most gentle gentleman ever to roam the earth. It was time to go to the source, to the land of Dixie.

7

The Gentlemen's Club

Gentle man: an oxymoron if ever there was one. Granted, modern men do come in all flavors — some are cute and cuddly, but most of them are rough and tough, and some are just plain pirates. I encountered a good example of this while directing an episode of *Hercules: The Legendary Journeys* in New Zealand. The Kiwis are a very hearty bunch. The Down Under men are manly, fearing nothing except their wives, girlfriends, and elderly aunts.

Through idle conversation between shots, I became friendly with a grip on the crew. He was a very nice fellow, but you wouldn't know it by his rough look. He was tall and wiry, and sported a plethora of scary-looking tattoos. He even had a gold patch over his right eye, and it fascinated me. Eventually, I became familiar enough to ask the fateful question:

"Hey, Rod, how'd you get that patch over your eye?"

"Oh, no big deal," he said with a wry smile. "I used to inject cocaine into it. Goes straight to the brain that way. 'Course, after a while, the cornea wears out, doesn't she?"

I stared at Rod in horror. It was one of the most hideous stories I had ever heard. "Sorry I asked."

"No worries, mate."

But trying to focus on a genteel portrayal of Foyl Whipple meant putting away such macho memories. I had to erase the images of an overly aggressive modern man, a species bursting at the seams with testosterone, and replace it with the more restrained sensibilities of a Southern gentleman.

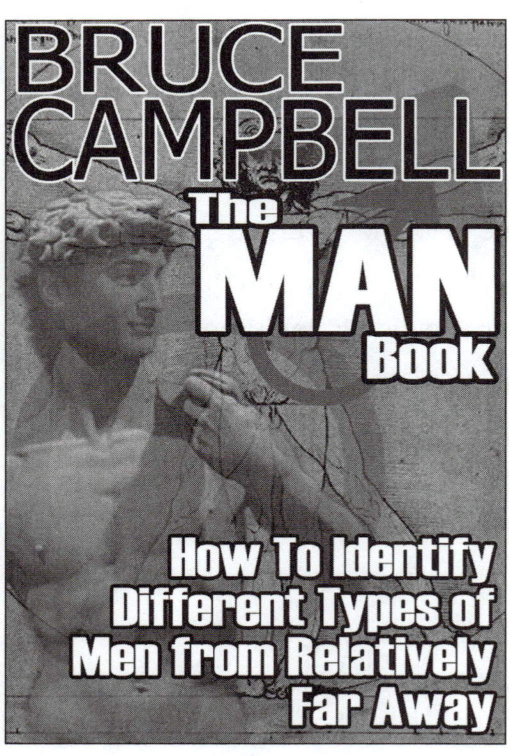

The Richmond Gentlemen's Society was housed in an antebellum mansion on Cotton Gin Lane. This grand estate wasn't just a place to stay, it was a living museum — a pristine link to a more mannerly time.

A dapper man of about thirty opened the door with a flourish. His Southern drawl was soft and long and syrupy. "Good afternoon, Mr. Hightower. We've been expecting you."

"Good afternoon to you, sir," I replied, my "sir" sounding more like a "suh."

I had decided to visit this mucky-muck establishment posing as a prospective member.

"Allow me to introduce myself. My name is Charles Butler, Associate Director. On behalf of the Richmond Gentlemen's Society, I'd like to welcome you. Please come in. Mr. Lee is expecting you."

I looked around. The foyer alone had more square footage than most homes.

"May I take your hat and coat?" Charles offered.

Fortunately, my wife, Ida, used to be a costume designer. Before I headed south, she outfitted me like a southern dandy from the old movies, right down to the spats. I handed over my top hat and coat.

Charles led me toward a substantial oak door at the end of a long, tongue-and-groove hallway. We walked past portraits of other famous southern gentlemen — Winfield Scott, Jefferson Davis, and Dale Earnhardt — all proud and firm in their resolve.

Charles opened the door and announced me. "Mr. Lee, may I present Mr. Hubert Hightower, from Savannah."

The paneled oak room was dark and plush and smelled like leather. Stuffed animal heads, plaques, and diplomas dominated the walls. But the real character of the room came from the two southern gentlemen who waited for me behind a large antique desk. One of them was Robert E. Lee. The other was his great-great-grandson, who was seated directly beneath the huge portrait of his famous ancestor, smiling approvingly.

"Mr. Hightower, I am honored to make your acquaintance," said Phineas T. Lee, coming around from behind his enormous desk, hand extended.

"The honor is mine, Mr. Lee," I said, trying to keep pace with his enthusiastic handshake.

"I understand you're interested in becoming a member of the Society."

"Yes, sir, most definitely. I feel as though my skills as a gentleman have diminished in this crude world of ours, and that your institution may very well be my salvation."

"Where is your family from, Hubert?"

"Virginia, originally, sir. My father is Major General Zachariah 'Zeke Hightower, now retired."

"A military family," Phineas nodded approvingly. "Did any of your ki serve in the War for Southern Independence?"

"Of course, sir — we served with pride in the Seventh Virgini Regiment. Many of my family were lost at Antietam, Shiloh, Gettysbur uh, Massa —"

In mid-word, I had forgotten the name of any more Civil War battles so my mind flashed to the first Native American name I could think o "Massapaquappa." It wasn't even a real Indian name, but that's wha came out.

"Massa — ? I'm sorry, Hubert, I can't quite get that out."

"It was a…a little-known skirmish. Several of my kin were attache to a group called the Wart Hogs — special ops. Even to this day, I'm no allowed to discuss it, sir. Being a military man, I'm sure you under stand."

"I see. Well, most honorable, son," he said, accepting my line of bul "You come from good stock."

"From what I understand, sir, you yourself enjoy a heavy dose o pedigree in your lineage."

"Oh, I don't like to broadcast such things, but I suppose one coul come to that conclusion."

"It's fitting that you should be the president emeritus of such an insti tution," I said, referencing the great Civil War general, "since Mr. Le himself, ol' 'Ace in the Hole,' ol' 'Uncle Bobby,' was the mother of a Southern Gentlemen, if I may."

"And at the risk of sounding expansive, the distinction of our famil goes back a wee bit further. Robert E. was the seventeenth direc descendant of Robert the Bruce."

"Of Scotland?" I asked, trying to hide my shock. I had been named after Robert the Bruce, and my relatives go back to those same misty Highlands.

"That makes me the twenty-first direct descendant," Phineas added with notable pride.

Holy shit — am I related to this windbag? I wondered.

"Do you have a family yourself, Hubert?"

"I do, sir. I'm married to, uh..."

And then it happened again — I blanked on the name of Hubert's wife and kids.

"Uh…Mary Todd Hightower. And I have three wonderful sons — Jeb, George, and Jethro — two of whom do the Hightower name proud."

Hubert's Confederate ancestor, Slim Hightower.

"And what occupies your time, Mr. Hightower?"

"Cotton, mainly."

"A textile man. How wonderfully traditional."

"You will find, sir, that the Hightowers are steeped in tradition. My ancestors had a hand in something called the cotton gin. You may have heard of it."

"My goodness gracious, I should say I have," Phineas said, laughing. "I should say I have! Mr. Hightower, it will be my pleasure to introduce you to the ways of the gentleman. But first, a few formalities," he said, rummaging through a lower desk drawer.

He produced a small box and opened it. "Since you're not a member — yet — I must ask you to wear this medallion around your neck. It will let the members know that you're a guest, and to afford you such treatment. It also grants you, as a true son of the South, full access to our activities today."

"I'll wear it proudly, sir."

Southern gentleman, Phineas Lee.

Phineas draped the thick medallion, supported by a fine silk ribbon around my neck. "And if I may, Mr Hightower, the fundamental rule for behavior in a club of this sort is the same as in the drawing-room of a private residence. In other words, heels have no place on furniture, ashes belong in proper receptacles, and there is to be no spitting or cursing."

"My good Mr. Lee," I said with a click of my patent-leather heels, "I shall comport myself in a manner that will uphold the dignity of this establishment and its esteemed membership."

"Very well, sir," Phineas said, digging a pocket watch out of his vest. "I'm due to regale the members on manners pertaining to manhood and courtship this very minute. Shall we?"

Phineas took me by the arm and led me to the parlor of his grand i slightly crumbling estate. The light was dim, and the air was thick with cigar smoke. Liquor flowed freely, and there was a lot of backslapping and friendly ribbing and a general air of masculine energy. Most of the members appeared to be well over sixty and carried themselves with the self-assurance of those already well established in life.

Charles Butler, upon noticing Phineas's arrival, addressed the gathering. "My distinguished associates, if you'll find a comfortable seat, we may enjoy the musings of our founder emeritus, Mr. Phineas T. Lee."

The men applauded respectfully and settled into overstuffed chairs as this leader of gentlemen walked to the front of the parlor. He orated like in the old days — by simply speaking loudly, though he was, in fact, an excellent speaker.

"Good afternoon to you, fine gentlemen."

"Good afternoon to you, Dr. Lee," came a perfect chorus.

"I wish to share a few precepts my grandfather passed along to me many decades ago. One morning, as I sat on his knee under a magnolia tree, he said, 'My boy, the honor of a gentleman demands the purity of his word, and the incorruptibility of his principles. He is the defender of the defenseless, the champion of justice — or he is not a gentleman.'"

A polite applause scattered across the room, with a few shouts of "here, here" thrown in for good measure. Dr. Lee hooked a thumb in his vest and began to stroll across the room.

"As a gentleman, you are a direct descendant of the knight. Your code of honor, particularly as it pertains to the matter of courting, must guide your motives. A gentleman, in the company of a female, will never be ostentatious or overbearing. These attributes are never to animate a well-bred person. Courting demands the utmost application of etiquette, which includes ethics as well as manners. This great association of ours, an association of gentlefolk, provides the necessary tools for us to apply good form in speech, charm of manner, and instinctive consideration for the well-being of others."

The men applauded vigorously. I threw in my own little "here, here" just for fun, and nobody seemed to notice. I was starting to feel good about my performance. If only Mike could see me now, he'd forget all about Danny Bonaduce!

"My good men, before we apply good courtship skills, I would like to make you aware of a distinguished visitor. Mister Hightower, make yourself known," Phineas announced, unable to find me in the hazy room.

I raised my hand and the men turned their attention to me.

"Please welcome Hubert Hightower to our society. He is a man of impeccable character and background. I know that you will treat him as one of our own."

I nodded at the friendly, welcoming applause, embarrassed that the old fart had to make such a fuss.

Phineas worked his way to a nondescript black door and gestured grandly. "And with that, I bid you an afternoon of gentlemanly delight!"

He opened the heavy door and two dozen women worked their way into the room. There was a general hubbub of agreeability upon their entrance, and let me clarify why — these were strippers, dressed (albeit temporarily) in what looked like prom gowns. My suspicions were reinforced by a subsequent change of mood in the room — the genteel classical music turned into a pounding disco beat, and the light went from a lazy straw color to a pulsing white and blue.

Holy Plantation! This gentlemen's club really was a *gentlemen's club*!

Charles managed to find me amid all the activity and took me by the arm. "Before too many of our gentlemen become 'otherwise engaged,' Mr. Lee would like for you to join him in pontification."

"Pontificate away," I said.

We found Phineas, ever the teacher, addressing a small group of men. "As you can see over here," he said, gesturing to two pop-eyed club members ogling a curvy stripper, "these gentlemen are exhibiting perfect etiquette through proper introductions."

Chivalry is indeed dead, and it's buried in Virginia.

One of the gentlemen bowed slightly from the waist. "Good evening to you, ma'am. Allow me to introduce myself. I'm Sheriff Jimmy Jones."

"Notice how he didn't presume to offer his hand?" Phineas observed. "Strictly speaking, it is always the woman's place to offer or not, as she so chooses."

"Good evening," the brazen woman said. "My name is Scarlet." She then offered her hand to the next gentleman, who smiled and took it willingly.

"Evening, Miss Scarlet. Mayor Lloyd Dickweed. It's a real pleasure to make your acquaintance."

Scarlet took the Mayor's hand and winked at him. "It's going to be a pleasure making yours...." And she led him away through the crowd.

"Now there, we have a fine example of what happens when you apply what I call the three *P*'s," Phineas said with a nod. "Patience, poise, and persistence. Mayor Dickweed exhibited these three qualities in a fine manner, and his gentlemanly ways are being rewarded this very minute."

There was polite applause from the group of rapt men. Phineas made

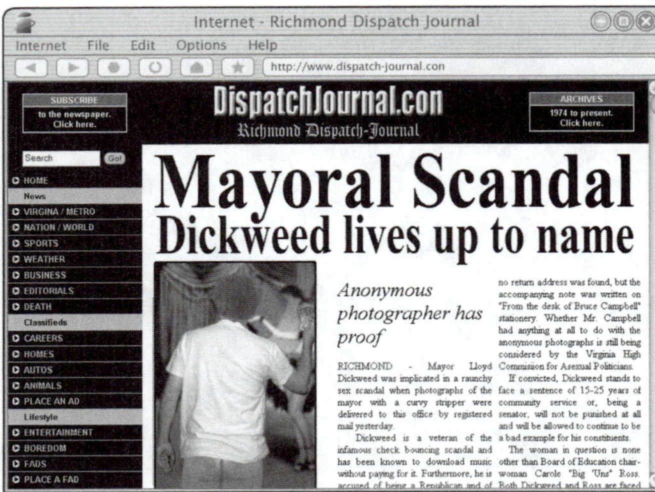

Internet - Richmond Dispatch Journal

Internet File Edit Options Help

http://www.dispatch-journal.con

SUBSCRIBE to the newspaper. Click here.

DispatchJournal.con

Richmond Dispatch-Journal

ARCHIVES 1974 to present. Click here.

Search Go!

HOME
News
VIRGINIA / METRO
NATION / WORLD
SPORTS
WEATHER
BUSINESS
EDITORIALS
DEATH
Classifieds
CAREERS
HOMES
AUTOS
ANIMALS
PLACE AN AD
Lifestyle
ENTERTAINMENT
BOREDOM
FADS
PLACE A FAD

Mayoral Scandal

Dickweed lives up to name

Anonymous photographer has proof

RICHMOND - Mayor Lloyd Dickweed was implicated in a raunchy sex scandal when photographs of the mayor with a curvy stripper were delivered to this office by registered mail yesterday.

Dickweed is a veteran of the infamous check bouncing scandal and has been known to download music without paying for it. Furthermore, he is accused of being a Republican and of no return address was found, but the accompanying note was written on "From the desk of Bruce Campbell" stationery. Whether Mr. Campbell had anything at all to do with the anonymous photographs is still being considered by the Virginia High Commission for Asexual Politicians.

If convicted, Dickweed stands to face a sentence of 15-25 years of community service or, being a senator, will not be punished at all and will be allowed to continue to be a bad example for his constituents.

The woman in question is none other than Board of Education chairwoman Carole "Big 'Uns" Ross. Both Dickweed and Ross are faced

If this acting/writing/directing/producing thing doesn't work out, I've always got my camera.

his way over to me as his entourage sauntered about the room, taking in the raunchy proceedings. "You see, Hubert, the value of these exercises to a gentleman is priceless. Here, he can hone his etiquette skills so that he may present the best of himself back home later."

"To his *wife*, I presume?"

"A gentleman never presumes, Mr. Hightower. And his presumptions are best kept to himself."

With that, Phineas walked into a dark lounge. This was where the old-time booze still flowed. None of that frozen daiquiri crap — these guys were sucking down top-end bourbon and whiskey. Every man in the place made sure to smile, nod, or wave as Phineas passed — he was the head honcho and everyone knew it.

"I'm quite pleased with the level of etiquette I've seen displayed so far. There is a hairbreadth between rudeness and reserve, you know," Phineas said, waving a finger in the air.

Then, from across the room, a Rebel yell caught everyone's attention. We looked up in time to see a burly man wind up and spank the rear of a full-figured stripper. "I'm gonna enjoy ridin' you tonight, darlin'!"

The woman turned to smack the lug, but she stopped short, because she could see what her aggressor couldn't — Phineas approaching from behind.

"Kind sir!" he bellowed.

The sweaty guy jumped out of his skin and turned to Phineas.

"Drummond, isn't it?" Phineas demanded.

"Yes, sir, Hank Drummond, but what did I do? I was just having some fun with the little lady."

"Hold your tongue. If you're a Drummond, then you know right well that it's not proper to slap a woman on her bottom side unless duly warranted."

"Yes, sir, I unnerstand," the man said, contritely. "Thank you, sir."

Phineas approached the woman Hank had slapped. "What's your name, my dear?"

"Ginger, sir."

"Now, we all know that a dusting on a woman's posterior is a sign of affection, even playfulness," and Phineas demonstrated with a light fanny tap on Ginger. "Now, ma'am, did I harm you in any way?"

"No," Ginger said, rolling her eyes.

"With regard to force, temperance must be the rule. A woman is a delicate flower." Phineas turned back to Hank with a little more fire in his eyes. "Let's have that apology, son. Say you're sorry to Ginger for your ungentlemanly behavior."

Hank rubbed his sweaty palms together and cleared his throat. "Miss Ginger, I'm sorry for what I done — powerful sorry."

"I accept your apology," Ginger said, and kissed Hank on the cheek.

Phineas clapped his hands together. "And there you go. Hank thereby redeems himself as a gentleman, and all is forgiven."

There was a joyous response, and Hank was rushed by his fellow gentlemen, welcoming him back into the charmed circle.

Phineas turned his attention to me. "I'm sorry you had to see that, Mr. Hightower."

"It's quite all right, Mr. Lee. The price you pay to be a gentleman, I reckon."

"A price that all must be willing to pay, without exception."

"Now, don't get me wrong, here, Mr. Lee. This is a fine institution to be sure, but I suspect that a man who spends too much time here will create troubles of his own at home."

"Son, I'll simply say this: men do what they do at this establishment, so as to avoid the need for such rambunctious behavior at home. We have, on many occasions, gotten letters from wives of thirty-five years, praising our name to the heavens for what we have done to tame their husbands and fiancés and sons. We are to be commended, Mr. Hightower — not questioned — for our service to society."

Phineas pivoted away from me as a means of politely changing the subject. "Another of the gentlemanly arts we encourage among our members is the art of conversation. Witness what we have over here."

I looked in the direction of Phineas's gesture and jumped at the sight: an octogenarian with a bad toupee being lap-danced by a red-headed bombshell. The man's face was breast height as he addressed her.

"I declare, Miss Tiffany, wasn't today the most ideal scenario for a walk in the park?"

Miss Tiffany giggled. "Why, Judge Green, the sun came through the clouds like a ray of hope upon the land."

"Your amplitude leaves me in arrears," the old geezer cooed to Miss Tiffany, who faked another giggle. "If I were to become one with your amplitude," he continued, "I fear that I may become hopelessly lost."

"You see?" said Phineas. "It is possible, even in this crude world of ours, to comport oneself with grace and aplomb."

Then, from across the bustling room, at a volume reserved for sporting events, we all heard, "Oh, my God, it's Ash!"

This incongruous shout caught everyone's attention, and we turned with great curiosity to the culprit: a busboy, bright red from embarrassment. "I am so sorry, but that's the guy from the *Evil Dead* films!"

"Hold your tongue, boy!" Phineas shouted, and the room fell silent. "Evil…Death?"

"*Evil Dead*, sir," he nervously corrected.

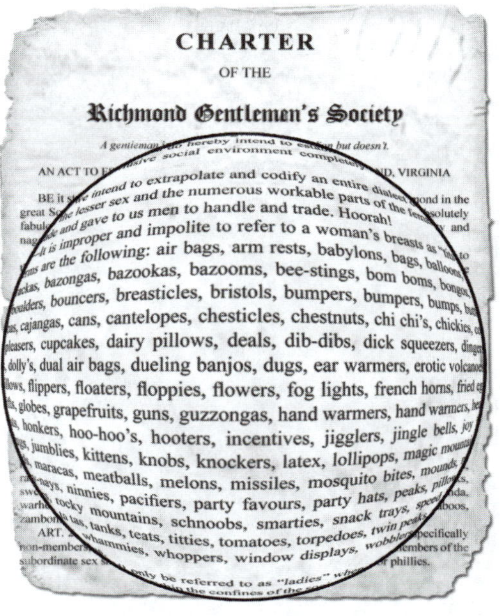

The abridged version.

"What could those words have in common with this institution?"

"Uh, well, B-B-Bruce Campbell, sir," the pimply kid stammered, pointing directly at me.

Phineas didn't follow the kid's line of reasoning. "Why, we all know that he's Hubert Hightower, from Richmond," he said confidently, then — eyeballing me: "*Aren't* you, son?"

I was busted either way, so I decided to throw in the towel. How bad could it get? "Well, sir, not exactly," I said, minus the hokey Southern accent. "I'm an actor researching a role for a film."

A hushed murmur began among the men, and those that so easily brushed shoulders with me seconds ago stepped back.

"You're from Detroit, aren't you?" the busboy asked.

"Detroit!?" Phineas blurted indignantly, as if the city was from another planet.

"Yeah, that's right," I confirmed. "Outside the city."

Fan boy Skip Lee.

"You went to Groves High School. I went to Seaholm."

"Really? You were a 'Sea-Foamer'?"

The kid chuckled and relaxed a little bit.

"What's your name?" I asked.

"Skip."

"Where you from?"

Phineas took in our exchange with building indignation. Skip held up his right hand, fingers together, creating the shape of Michigan — a sure sign of a native Michigander. He pointed to a spot just "east" of the tip of his pinky.

"Northport Point."

"Holy crap, I went to camp there!" I said.

"Enough!" Phineas demanded, approaching menacingly. Two dapper men, sporting bouncer physiques, suddenly appeared on either side of me. "Sir, is it true that you are not the selfsame Hubert Hightower and that you are, in fact, an actor named Bruce Campbell?"

There was a courtroom feel to his questioning and I couldn't help myself. I took the bait. "Right-a-reeno, Mr. Lee."

"What? Ho! Say no!" the men cried out in agonized shouts.

"And is it also true, *Bruce Campbell*, that you are not from the great city of Richmond, the siege city, and that you are, in fact, from...Detroit?" he asked, having trouble even saying the word.

I puffed up my chest as I delivered the answer. "Yes, sir, it is true.

Every bit of it. I'm from Detroit, and Detroit can kick Richmond's ass any day of the week!"

"Damn straight!" Skip shouted in support. Several men nearby began to reprimand him for his impertinence, but he knew his job was already toast, so he peeled off his waistcoat and flung it high in the air. "And you know what, you old farts? You can kiss my pimply, red-rashed ass, 'cause I quit this shit!"

Without warning, Skip dropped his pants and shot that roomful of stately men what was indeed a pimply, red-rashed ass of a moon. The ensuing dynamics were very strange. Members shouted and scolded and wagged their canes at Skip as he walked slowly out the door, tossing his fake bowtie into a trash bin.

"Order! Order!" Phineas bellowed above the din. The room settled somewhat, their attention returning to the inquisition. Phineas was red in the face, but the bluster was gone, and he was all about resolution.

"In light of the fact that, in front of many witnesses, men of impeccable character, you willfully and purposefully presented falsehoods, thereby disgracing not just my honor, but the honor of this establishment, and the honor of Southern gentlemen everywhere, I hereby challenge you to a duel on the front lawn!"

The men cheered with great force. Their tone was changing too, from outrage to calls for action.

"A duel?" I asked in disbelief. "Get real, Phinney. I'm out of here."

"Mr. Butler, may I have my pistols, please?"

Without realizing it, I had become enmeshed in the workings of an ancient and deadly protocol. As Charles Butler walked toward Phineas's office, the men parted like the Red Sea — doors opened, feet shuffled, keys jangled.

I started to get creeped out. "Hey, you know, this has been fun, Mr.

Lee, but your little joke is over. Where's the hidden camera?"

Phineas responded by nodding to his aides, who each placed a "you're not going anywhere" hand on my shoulder. Charles made his way toward a glass and mahogany cabinet. Inside, half submerged in a crushed velvet lining, two eighteenth-century flintlock dueling pistols glistened in the amber light.

"Mayor Dickweed, may I have the key to the dueling cabinet, please?" Charles asked, now more formal than ever.

The mayor, somewhat ruffled from his dalliance with Scarlet, fumbled with the keys, but eventually got the job done, and the cabinet doors swung open.

I was hustled outside by an increasingly unruly mob of old men and marched into place under the shade of a centuries-old magnolia tree. My senses sharpened by adrenaline, I found myself momentarily distracted by the manicured lawn. Their diagonal mowing process would be the envy of any golf course.

Standing twenty feet from me, Phineas removed his overcoat. He was sweating profusely, but kept his composure. One thing about these old freaks — when they commit, they *commit*. Phineas's two goons pulled my overcoat off, leaving us both in vests. As I looked around at the haranguing crowd, now formed into two rows on either side of us, I couldn't help but appreciate the authenticity of it all. This would have been a great plot for *Jack of All Trades*, I thought.

But the flintlocks brought me back to reality. Charles escorted them on a velvet pillow to a position directly between Phineas and me.

"We, as gentlemen, hereby agree to the guidelines set forth in the Dueling Code," Charles stated, as if he'd said those actual words before.

"In case you're interested, I didn't agree to anything," I shouted, so all could hear.

"Quiet!" "You've had your chance!" "Bah!" were the various gentlemanly responses.

"As the presiding officer, I, Charles Stonewall Butler, shall lead the proceedings. Will the challenger and the challenged please step forward?"

Phineas and I stepped forward. He wiped a sweaty hand through his hair. I responded by adjusting my visitor medallion.

"Bruce Campbell, you are hereby accused by the honorable Phineas T. Lee to have perpetrated a grave fraud on this society, and shall therefore be subject to the measures of justice this society sees fit and fair to administer. At the behest of Mr. Lee, this society therefore sanctions the use of pistols as an accepted method of resolving disputes, and shall commence imminently."

"Can I interject?"

"Not at this time, sir," Charles said, like an official at Wimbledon. "Not according to the rules."

Try to remember that violence never solves anything. Flintlock pistols, on the other hand, can solve almost anything.

Avoid potentially offensive phrases such as *redneck, cracker, hick, hayseed, hillbilly, democrat,* or *Detroit.*

If you happen to have a gift certificate for a local restaurant, offer it to your opponent.

A surprise punch to your opponent's nuts can work wonders.

Aim for the head. That way, if your opponent turns out to be a zombie, you still win.

If None of the Above Works...

Accept death. Only after you face the fact that you are going to die can you really begin to live. Unfortunately, given your current predicament, you probably only have a few minutes to live life to the fullest.

If time allows, moon your opponent.

"This is barbaric."

"On the contrary, my good man, this is tradition. Choose your weapon."

"I choose a grenade."

"Choose a pistol please," Charles repeated.

"Eeenie, meenie, miney —"

"Get on with it, man!" Phineas blustered.

Charles grabbed the nearest pistol and pressed it into my palm. He was obviously way more hip to these dueling rules than I.

"Point the pistol toward the sky, please, Mr. Campbell," Charles instructed with such assurance that I started to wonder how many duels he'd presided over.

Phineas took the other gun and we stood facing each other, barrels pointed in the air.

All I could think about was the state of my underwear.

"Turn away from each other."

Phineas and I adopted the desired position while Charles ran down the rules: "On my command, you will walk twenty paces in the direction in which you are presently facing. On my next command, you shall turn upon your adversary and fire. Your pistols each have one ball with which to inflict a mortal wound. Doctor Strom Tollison, are you present, willing, and able to administer to the dead and dying?"

A rickety man, easily a hundred years old, hobbled into view with his faded medicine bag. "Present, willing, and…what was that last one?"

"Able, sir."

"I am," said the doctor, hoisting his cane, and the surrounding men gave him a rousing cheer.

"When both adversaries have fired their shot," Charles continued, "the aforementioned disagreement shall be constituted null and void, and both parties, dead or alive, shall no longer carry the grievance forward. Are there any questions?"

"Yes, what's the difference between null and void?" I asked, stalling like a son of a gun.

"That is not a valid question, sir!" Charles snapped.

"I am prepared to settle this matter," Phineas stated with old-time resolve.

"Prepare to pace."

I tried to ready myself, but who was I kidding? If I could go out without soiling myself, that would be heroic enough.

"Forward — pace!"

You've done a lot of dumb-ass things before, I scolded myself, *but at least they were on film. My family won't even get the pleasure of watching me die, in slow motion, on national TV over and over and over. Okay, Mr. Actor Boy, You'd better run through all those cheeseball action films you were in, and think of some way to win this gunfight.*

As I paced off the twenty steps, I cursed the fact that I had never actually owned a gun. I didn't know how to aim that clumsy thing to save my life, despite the fact that that was exactly what was at stake. Pretty much every fight I'd ever been in had been resolved through stuntmen, sound effects, and judicious editing.

Being in films like *McHale's Navy* didn't help either, because I had used a fifty-caliber machine gun as a weapon, not a flintlock. The same reasoning applied for films like *Moontrap, Assault on Dome Four*, and *In the Line of Duty: Blaze of Glory* — in each case, I used a semi- or fully automatic weapon. Even in *The Adventures of Brisco County Jr.*, a western, I fired a single-action six-shooter, and you at least had six tries to kill the guy.

What I wouldn't give for that sucker, right now, I lamented. *I knew I should have purchased it on eBay last year.*

"And halt!" Charles yelled to us, now farther away.

Okay, okay, think — what would my stunt pal Johnny Casino do right now? He'd drop to the ground and gut-shoot him, or he'd throw up some dust, just enough to cloud the opponent and give him that extra second to aim, or he'd scream and charge straight forward, freaking the guy out, forcing him to take a poorly aimed shot. It's a gamble, but if he missed, you'd have a huge edge — he'd be out of bullets, and by the time you shot back, you'd already be ten paces closer to the mark.

"Prepare to fire!" Charles shouted with a terrifying seriousness.

Though I still hadn't figured out what I was going to do, my thoughts grew unusually lucid, particularly for an actor. Why must we always resort to violence when resolving disputes? Even though anger is a strong emotion and crimes of passion are many, we all know that violence only breeds more violence in an endless cycle of misery. That's it! I just won't take part in it. I'll do what Martin Luther King, or Jesus, or Gandhi would do — I'll resist violence, no matter what the cost.

Charles sucked in his breath and shouted, "Fire!"

As I turned, I made no attempt to raise my flintlock. Instead, I chose to greet my adversary with a smile. Even as Phineas T. Lee raised his flintlock in anger against me, with the full intention of inflicting great harm, I just looked at him, eye to eye, man to man, and hurled thoughts of peace, not a lead ball made in some death factory. I knew that even if my mortal body was taken away and forgotten in days to come, my gesture of peace was spiritual, and would remain undimmed forever.

The bastard fired his flintlock anyway. The ball hit me square in the chest, blowing me off my feet.

"Wooooh!" a unified cheer rang out. The men were very pleased with the outcome. Phineas threw his arms into the air, and a mob of joyous members rushed toward him in congratulation.

"Good gentlemen, in accordance with the rules and regulations of this society I, Charles Butler, hereby terminate this dispute. Phineas T. Lee shall go on record as the moral victor, and the name of the imposter, Mr. Bruce Campbell, who willfully misrepresented himself to be one Hubert Hightower, shall be stricken from the records so as not to sully the storied history of our esteemed organization!"

"Hurrah!" the men shouted in unison, many launching their top hats into the air. Phineas was hoisted up like a victorious football coach and paraded about.

My senses began to shut down, as if someone had wiped Vaseline over my eyes and shoved cotton in my ears. As I struggled to stay conscious, I saw a blurred image of the old doctor, kneeling down to attend to me. As he squatted, he couldn't help but release a healthy fart.

"Pardon me, young man," he said, rummaging through his bag for a stethoscope. "Of course, you've got more to worry about than an old man's flatulence, I'll tell you that."

I could make out the shine off the doctor's naked head, as he listened for my heartbeat. After a moment, suspended in time, he slowly shook it in resignation. "Not much I can do for him."

Losing strength, my head fallen to the side, I got a wonderful whiff of the freshly cut grass, always one of my favorite smells. *My lawn in Oregon never looked this good,* I thought.

Then, everything went black.

Beep-beep-beep — the EKG machine marked out time with my heartbeat. It was weak, slowed by pharmaceuticals and trauma. My mouth was so dry, my tongue had fused to the side of my mouth. I opened my eyes to see a dark, bland hospital room. I assumed that this was better than being in an operating room with five worried doctors racing about, pounding away on peoples' chests, yelling things like, "We can't just give up!"

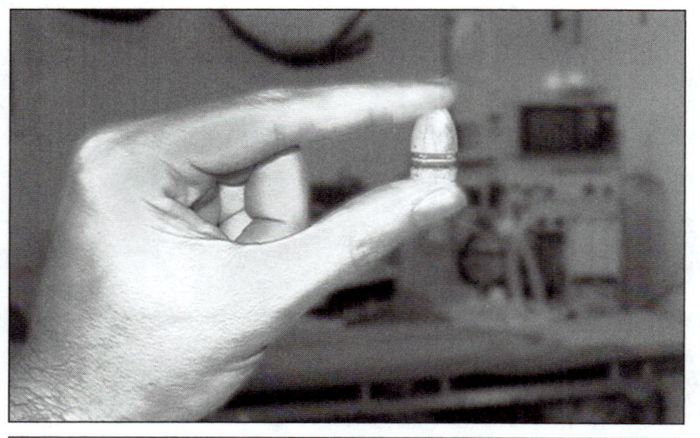

Now, acting isn't the only thing I have in common with Ronald Reagan.

In movies, the hospital room is also the place where you get the "you've got seven minutes to live" news, or the "I did everything I could, but..." news. That day it was the "you're a very lucky man, Mr. Campbell" news.

"How do you figure?" I asked. "I've been mortally wounded. I'm dying in a hospital."

"Well, you *are* in a hospital," said the attending doctor, "but your wound isn't exactly mortal, and you're nowhere near death."

I looked around the room again, this time with a clearer head. There were no sobbing relatives, no Billy Graham, and thankfully, no lawyers. "How come I'm not dead? Last time I checked, I was inhaling grass clippings and the big light was coming."

"You've suffered a major trauma, no doubt, but what I mean by lucky is that the ball from Mr. Lee's pistol glanced off your metal medallion. It didn't even break the skin."

Saved by the fact that I wasn't a member, I thought, smiling. "Then why do I feel like I've been hit with a baseball bat?"

"That's essentially what happened. The force of the bullet pushed the medallion into your chest and fractured your sternum."

"My sternum? How long is that going to take to heal?"

"It's not really broken, but you're not going to want do a whole lot for a couple of weeks."

"Is it always going to be this painful?"

"Only when you breathe."

"Excuse, me, doctor?" a nurse said from the doorway. "Mr. Campbell has a visitor — a very distraught young man. He says he only needs a minute."

The doctor looked back to me for approval and I shrugged. "What the hell, as long as I'm not dying."

The "young man" happened to be Skip, the hapless busboy whose sharp eye and big mouth had precipitated my current condition. He entered the room, trembling. "M-m-m-mister Campbell," he said, eyes red from crying, "I am *soooo* sorry about all this. If I would have known that I, of all people, was responsible for you getting killed —"

"It's all right, Skip, I'm not dead yet."

"If there's anything you need here, any kind of treatment at all, you just let me know, and I'll make sure you get it."

"What, do you own the place?" I asked, not even trying to hide my smirk.

"No, but my dad does," Skip said, casually pointing to a sign which read Phineas T. Lee Center for Advanced Medicine. "And if it's any consolation, he feels pretty bad that he actually shot you."

"Wait a second," I said, with enough agitation to cause the *beep-beep-beeps* on my heart monitor to speed up. "You mean to tell me that Phineas Lee not only owns this hospital, but you're his son?"

"Right on both counts."

"I thought you said you were from Michigan?"

Skip hesitated for a moment. "Well, see, I'm his *other* son," he whispered, "the one he doesn't talk about. But he takes pretty good care of me, so you just say the word if you need anything."

"I sure will, Skip. Thanks."

"So, no hard feelings?"

"No," I said, reassuring him.

Skip's mood improved dramatically and he actually smiled. "Cool, then if it isn't too much trouble, could you sign my *Army of Darkness* poster?"

My first inclination was to tell this fan boy where to shove his poster, but I recalled the advice of Skip's old man, Phineas T. Lee himself, about what a true gentleman would do in this situation.

"Sure thing, Skip," I said, flexing my signing hand. "It's the gentlemanly thing to do."

8

A Dash of Dash

I was having one of those phone dreams, the kind where the phone keeps ringing, but you know it's just a dream so you don't answer it — until you realize that it's not a dream.

RRRRRIIIIIIINNNNNNGGG!

I swatted at my cell phone, trying desperately to launch it off the nightstand, but the room was pitch black, and I didn't even know what state I was in. After about a minute of flailing with the covers, searching for a light switch, and swearing loudly, I managed to locate my cell phone.

"Okay, who died?"

"I'm sorry, did I wake you?"

I glanced at the clock. "At four o'clock in the morning? Hell no, I'm usually on my second breakfast by now. By the way, who is this?"

"Richard."

"Gere?"

"Yes. I'm sorry to call this early, but I had to talk to you about something."

"Okay...."

"I'm worried about scene forty-one A."

"Oh, I've got it right here," I said, snidely. "Hang on, lemme find it."

I lumbered groggily through my disaster of a hotel room. Weeks on location can be devastating, creating logjams of personal stuff in a room that always feels like it's shrinking. Rounding the foot of the bed I bashed my knee on a protruding piece of luggage, then limped to my "executive desk," where the *Let's Make Love!* screenplay lay under a stack of unpaid bills.

"Okay…I'm back," I announced, returning to bed, but there was no response. "Hello?"

SpentPCS

Charges for: BRUCE CAMPBELL
555-555-5555
bcact@aol.com

	Date	Time	Phone Number	Call Destination	Caller ID Alias	Duration
36	4/15	10:12 PM	310-555-4373	Incoming	Gere, R	10
37	4/15	11:48 AM	310-555-4373	Incoming	Gere, R	32
38	4/16	12:39 AM	310-555-4373	Incoming	Gere, R	1
39	4/16	12:46 AM	310-555-4373	Incoming	Gere, R	8
40	4/16	1:28 AM	310-555-4373	Incoming	Gere, R	5
41	4/16	1:37 AM	310-555-4373	Incoming	Gere, R	10
42	4/16	1:47 AM	310-555-4373	Incoming	Gere, R	2
43	4/16	1:49 AM	310-555-4373	Incoming	Gere, R	4
44	4/16	2:14 AM	310-555-4373	Incoming	Gere, R	5
45	4/16	2:25 AM	310-555-4373	Incoming	Gere, R	3
46	4/16	2:33 AM	310-555-4373	Incoming	Gere, R	1
47	4/16	3:11 AM	310-555-4373	Incoming	Gere, R	9
48	4/16	3:23 AM	310-555-4373	Incoming	Gere, R	9
49	4/16	3:44 AM	310-555-4373	Incoming	Gere, R	4
50	4/16	4:10 AM	310-555-4373	Incoming	Gere, R	7
51	4/16	4:27 AM	310-555-4373	Incoming	Gere, R	3
52	4/16	4:55 AM	310-555-4373	Incoming	Gere, R	1
53	4/16	4:56 AM	310-555-4373	Incoming	Gere, R	10
54	4/16	5:07 AM	310-555-4373	Incoming	Gere, R	6
55	4/16	5:29 AM	310-555-4373	Incoming	Gere, R	123
56	4/16	8:03 AM	310-555-4373	Incoming	Gere, R	5
57	4/16	8:36 AM	310-555-4373	Incoming	Gere, R	43
58	4/16	10:01 AM	310-555-4373	Incoming	Gere, R	4
59	4/16	10:05 AM	310-555-4373	Incoming	Gere, R	201

"I'm here," Richard said. "I was just meditating. Do you meditate, Bruce?"

"Not really. Whenever I try, I fall asleep."

"Then you're not concentrating hard enough."

"My mother said the same thing. Hey, so, scene forty-one A...."

"It's where I pick up Debbie for the first time."

"Yeah, it's kinda cute. What about it? I'm not even in it."

"I'm just not sure if I can pull it off."

I clicked the light up another notch and glanced at the scene.

"What's to pull off? You're calm and cool, you've got some good lines and you sweep her off her feet. You'll be out of there by lunch."

"It's not that simple. I've never picked up a woman before."

I held the phone away from my face. Sometimes you have to do that to get enough perspective during weird conversations. "Are you saying what I think you are, Richard?"

"I'm saying that I've never had to *try*."

"Oh, meaning that you never had to pick up a woman, because they were always picking you up."

"Exactly."

"Never?"

"No."

"You're breakin' my heart."

"Bruce, this really is an issue," he explained sincerely. "I never planned for my life to turn out this way, but there's nothing I can do about it."

"But, you know, Richard, the words are on the page for you, it's not like you have to make it up or anything. That's the beauty of being an actor — somebody else does most of the work for us."

"Then you don't know Mike Nichols," Richard said firmly. "A script to him is a rough guide. I know what's going to happen — after the first take, he's going to see right through my charade, and he'll throw out the words and force us to ad-lib, and I'm gonna be dead."

I didn't respond to Richard right away because I was too busy being amazed that even big actors have the same, silly fears that little actors do. It was both reassuring and terrifying at the same time, because Mike had essentially threatened me the same way.

"Now, your character would help me, Bruce," Richard continued. "And if you take this film seriously, you'll help me too."

"Okay, sure, but help you do what? Ad-lib?"

"No, help me pick up a woman."

I let that one hang in the air for a beat or two. "You're serious, aren't you?"

"I called you at four in the morning, didn't I?"

"Good point. But, you know, if you're looking for advice on how to snag a babe, you're better off talking to your real doorman, because I don't know shit about that world — just ask my wife."

"It's okay, you can still help," Richard said. "I need to find an expert, and I hear you've been running rings around us all in the research department."

"Oh, well, uh, what's your budget?"

"It doesn't matter, I'm dyin' here...."

"Okay, I'll get back to you."

I gave Richard a lot of credit. The majority of men are cowards — they're afraid to admit that they don't know their way around women. Mostly, they love to brag about their conquests, and while these boasts are almost always highly inflated — if not completely imaginary — not long ago, I had met a guy from Las Vegas who appeared to have some legitimate claim to the title of "King of all Ladies' Men."

I'd been to Las Vegas a bunch of times, hawking everything from horror DVDs to a western TV show, mainly because it's a popular place to hold conventions and stage huge promotional events. People love to mix business with massive quantities of gambling, booze, and sex, and Vegas is popular because it makes all three very convenient.

As a city, it's all about contrast — streets that are inconceivably hot, and casinos that are unfathomably cold. My emotional response to Vegas always takes the same form: horror, exhilaration, disorientation, amusement, then finally circling back around to horror. All in all, I can ake or leave the place, but it's perfect for a guy like Dash Darwin.

I met Dash when I was in town to premiere an Elvis/mummy film :alled *Bubba Ho-Tep* at the Las Vegas International Film Festival. At a ›ost-screening "afterglow," Dash had cornered me in order to pitch a novie based on his lifetime of sexual exploits. I thought he was perhaps he biggest B.S. artist I had ever met, but by the end of the night, almost ›very woman in the room — and there were some outstanding exhibits – had stopped to pay their respects.

The man had been *around*. I had to give him that.

Dash was the perfect teacher for Richard, but Richard wasn't the ›erfect student for Dash — mainly because he was too perfect. The :hiseled jaw, the rugged chin, the molten eyes — if I was going to help iim experience what it was really like to try and pick up a woman, he'd iave to undergo an "extreme makeover" — *in reverse*.

Fortunately for Richard, I could, in fact, help him out. Having undergone special effects makeup of all sorts over the years, I had a few ;trings to pull.

Melanie Tooker, Richard Gere — Richard, Melanie."

"Mel" extended her hand oward Richard Gere. As ı special-effects makeup ırtist, she had worked with nany "name" actors, but I :ould tell she was nervous around this particular one.

Just one of the ways Dash Darwin gets some ass.

"Charmed," Richard said, kissing the back of Mel's hand.

We had gathered in Mel's converted warehouse in Chatsworth, California, home of her "Ten Thousand Faces" workshop, to assess the situation.

Mel smiled unabashedly as she studied Richard's face. "Gee, in all the years I've done this, I never had to make a gorgeous man average."

Richard blushed, which is perhaps one of his many attractive qualities to women. It caused Mel to blush, and I must admit, even brought a little color to my face.

"Okay, Melanie, so the idea here is to make me look, not ugly, per se, but just not at all like myself," Richard explained. "Like I could sell insurance or something."

Mel walked us to a nearby computer, with a scan of Richard's face on the screen. "When I heard you wanted to do this, I did some renderings, and morphed your image with a picture I had on file. So we would go from this, to..."

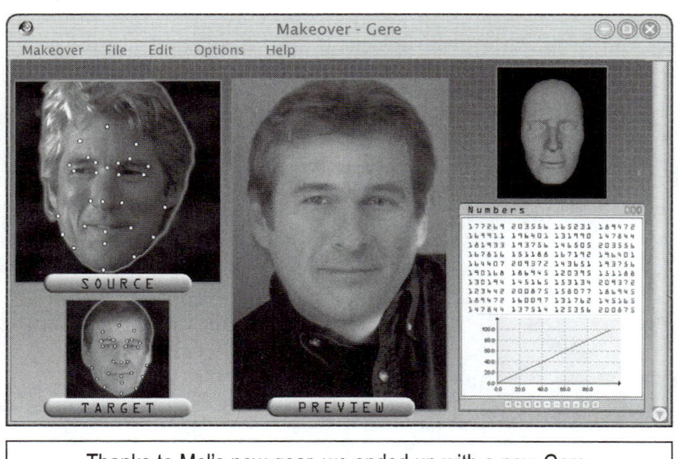

Thanks to Mel's new gear, we ended up with a new Gere.

Mel double-clicked on an icon, and a wonderfully bland version of Richard popped up on the screen. His features were similar, but dulled down enough to make him completely forgettable.

"...this."

"That's amazing, Melanie," Richard remarked, impressed. "Who did you combine me with?"

"An old boyfriend. And just so you know, he couldn't get laid to save his life."

"Perfect," Richard nodded. "Let's do it — make me unlayable!"

The amazing Dash Darwin swung open the door of his penthouse.

"Dash Darwin, you old dog," I said, offering my hand. "Great to see you again."

"Lemme see," Dash calculated, "that was about three hundred and fifty-two women ago...."

"Hey, that's between you and your STDs."

Dash laughed, then looked at Richard, who until now had been invisible.

"Is this our guinea pig?"

I pushed Richard forward. "Sure is — Little Dickie Simpson is his name."

Richard shot me a look like he was going to murder me in my sleep, but we hadn't thought of a name for him and I had to act fast.

"People call me... *Richie*," Richard added.

"Hey, Richie, Dick, it's all the same to me," Dash chuckled, slapping Richard on the back. "C'mon in, let me fix you boys a martini and show you the pad."

As Dash led us to his wet bar, which was outfitted like Appleby's, I cased out his biggie-size bachelor pad. The place fit right in with Las Vegas because everything about it was exaggerated.

"If you don't mind my asking," Richard asked meekly, "how did the label 'Mother of all Ladies' Men' come to be?"

"*Macho Magazine* labeled me that," Dash said, maneuvering behind the bar like a pro. "They took a poll of women in fifty-five cities who they thought was the best date they ever had — and I had the most votes. Two hundred and forty-four different women recommended me That was a record," he said with pride, pouring tall martinis. "Hey, how about we take the nickel tour? For starters, we're in what I call the Entertainment Room. I designed it so the sound system can be different levels in different parts of the room."

Dash walked to a massive electronic control panel. "Atmosphere is the key," he said. "To woo a woman I need three nights. That requires three progressive programs, because each mood needs visual, audio and sensory support. Check out program number one."

Dash hit a button and recessed lights came up full. The room really sparkled. Richard had a little notebook and was writing furiously.

"If you are meeting a woman for the first time, the room has to be light and bright. Safe. I use no filtration at all. She looks around and sees that the place is clean and that I have nothing to hide — except the *Playboy*s. And those go here...."

Dash walked to the garbage can under the wet bar and pulled up the plastic bag.

"Under the trash bag in the garbage can. No first date will ever look there."

Dash closed his eyes. "Notice the music? It's upbeat, progressive harmless. She's going to feel good about herself, pumped by the music I also cool the place down, to maybe sixty-eight degrees. It makes my lady feel like it's okay to keep her clothes on. Anything less can restrict blood flow, and I'll say no more about that."

"Dash, what's your theory on first-date libations?" Richard inquired.

"I'll offer her an iced tea, or maybe a nice buttery chardonnay. You have to match the mood. As much as I like vodka and tonic, I'm not gonna be pushing that right out of the gate. Men are notoriously impatient. I have found that if you show even a little restraint, she'll be a over you. For the second date, program number two."

Dash hit a button, and the lights dimmed selectively. The mood was decidedly subdued.

"To achieve this 'warm' look, the lights are filtered with an amber gel. This tells the woman that the place is not only safe, but it's comfortable. She can kick off her shoes and spend an evening chatting in front of the fire. We talk about more personal things, about hopes and dreams. We get past the basics."

"And the music would be different too," Richard assumed.

"The music is still going to be progressive, but slower. It's not going to pressure her to feel sexy, but it's going to relax her. I'll turn the temperature up to seventy-two. As a libation, I would move into the red wines, maybe a nice port after dinner. She gets a little tipsy, but she's still in control."

Richard, an apt pupil, was like a sponge. "And phase three?"

"For the third date, otherwise known as the move-in-for-the-kill date, I pull out all the stops."

Dash hit several new buttons and the lights lowered half as much again. The room was transformed before our eyes.

"It'll take about thirty seconds for your retina to adjust," Dash said, walking around his love nest, gesturing. "For Date Number Three, I use darker colors. Reds and blues now take over the amber hues. The music is full-on Barry White–style seduction. She

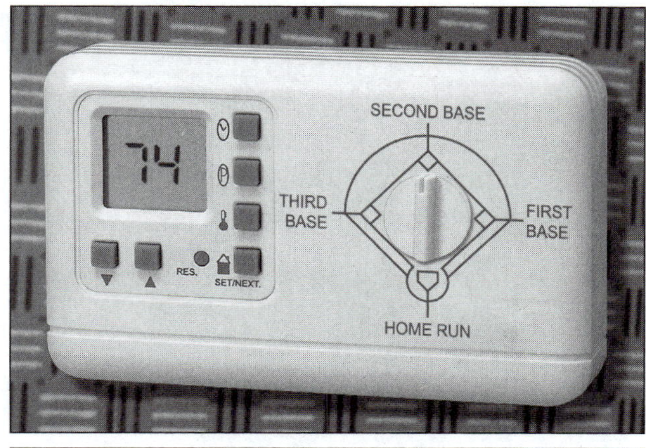

The real reason your father never let you touch the thermostat.

sees that I'm not in a hurry, but she'll know that I'm also a man with needs like every other man. The temperature will rise to seventy-four clinically proven to feel comfortable in lingerie. To calm her nerves, I'l go for the full-strength drink. It'll be something dark, like the room — maybe an aged whisky."

Richard nodded. I couldn't tell if he was impressed, or simply bewil dered by the human condition. "Looks like you have it all figured out Dash."

"Maybe not all, Richie, but I have created a 'romance pattern' tha works for me."

"Do you take the same amount of pains with your clothes? I noticec that your robe is quite elaborate. Is that silk?"

Richard was referring to his fire-engine-red satin bathrobe with Larry King–style padded shoulders, black piping, and deep pockets on each side.

"Satin, actually," Dash correct ed. "Silk gives me a rash. I had i tailored special. Ladies like it wher a man puts himself together."

I couldn't help but ask, "Bu what's the distinction between 'pu together' and 'overdone'?"

"I'll put it to you this way: mos men can't match colors, fabrics, o layers, so they just don't do it Women have had to lower thei standards over the years as a result. If a man puts himself togeth er — his socks match, he has a belt, there are no stains on his shirt — he will distinguish himself from the others."

Richard raised a finger. "Excuse me, is blow-dried hair necessary?"

"You bet. That's why I installed a 'preparation zone.'"

Richard began to write on the back of his spiral notebook pages as we moved from Dash's three-program entertainment room to his elaborate bathroom. The lights revealed an oversize personal hygiene bunker with all the trimmings.

"This is where the magic happens," Dash said, gesturing to the dual-head, multispray contraption. "A night out all begins with a good shower. I take three a day. Cleanliness is rule number one with chicks. If a guy stinks, he's history. That's why I use a hypoallergenic, antibacterial, antifungal soap."

Ever since moving into the bathroom, with its surgical lighting, I couldn't take my eyes off Dash's hair. That mane belonged to another species. The color wasn't just black, it was a raven blue-black, the color Richard Burton used in *Exorcist II* to look young and vibrant again. It's also impossible for humans to have that color naturally.

"How do you get your hair into that shape?" I realized it was something like the style used by the Big Boy restaurant mascot — equal parts Superman and Jethro.

"This? I've been practicing good hair technique since I was a teenager. I've got this down to about forty-five minutes."

Dash looked at Richard and cocked his head in thought. "Can I be frank with you?"

"Sure."

"Let's fix the hair," Dash said, gesturing to the mirror in front of Richard. "What kind of a style is that? Snoresville, that's what. For starters, you have nothing in it. You can't manage hair without product of some sort," he said, opening one of his many cabinets to reveal every hair product ever manufactured.

"Richie, your hair isn't going to be the same every day, and your hair needs aren't going to be the same either. But you can fight it with science. If your hair is feeling listless, you can perk it right up with KUP2 firming gel. If your hair is getting thin, you can fatten it up with Largess. If you're going outside, and it's going to be bad weather, you can set it in place with Perm-HLD fastening treatment."

Dash pulled out a tube of Natra-Gel, squeezed some of the clear goo into his hand, and massaged it into Richard's limp hair.

"Tonight, let's go with a look that says I just played half court with my pals — and now, I want to hang out and meet some ladies."

"A hair goo can say all that?" Richard marveled.

"The right one at the right time can," Dash said with a wink of assurance. "Something for every mood. But enough about hair...."

Dash flung open a new cabinet. Inside were a number of colognes. "A man's scent is as important as anything."

"Whoa," Richard said, reeling from the waft of aromas.

I stifled a sneeze.

"Cologne is the front line of communication between the sexes. What essence do you want to present to the woman you are dating?"

"That I'm...relatively clean?" Richard guessed.

"No," Dash insisted. "Tonight, you want to exude confidence, humor and a wild spirit, yet with responsible undertones."

"One single scent can do that?"

"I shit you not," Dash said, producing a vintage bottle of Bru cologne. He held it up like a successful lab experiment. "The scent of kings."

Dash unscrewed the lid and held it toward Richard's nose. "Don't tel ne you never wore Brut?"

"I did wear it — once," Richard admitted. "But Brut made me feel ike a loser."

"You mean a loser like Elvis?" Dash asked, challenging.

"He wore Brut?"

"And Hai Karate for a while, during his Hawaii comeback phase."

"But, Dash," Richard interjected, I guess that what I still don't understand is, do you wear things, n this case, cologne, because you ike it, or do you wear it because 'ou think a woman will like it?"

"It depends on the type of woman I want to snare."

"You sound like you're going hunting."

"In a manner of speaking, I am. I use Brut primarily because it vorked for the King, and I happen to enjoy the smell. If I just want to ave sex, I'll wear yak scent."

Dash pulled a small, blue-tinted bottle out of his scent repository and ook a whiff. "In very small doses, the scent a male yak emits when he's ooking for a mate drives the chicks wild. Take my word, it works. I just lon't care for the smell."

"I'll pass on the yak."

"I would too," Dash agreed. "Saturday night in Vegas. You don't need he big guns — dames are gonna be falling out of the trees. Oh, I lmost forgot — the medicine cabinet."

Dash opened a hospital-style dispensary near the sink. Inside was every form of male "booster" in liquid, powder, and pill form.

"Time for my fun pack. I start with adrenal gland — it gets the testes going. Yohimbe is next. It's a bark from Africa. Shwing, shwing, ba-da bing!"

Dash emphasized his point with a stiff forearm in the air, fis clenched. Richard turned to me with a look of horror. Dash popped the pill and turned his attention back to the cabinet.

"Siberian ginseng — the root for *your* root, as they say. Tons of gar lic. It gets the blood pumping, know what I mean? And zinc to keep the reproductive chemicals in balance. Plus a buttload of vitamin E because a guy has to have something to show for his manly efforts doesn't he?"

"Are you referring to your 'essence'?" Richard asked, mildly appalled.

Dash winked and saluted. "On standby to replenish, sir," and he popped the pill. He then pulled a small vial from the top shelf of the cab inet and shook a substantial blue pill into his palm. "And finally," Dash said, checking his watch, "timing is everything with this little puppy."

Dash's lion's den.

"Oh, my, you have the Big Blue," I said, gawking at what was surely Viagra in Dash's hand.

"Harder by the yard." Dash downed the blue wonder pill and smiled. "I'm a slam dunk to have a little filly back here in two hours."

"And if not, you'd better crack open the *Playboys*," I said, "because you've had enough male stimulant to raise the dead."

Dash didn't want to talk about it anymore. "Come on, boys, we're trying to get Richie here a lady, and we haven't even gotten to clothes yet."

We followed Dash to his adjoining bedroom. I walked behind Richard, which proved difficult, because the Brut had removed all oxygen in its wake.

"This is my lair."

Dash wasn't kidding — his four-poster bed had lion heads on each corner.

"Lions are a symbol of masculinity."

"Where's the deer head?" Richard asked, half joking.

"Behind you."

Sure enough, we turned to see an enormous elk head with a twelve-point rack hanging above the bathroom.

Dash stepped into his walk-in closet. Outside, I heard a very muffled "Come on in."

He had an entire room devoted to the maintenance and storage of clothes. It was almost a closed-loop clothing operation with items you could only find in professional dry cleaning operations: a deluxe washer/dryer, a large folding table, a professional-grade pressing machine, ironing board, steamer and even a shoeshine machine.

"Level with me, Bruce," Richard whispered to me, half impressed, half horrified. "Are we on one of those reality shows? Am I being…what's the word? 'Punked'?"

Dash slid back a mirrored door to reveal a collection of undergarments that would rival an Asian sweatshop. "If you feel good underneath, you feel good on the outside."

"You aren't one of those purple minibrief guys, are you?" I asked.

"I wear an assortment of underwear. Am I fond of briefs? Yes. Why, you're a boxer man?"

"Not really, I like a good hybrid. I don't like the cheek squeeze of briefs, but I also don't like the wrap-around-your-leg effect that boxers have."

Dash pulled out a small pair of black briefs. "I hear you, but I need something to keep my package in line."

"Didn't I hear something about briefs and lowered sperm count?" Richard challenged.

Dash shook his head. "That was just propaganda from Fruit of the Loom." He plucked out a black tank-top T-shirt and tossed it at Richard. "Put that on under your shirt. It'll give you a multilayered look. You'll appear more fascinating — one part of you is loose and light, the other is tight and dark."

Richard rolled his eyes, but he took off his dress shirt and put on the black T.

Dash walked over to a huge Lazy Susan and spun it around until he found a pair of black socks. "Socks have to be as slim as possible," Dash explained. "I want to be able to slip out of my shoes fast, because the last thing you need when some hot momma is ready to party is clingy loafers!"

Dash walked to the next and revealed a row of slacks, a row of sport coats, and a row of shirts, half of them dress, half of them Hawaiian.

"Tonight, we're going to the Pink Flamingo. It's not a formal place. I did some recon ahead of time. It's mainly bright colors, with an international flair. No sweat."

Dash pushed a button, and the row of pants started to move. He snagged a black pair off the rack and tossed it to Richard over his shoulder. "Those will look sharp." The Hawaiian shirts swung around, and Dash picked out a solid pink one, with black piping down the front. He held it up against Richard and the combination was suitably cheesy.

Having taken care of Richard, Dash assembled his own duds. Fully dressed, he looked like he was on his way to a Hamptons garden party — every article of clothing white, from head to toe, including the belt. The only exception (a glaring one) was a black T-shirt.

"The Flamingo is international, so in case you do some dancing, let's get you a shoe with a boxier toe — it's the rage." On the opposite wall, Dash revealed five rows of shoes.

"Are you related to Imelda Marcos?" Richard asked.

Dash, ignoring the jibe, slid back yet another mirrored door, exposing shelf after shelf of hats. "A man is put together from head to toe, my friend," and he picked out a matching pink Frank Sinatra fedora and tried it on Richard.

"Richie" looked put together, in that his pants were a little too tight and a little too short; his shirt was a little too open at the top and a little too wide at the collar and his shoes looked boxy and uncomfortable.

Dash grinned and put his arm around Richard. "Ladies of Las Vegas, watch out!"

The Pink Flamingo Bar was one of those ridiculous Vegas joints where the combination of money and grand ideas don't always go together.

Personally, I think the decision to put a forty-foot-tall pink flamingo in front of this place was premature, but as a navigational aid, you can't beat it. I bet one hears, "Turn left at the big flamingo" a lot around here.

Inside, The Flamingo was a meat-market extraordinaire of mostly twenty-somethings but, because it was Las Vegas, plenty of forty-somethings as well, looking for a fling.

The ratio of women to men was really high, maybe sixty-five to thirty-five. Most of the women wore very little clothing, but compensated with lots of makeup. The men sported clothes from the casino gift shops and fresh burns from an afternoon at the martini-shaped pool.

Horribly Ineffective Pick-Up Lines

WARNING: These DO NOT work!

- How'd you like gain 165 pounds for about six minutes?
- Is your father an astronaut because I sure am horny.
- Drunk yet?
- I may not be the best looking guy in here, but I'm the only one talking to you.
- They just called last call, and I'm out of options.
- My apartment is being fumigated. We should screw.
- Quick while my wife's back is turned!
- Your name must be Daisy because I sure am horny.
- So, are you the fat friend or what?
- Anybody else here live with their parents?
- Personally, I found *The Fountainhead* to be a bit pedestrian.
- I designed Bruce Campbell's website.

We walked toward the expansive bar. Dash was in his element. "Right off the bat, Richie, you gotta become the bartender's best friend, and the best way to do that is grease their palm." Dash slapped a twenty on the bar. A cute bartender spotted it and hustled over. Dash winked at me.

"Evening, gents, what can I get for you?" she asked.

"A cold drink and a hot bartender. What's your name?" Dash asked smoothly.

"Misty."

"You can play me all night, sweetie," Dash said with surprising charm. Like any good salesman, Dash believed every word he said.

"What can I get for you?" Misty repeated, not changing her tone.

"A Pink Flamingo, baby," Dash said, winking.

I looked at my watch. Thirty minutes had passed already since he dropped that Blue Bomb on his system. He was going to be doing a lot more than winking pretty soon.

"What's in a Pink Flamingo?" Richard asked.

"It's the house specialty," Dash said, smiling. "Rum, vodka, gin, scotch, bourbon, triple sec, and a dash of bitters."

"Sounds like a heap of hurt to me," I said. "I'll take an Amstel Light."

Dash immediately went into scope mode. "I like this place because the bar is a semicircle. Do you know what's good about that?"

"You can see every lonely guy across the way?" Richard guessed.

"If your glass is half empty you will," Dash scolded. "No, you can see all the available chicks."

Dash was right on this occasion. Circling around us was an impressive array of women, mainly grouped in twos and threes, though scattered among them were also plenty of singles.

Richard turned to Dash, all business. "Okay, so Dash, let's have it. What's the secret of the pickup?"

"I'm not gonna tell you, Richie, I'm gonna *show* you. Okay, see that blonde over there?"

Dash pointed to a woman who was very tan, very blonde. Her clothing and makeup were both sparkly. She seemed a likely target.

"I'm gonna do the ol' bait and switch."

Richard furrowed his brow. "Is that a card trick?"

"No, it's where I'm *not* gonna try and pick her up. Here, watch. I'm gonna talk about anything other than her or me. I'll sit on her left. You go around the other way and sit on her right — and get your little notepad out."

Dash looked at his watch and took a shot of breath spray. Richard circled around and sat to the right of the blonde, trying not to make eye contact. I parked myself nearby on a stool, strategically positioned to observe the play-by-play and help myself to a bowl of Chex party mix.

Dash took a seat on the blonde's left. She knew she was surrounded, but remained remarkably cool. Dash did his best to mind his own business, so the threesome sat, ignoring each other.

Eventually, the blonde spoke first and, surprisingly, to Richard.

"Well, hello," she said, in a very friendly tone.

The way she added "well" in front of "hello" gave it a slightly different meaning. Richard made contact with her piercing blue eyes.

"Good evening," Richard said, trying to be Mr. Regular Guy in a Bar.

"Where's your ring?" the woman asked.

"That's a mighty big assumption," Richard said, truly surprised. "I'm Richie, by the way."

"Richie what?"

"Richie Gere-er-ing," he stumbled, trying to ad-lib a last name.

"That's nice. What brings you to Vegas?"

Dash shot Richard a "why are you talking to her?" look.

"Oh, I'm just here visiting friends," Richard explained casually. "What is your name?"

"Tonight, my name is…Anastasia, Richie," she said, placing a delicate finger on his lips. "I love the way my lips move when I say your name. Riccchhhiee," she whispered, puckering up lasciviously.

Over the blonde's shoulder, Dash was giving the hunched, palms in the air, "what the fuck?" look.

Richard stared for a moment at his stunning blonde friend, glanced at Dash, and said something that (for him) was an utterly foreign phrase. "Will you…come home with me?"

"I'll get my purse," "Anastasia" said, halfway out of her chair.

Richard smiled infectiously and mouthed "thank you" as he passed me.

Dash watched in shock and awe. "That son of a bitch shattered my land speed record of 2 minutes and 38 seconds."

I watched "Richie" and his date leave the Flamingo, and marveled. "Well, Dash, don't be too hard on yourself. After all, you lost out to Richard Gere."

"What are you talking about?" Dash asked, still miffed.

"My buddy Richie — he was Gere in disguise."

"Get out of here."

I nodded yes.

"Well no wonder he got the chick," Dash rationalized. "He's a god-damn Hollywood movie star — I can't compete with that."

Dash glanced at his watch nervously. More precious time had elapsed. "Shit, I'm about to turn into a pumpkin."

Dash scanned the bar like Robo Cop looking for a mutant sex offender. He zeroed in on a brunette, seated alone. "See that saucy little thing over there with the fabulous bags?"

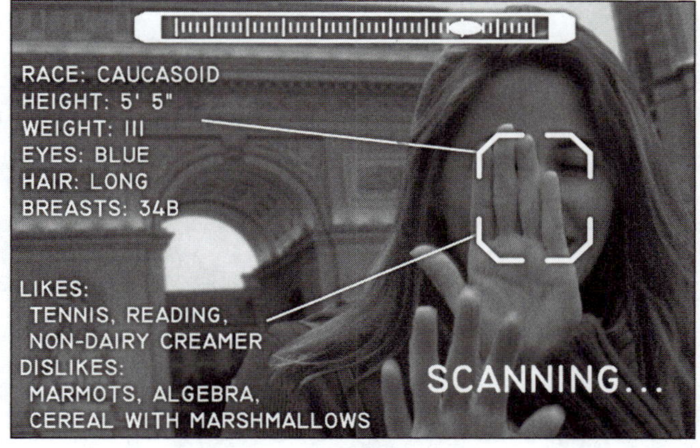

Dash's POV.

"The one with the low-cut dress?"

"Yeah. I'm goin' for the full-court press. Get ready to be impressed."

Dash went for his target, and I circled wide to view from afar. Dash parked it next to the statuesque woman and pulled out his Zippo lighter to fire up a cigarillo, the classy kind with the plastic tip.

"Do you always case out women?" the brunette asked, not particularly upset.

"Can you blame me? If I was you, I'd stalk myself," Dash explained smirking. "But hey, I'll just sit here and mind my own business."

Dash's master plan, of course, was to let his prey make the next move — and she did.

"Where do guys get shirts like that?"

"Oh, this? At the cool-guy clothing store."

"I'd have thought the Salvation Army, because it's so butt-ugly."

By now, any mortal man would have been thrown for a loop, but Dash was not exactly a neophyte at this game. "It's not the shirt that matters, sugar, it's what's *under* it."

And finally, Dash Darwin himself.

"All I see under it is a T-shirt. What's that for, to soak up your sweat?"

Dash was taken aback. This woman obviously had his number.

"And what's that stinky thing? A Tiparillo?"

"A Cigarillo."

"Whatever. It's not a cigar or a cigarette — it can't make up its mind. Christ, my *father* smokes those. He chews on the plastic tip for days."

"Your father is a great man," Dash said defensively.

"My father is a louse. And something smells like a medicine cabinet."

"It happens to be Brut."

"It happens to suck," she said without remorse.

"It was good enough for Elvis."

"Oh, I should have known by your hair — or is that a fright wig? When does the lounge act start, Wayne?"

"Are you referring to Wayne Newton?" Dash said, his hackles rising.

"I am."

"In a negative way?"

"Is there a positive way, Pompadour Pete?" the brunette said, her delivery devastating.

In the middle of this shooting war, I slid the Chex mix a little closer and ordered another Amstel Light.

"Hey, if you haven't got anything nice to say about the King, or the Prince of Vegas, maybe you shouldn't say anything at all."

"Maybe you're right, you hairsprayed, freeze-dried, limp dick."

The brunette grabbed her clutch and left without a further word.

Dash glanced at me, looking beaten and sheepish. "Heh-heh. What can I say? Sometimes it's a good news/bad news scenario: the good news is, she's talking to you — the *bad* news is, she's talking to you. You never know how it's gonna go down...."

Just then, a drop-dead sexy woman sashayed past, nearly giving us whiplash. Dash's reaction was more audible than mine, mostly because two hours had elapsed since he popped Mr. Blue Pill, and something biological was long overdue.

Dash got a look in his eyes that only guys can appreciate. It was the "I'm out of time" look. He pointed at his watch, and mouthed the word *trouble.* A waiter passed with an empty tray, and Dash yanked it from his hand to cover up his *bonis maximus*. As he ran away, a pretty full room got a good idea of why Viagra is regulated.

I decided to walk back to my hotel from the Flamingo. Las Vegas is best after dark, mainly because it's the only time you can walk around outside without feeling like an egg on a giant skillet. Lots of people were on the street, mostly en route to a bar or casino, and I wondered about the games they'd play tonight, trying to pick each other up.

Personally, I think guys like Dash — and we're all Dash to varying degrees — are idiots. His life would be so simple if he stripped off the fake hair, gave up the scents, the color coordinating, and the methodical planning, and never went to places that made him feel desperate. He'd never have to use pickup lines, per se, because he would never try to someone else. He'd save all kinds of money that he could put toward a hobby, which would enrich his life, not just his nightlife, and he'd probably meet someone within a year and settle down forever. Okay, that's not going to happen, but you know what I mean.

Back at the Best Western, I rounded the last corner on the fifth floor and came face-to-face with a polka-dot handkerchief wrapped around the doorknob of our shared room (in a mutual effort to keep the actor's "eye of the tiger," Richard and I decided to bunk together). The prearranged signal was clear: handkerchief on knob = "do not enter" or, in this case, "Richard got laid."

I was happy for him. From an actor's perspective, he really punched through a brick wall, and it was exciting to watch him grow firsthand. But I was so tired I couldn't see straight, so I did what any forlorn roommate would do — I sat my ass on the floor and began to root through the leftovers on his room-service tray. Fortunately, Richard is a classy guy, so there was really good stuff to scavenge — a third of a bottle of Dom Perignon, a half-eaten turkey croissant sandwich (the mayo was easy to scrape off), with white-chocolate-dipped strawberries for dessert. It wasn't easy, but somehow I managed to make it through the night.

9

Dial "M" for Marriage

The crick in my neck from sleeping in the hallway didn't keep me from meeting with Mike in New York the next day. The message on my voice mail was simply that Mike wanted to "talk." Being naturally paranoid, I assumed that I had done something wrong, and booked the earliest flight available.

"Thanks for coming, Bruce. Have a seat."

Mike had this infuriating way of being both cordial and demanding at the same time, but he never had to tell me twice. I sat in a plush chair to one side of his desk.

"Two things. First, thanks for Vegas," Mike said, choosing to remain standing. "Whatever the hell you and Richard did there worked wonders. Richard called me in the middle of the night, exploding with ideas. He's like a kid again. Second, and the main reason why I wanted to talk to you: have you had your 'woohoo' moment yet?"

"My…'woohoo' moment?" I asked, missing his point.

"Yeah. The big breakthrough — the moment when you've skinned the character alive and you finally see what's inside."

"Well, uh, I could lie to you, Mike, but no, I haven't exactly had that moment yet. I didn't know I was supposed to."

Mike took a few commanding steps toward me. He's not a big guy, but he carries himself well. "I don't want a woohoo-less actor in my cast, Bruce. We're getting damn close to shooting, and I want my actors to know where their characters came from, where they're going, and how they got there. Once that portrayal is committed to film, we're all going to have to live with it."

"Yes, sir," I said, sheepishly.

"Now get out there and find your woohoo moment!"

Mike made his point: I had fallen short, again. Foyl was supposed to be a relationship expert. He was happily married and a font of wisdom on that particular topic. I'm on marriage number two, and though I have been joined in matrimony for 18.5 years collectively, it doesn't mean I know the first thing about it.

I knew a horse wrangler one time who had the perfect plan for avoiding the institution of marriage altogether: "You treat 'em [women] real good until you hear 'em talkin' about getting married. When this happens, you gotta do something shitty — I mean *really* shitty — out of nowhere. It'll take 'em awhile to get back to marriage talk after that, and if they do, you just do it all over again. It's kept me out of marriage for years."

I couldn't envision Foyl Whipple dispensing that same advice to Richard Gere. For the sake of *Let's Make Love!* — and perhaps my career — I decided to crawl back into the womb of marriage and experience it with new eyes. I hadn't said a vow in fourteen years, so I figured it wouldn't hurt to get some insight from the pros.

"Let me get this straight, Mr. Campbell, you want to work with us as a wedding planner, but just for one wedding? Isn't that a little unusual?"

"I'm an actor," I said. "I'm just doing research for a part."

Neither Dick Patterson nor Reed White, co-owners of Patterson & White: Your Wedding Planners, seemed reassured. "You're not one of those damn actors who's only in straight-to-video sequels and Sci-Fi Channel movies, are you?"

What could I say? "I won't charge you for my services."

"Uh-huh. Well, that's a little more attractive, but there is the issue of training and capability and liability."

"I'll assume all liability, and as far as capability, you guys don't have a worry in the world."

Dick Patterson turned to his business partner. "Reed, can you believe this fellow wants to walk in here and plan one of our top-end weddings for no particularly good reason?"

"Sounds like a secret camera show to me," Reed said. "How do we know that this isn't some kind of *Caught on Tape* horseshit?"

"Lots of actors have reality shows these days," Dick added.

"Especially ones that haven't had anything new on the air in a few years," Reed said, looking directly at me.

"Hey, guys, this isn't a hidden anything," I explained. "I'm just honing my craft."

The men huddled and whispered to themselves while I continuec the hard sell.

"In fact, you can even video the whole process," I assured them "Use it as promotion for your company — but we'd have to talk if yo ever went national."

As the men talked, they gestured and nodded, sometimes witl emphasis. The overall length of their deliberation wasn't a positive sign so I assumed a no was coming. Suddenly, the intensity of the two mer dissipated. Their huddle relaxed, and Dick came toward me smiling.

"All right, Bruce, you're on board," Dick relayed with a smile. "But i you fuck us over, we'll kneecap you in the parking lot."

I looked at the two businessmen who had owned and operated, fo the past thirty-two years, Patterson and White Weddings in downtowr Columbus, Ohio. There was something very "Detroit" about their warn- ing, in that it also seemed very real.

"Sounds like a good deal to me, fellows," I accepted with a smile "Thanks."

A fan sent me this picture... a weird fan.

Without delay, Dick pulled out a thick folder. "Okay, you've got the Boils — Lance and Jackie. They're getting married Friday the twentieth."

"Holy cow," I blurted, looking at my watch. "That's only two weeks from today."

"That's pretty typical, kid," Reec said. "These bastards come in at the last minute and want everything fo nothing — fast, good, and cheap."

"'Pick any two,' is what I tel

clients," Dick chuckled. "Here's the lowdown: the bride — Jackie Troutman — her old man, Ed, made a ditchload of money by paving half of Columbus. The kid, Lance, doesn't know shit from shine-ola, but he works for her daddy and is next in line to be the paving king."

"Your job as a wedding planner is part sales, part planning," Reed added, playing the second half of the tag team. "This is a big day for these people, right, Dick?"

"Biggest day of their life," Dick shot back, with the timing found only in well-rehearsed routines. "If Daddy is going to spend money on any day in his life, it's going to be on his little girl's wedding day."

"It's actually why we're giving you this gig," explained Dick. "This one's a no-brainer."

"I can see what the kid wants from her," I reasoned, "but what does she get out of him?"

Reed became visibly agitated by my question. "Never do that, kid," he said, with a hint of reprimand in his voice. "Never bring it up. You're part defense lawyer, too. Your client is always innocent and perfect — unless the check bounces, in which case you sue the shit out of them."

"Cash-flow problems aside," Dick added, "the couple-to-be is always a great match. Your personal opinions don't count, and your job is never to question the pairing or the in-laws, just keep the wedding on track."

"It's like working air traffic control," Reed offered. "You don't care what airline they are, as long as they all land safely."

Dick and I looked at each other. Neither of us could make sense out of that scenario.

"It doesn't matter," Reed said, rummaging through his desk. "It's like Mickey Rooney once said: 'As long as the wedding takes place without loss of life, you've succeeded.'" He tossed a hefty wedding catalogue in my lap. "If you're ever having trouble sleeping, this'll do the trick. It's the ultimate marriage bible. You think marriage is about love and happiness? Think again. Marriage is about cakes and catering and stationery and limousines and gifts. Marriage is about moola."

"Marriage isn't a question of 'am I going to spend money?', it's a question of 'how much money am I going to spend?'" Dick said, unconsciously jingling the coins in his pocket.

"It's ugly," Reed agreed, "but it's all part of getting hitched in the modern world."

"For many, marriage is a dream come true," Dick said, walking across the room to me. "At this company, we help make dreams a reality. If our client wants rose petals falling from the sky as they walk down the aisle, even though later that night they're going to beat the crap out of each other, then by God, rose petals it is."

I never saw the dog-eat-dog sales play, *Glengarry Glen Ross*, but I imagined it was kind of like this.

"Sell!" Reed shouted, escalating the energy in the room.

"I will!" I said, pumping a fist in the air.

"Wedding!" Reed yelled.

"Best day of their lives!" I answered.

"Money!" Dick bellowed and the three of us danced around their stuffy office, pumping our fists in the air like the beginning of an Anthony Robbins infomercial.

Dick caught his breath and shoved a piece of paper in my hand. "That's the address to the Troutmans'. They're expecting you at six o'clock sharp for drinks, dinner, and a planning meeting."

"Uh, okay," I said, trying not to appear addled. "Who's going to be there?"

"Everyone."

I wasn't sure if they heard me gasp, but Reed put a reassuring hand on my shoulder. "We'll follow up tomorrow and see how you did. Now get out that door, son," he said, like Knute Rockne, "and plan us a wedding we can all be proud of!"

The Troutman estate had the longest black asphalt driveway I had ever seen — almost half a mile through the rolling hills of northern Columbus. Given Ed's vocation it made sense, but I could have done without the antique Caterpillar bulldozer at the entrance, elevated six feet on huge footings as a monument to the paving industry.

Ed Troutman's house was a sprawling, L-shaped ranch, mid-sixties in its sleek styling. As I swung up in my bug-splattered Ford Explorer, the proprietor himself was the first one out the front door.

"Hey, friend, I didn't hear anything about a Ford coming on my property."

"I'm sorry, are you Ed Troutman?" I asked.

"I am," he said, "but we're not talking about me, we're talking about the Ford, son."

Before Ed could get up to speed, his daughter Jackie, a cute, bubbly young woman of twenty-four, hugged her father from behind. "Oh, Daddy, how would he know we're a Chevy family?"

"He could have called ahead and asked," Ed said, indignant.

Ed Troutman with the occasional mid-grade celebrity.

"I'm Jackie, and this is my daddy, Ed Troutman," she said to me with a smile. "You are most welcome here."

"And hello to you," I said, getting out of the Explorer and offering my hand. "I'm Bruce Ca —" And then it happened again, I realized I hadn't bothered to come up with a fake last name. "I'm Bruce... *Carlson*, I'm the wedding planner."

"We know who you are," Ed said. "Now, pull that car around to the side. I don't want anyone to see a Ford in front of my house."

"Are you from Detroit, sir?"

"Why do you ask?"

"Well, that's where I'm from, and we used to talk like that. Some folks were Ford families, others were Chevy or Chrysler. I know where you're coming from. I came from a Chevy family, too."

"Then why are you driving a goddamn Ford?"

"I bought it off my neighbor in Oregon when the weather was really bad. I lost my head, I wasn't paying attention. I'm sorry, sir."

"You can't do that to your brand, son. It just ain't right. Besides, I'm on the Columbus city council, and Chevy is the largest employer in the metropolitan area, if you catch my meaning. So, pull it around to the side, then come on in and I'll pour you a tall one."

As I walked back to my "goddamn Ford," Jackie gave me a withering smile as if to say, "I know my daddy's an asshole, but he's the only daddy I've got."

Ed Troutman had money, and he knew how to spend it. After meeting his diminutive wife of few words, Pearl, I got a ten-dollar tour of the house from Jackie while Ed supervised the makings of a Tom Collins.

The Troutmans enjoyed a state-of-the-art entertainment room, a big-game trophy room, a wine cellar, sauna, walk-in closets, bathrooms around every corner, and pictures of Ed with politicians, athletes, and the occasional low-to-mid-grade celebrity.

I admired the one with Sonny and Cher. "This one's my favorite. Your dad looks like Clark Gable."

"That's Ed Troutman, he's just larger than life," Jackie sighed.

"How is Lance adjusting?"

"That's an interesting word. I guess I'd say it's a process," Jackie said politely.

This was not the type of family to come out and say, "Lance is a dweeb, Dad is an asshole, and Mom won't say anything about anything."

"Are the Boils due to arrive soon?"

"Yes, we're waiting on the Boils," Jackie said. "We're *always* waiting on the Boils."

=Ding-dong=

Jackie raised her eyebrows. "Not anymore."

The Boils, father Vic and second wife/stepmother Tina, pulled up in a Chevy Nova. I'm sure Ed was very happy about that. Son Lance was right behind in his Pontiac Trans Am. His car wasn't a Chevy, per se, but at least it fell under the General Motors umbrella.

Vic Boil, sporting a thin moustache and a serious comb-over, was a tool-and-die shop manager. Tina, an overweight secretary, worked for the mayor's office, which apparently was a source of friction between her and Ed.

Lance Boil, twenty-seven, and going in every direction at once, was a doofus. He worked as "vice president of sales" under Ed. It wasn't a job he excelled at, but then, he didn't really have to.

As the Boils and the Troutmans converged in Ed's family room, could sense the clash of styles, tastes, and social standing. The Vic Boils of the world tended to hate the Ed Troutmans. Whenever Vic could get in a cheap shot at corporations he would, while Ed was more than happy to lob back insults about the "lazy-ass" working class.

Tina and Pearl never really gelled either. Tina was, in Pearl's eyes a "step" parent, and always would be. In fact, of the two families, the only positive dynamics were between the bride and groom, who seemed to genuinely enjoy each other's company.

"A Collins, Vic?" Ed boomed across his wet bar, which was decorated like a NASCAR pit stop.

"A Bud'll be fine, Ed, like always," Vic said, taking a seat on a bar stool. "How's business?"

"We're paving the way to the future, Vic!"

"I walked right into that one."

"How about you, Bruce? A Collins to get your engine running?"

"No thanks, Ed, I'm working tonight," I said. "Do you have Dr Pepper?"

"Mr. Pibb all right?"

"Sure."

"Hey, dumb ass!" Ed bellowed.

I wasn't sure whom he was insulting, but then I saw Lance, hugging family members in the foyer.

"Yo!" he yelled back.

"Want a Tom?"

"You know it, boss man."

"How about you, Tina girl?" Ed urged.

"Diet Pepsi, thanks," she said, joining the group at the bar.

Ed grabbed a soda from his fully stocked fridge and popped the top. "How's life with numb nuts?"

"If you mean 'how is working for his honor the mayor,' it's just fine," sniffed Tina, "and a lot more friendly than the snake pit down there at the city council."

"It's where the rubber meets the road, darlin'."

"And we'll provide the road," Lance blurted out, joining them.

Ed jammed a drink into his hand.

"Keep the wedding on track," I heard Reed say. "I propose a toast!" I said, raising my Mr. Pibb high. "To Lance and Jackie: a terrific couple. I'm look forward to this wedding, I'll tell you!"

"I'll bet you are," Ed mumbled to himself.

In a delivery that would make my employers proud, I announced: "It's a once-in-a-lifetime day, isn't it?"

Lance kissed Jackie and there was sporadic clapping.

Ed forced a smile. "So when do we get to hear them big ideas, Bruce?" he asked.

"I'll be making my presentation after dinner."

"Why wait?" Ed insisted. "What else are we here for? We can eat dinner any ol' time. Someone get Pearl in here."

"I've been here the whole time, jackass," Pearl barked, startling everyone from a dark love seat in the corner.

"Sorry, honey, you're so damn quiet sometimes. . . ."

I knew my time was at hand. "Folks, I'd love to share some life-changing ideas with you."

The family migrated across to the Ethan Allen Mt. Vernon family-room set and formed a semicircle, with Jackie and Lance in the middle. Ed, too nervous to sit, paced behind them. I took a sip of my Mr. Pibb and recalled what Dick and Reed told me: *"Always have three wedding pitches ready, because the first two are going to get rejected."*

"Lance, Jackie, you're a young, dynamic couple," I said, subtly flapping my hands behind me, trying to make the sweat dry. "But getting married is a big step. It's more than that — it's a leap, actually. And what better way to demonstrate that than by skydiving your way down to the wedding?"

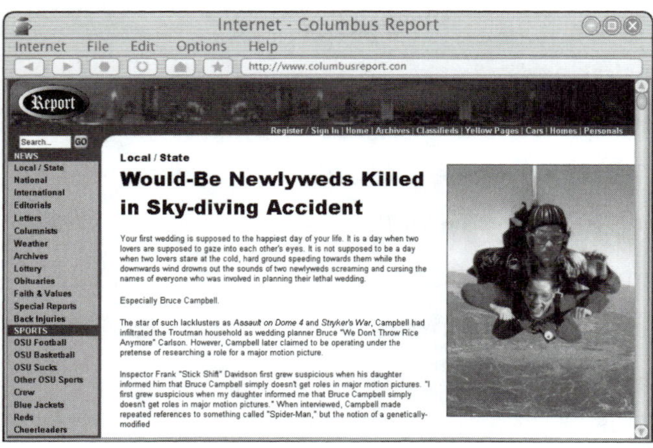

Internet - Columbus Report

Internet File Edit Options Help

http://www.columbusreport.con

Report

Register / Sign In | Home | Archives | Classifieds | Yellow Pages | Cars | Homes | Personals

Search... GO

NEWS

Local / State
National
International
Editorials
Letters
Columnists
Weather
Archives
Lottery
Obituaries
Faith & Values
Special Reports
Back Injuries

SPORTS

OSU Football
OSU Basketball
OSU Sucks
Other OSU Sports
Crew
Blue Jackets
Reds
Cheerleaders

Local / State

Would-Be Newlyweds Killed in Sky-diving Accident

Your first wedding is supposed to the happiest day of your life. It is a day when two lovers are supposed to gaze into each other's eyes. It is not supposed to be a day when two lovers stare at the cold, hard ground speeding towards them while the downwards wind drowns out the sounds of two newlyweds screaming and cursing the names of everyone who was involved in planning their lethal wedding.

Especially Bruce Campbell.

The star of such lacklusters as *Assault on Dome 4* and *Stryker's War*, Campbell had infiltrated the Troutman household as wedding planner Bruce "We Don't Throw Rice Anymore" Carlson. However, Campbell later claimed to be operating under the pretense of researching a role for a major motion picture.

Inspector Frank "Stick Shift" Davidson first grew suspicious when his daughter informed him that Bruce Campbell simply doesn't get roles in major motion pictures. "I first grew suspicious when my daughter informed me that Bruce Campbell simply doesn't get roles in major motion pictures." When interviewed, Campbell made repeated references to something called "Spider-Man," but the notion of a genetically-modified

Lance began to smile like an idiot, and Jackie was definitely intrigued, but the look between Pearl and Ed spoke volumes.

"That sounds like a great idea. I'm for it," Lance said, looking around for support.

"Uh-uh," Pearl uttered, shaking her head from side to side. "No way on God's green earth."

"I paced it out," I interjected. "Ed, you've got twenty acres here, am I right?"

"Give or take."

"That's plenty of land, even on a day with light to moderate winds."

"Shit, boy — jumpin' out of a damn airplane?" Ed exclaimed. "That's my *daughter* you're talking about."

"It might be fun, Daddy," Jackie responded.

"Fun? You seen them power lines on the south end of this property? I can't let my daughter, let alone my vice president of sales, get strung up and fried on their wedding day," Ed said as he walked back behind the wet bar.

"I don't like the idea," Tina said, "but I must say, you could only consider something like that with the current zoning laws Mayor Coleman supported."

Ed blew a raspberry at Tina as he loaded up the stainless-steel blender. "It's just a bad idea all the way around."

In my two hours of formal training, one thing Reed said really stuck with me: *"If you bomb, kid, just make a joke out of it. Keep tap dancing."*

"Hey, I'm not *married* to it," I chuckled. "This has to work for everyone."

"I was…all right with it," Lance said, defeated.

"Why don't you tell us what you really had in mind," Ed called out.

"I'm glad you asked, Ed," I said, turning to the newlyweds-to-be. "Lance and Jackie, I've done some research on you two. You both went to Ohio State, one graduated, and Lance, you once played side by side with the great football coach Woody Hayes."

I conveniently left out the fact that Lance had been a third-string defensive end on the kickoff return team. "Ed, you and Pearl have Buckeye fever, am I right?"

"Class of sixty-six," Ed acknowledged, raising his Tom.

"So what better way to share your love than to get married in the stadium?" I proposed.

The men in the room perked up, particularly Ed and Lance.

"Right on the field," I continued. "The same field as the 2002 National

Champions. But that's not all. The colors of the wedding will be scarlet and gray, the school colors. If it's been good enough for Ohio State since 1878, then it's good enough for Lance and Jackie."

Jackie wrinkled her nose at this idea, but I kept the sales pitch moving. *"Never let a lack of enthusiasm slow you down,"* Dick Patterson's voice echoed in my mind.

"The bride and groom enter the stadium through a victory arch formed by the members of the wedding party."

"That would be beautiful," Pearl imagined.

"Almost as beautiful as the day you met Ed in the stands in 1963," I said, closing in on Pearl. "He was the most handsome field maintenance man you'd ever seen."

Pearl blushed. "It's true, you know."

"Shit," Ed said, waving her away with a smile.

I started to get a good feeling about this pitch. The right people were responding. Vic and Tina were noncommittal, but Vic never had much to say anyway. Jackie, for her part, seemed to have become strangely unengaged in the process.

"And who is on the field to greet them, in formation, but the Ohio State marching band! And I don't need to tell you what T-B-D-B-I-T-L means...."

"The Best…," Ed started.

"Damn Band…," Lance continued.

"In the…," Pearl added.

"Land!" The three of them pounced on the final word together.

"That's right," I said. "And after the ceremony, instead of the traditional scripting of Ohio, the marching band will spell out 'Lance and Jackie' in cursive, and play the 'Buckeye Battle Cry,' rewritten by a former *Simpsons* writer."

Reaction in the room had been building, and my pitch was met with enthusiastic hoots, clapping, and laughter.

"Shadddap!" A voice boomed.

Ed and the other merrymakers stopped to look at Vic, who had shouted. "I'm sorry, folks, but I'm gonna have to put a kibosh on that one."

I stifled a cough. Lance sat back in his chair with a "whoa." Ed came from around the bar.

"You been sitting there pretty quiet until now, Vic," he said. "What's the matter?"

"I'm just the father of the groom," Vic responded. "So, what I think doesn't really matter a damn in the whole marriage deal, but I marched in the University of Michigan marching band — class of '68 — and I don't think my son should participate in a ceremony that is so obviously slanted."

"Slanted? I went to college there," Lance said.

"So did I," Jackie added.

"I understand that," Vic said, trying to remain calm, "but you were never on the other side like I was. Even before the game, dressed in our maize and blue, little old ladies would spit and swear at us as we walked down the street."

"I never realized that," Pearl said, slightly alarmed.

"Believe it," Vic said, still agitated by the memories. "I been around, okay? I been in 'Nam. I didn't come home to no picnic then either, but I never come up against bigger assholes — you'll excuse me, ladies — than the goddamned Buckeyes and Woody 'chew your hat' Hayes."

Vic, I would later discover, was from Taylor, Michigan. There are only three things you do there: work, drink Budweiser, and watch University of Michigan football, arch rival of Ohio State.

"Watch how you talk about Woody in this house," Ed cautioned.

"Hey, I was tryin' not to say anything, 'cause I know how much you love that fat idiot, but enough is enough, Ed. There are two sides to this family."

An awkward silence followed, during which, little eye contact was made. Finally, Ed broke the impasse. "Okay, hey, I got no problem *not* paying to rent Ohio Stadium and the entire band," he said, clearly disappointed and pissed.

"All right, good," Vic said, with a nod. "Got any more Bud?"

"In the fridge," Ed gestured, not making any effort to get one.

Since I was now 0 for 2 in sales pitches, I assumed that this would be a good time for my third and final attempt.

"Lance and Jackie," I said pointing my finger at them as if I planned this all along. "You both went to Ohio State, but ironically you never met there — you met where?"

I not-so-subtly hinted at a huge banner for the Columbus Speedway above Ed's wet bar.

"The Speedway," Pearl said, her eyes lighting up. "I like that place. Those boys drive fast."

"That's right, Pearl," I said, playing the room. "And what were the circumstances?"

"Lance was a mechanic for a car Ed's company was sponsoring," Pearl said, fond of the memory.

"Jackie came down for a pit stop, and she never left — did you, baby?" Lance said through a Tom Collins smile.

"Nope," Jackie said, smiling back. "And it went from there."

"I'll say it did," I continued. "From humble beginnings to a full-blown ove affair for the ages, the race track has been your bond, the asphalt that has kept you two together."

"FYI," Ed blurted, "we resurfaced it in ninety-five. Helluva good contract."

"And what better way to cement your love," I asked, "than by standng in the middle of the oval track of Columbus Speedway?"

"Now you're talking my language, Jack," Vic added with renewed nterest.

"Each member of the wedding gets to race a lap against — and he's only a phone call away — none other than Jeff Gordon."

The idea of a NASCAR theme turned Ed around quickly. "Hey now, that would be a kick."

"The hell you say," Lance said, grabbing hold of Jackie. "My woman sn't goin' anywhere near Jeff Gordon!"

"The hell *you* say," Pearl said, getting everyone's attention. "He can eep me in the pole position any day!"

The men all burst into rowdy laughter. Nothing bonds drunken idiots ke sexual innuendo.

"Betcha I could take Gordon," Vic said, nodding. "Betcha I could."

"Betcha I could too," Tina said, winking at Vic.

"Can we get Garth Brooks to sing?" Pearl asked.

Lance and Jackie exchanged unexcited looks.

"Anything is doable," I said, snapping a finger. "We just have to make it worth his while."

"He hasn't had a hit in a few years," Ed chimed in. "He couldn't be all *that* much."

"Never know until you try," I said, smiling like Robert Preston in *The Music Man.*

"He can sing, 'Ain't goin' down 'til the sun comes up,'" Vic suggested.

"The best ideas sell themselves," Reed had said to me at the end of our "seminar." For all the crap he fed me in two hours, that notion made the most sense. As I looked around, the family members — the parents anyway — were excited enough to spitball their own take on what would make for the perfect NASCAR-themed wedding.

"You present the ring on the awards podium," Vic threw out, getting suddenly very verbal. "I've always wanted to stand up there."

"And for the big finale, I'd go for a mock accident," Ed added. "Hell, I could come zoomin' around, smash into Jeff Gordon, and he could bounce off the wall. You could even have some dummies and shit that go flyin', I mean, really blow the lid off that place."

"Did you know that the Speedway is wired to do closed-circuit TV broadcasts?" I asked.

"Could our friends in Iowa tune in?" Pearl wondered.

"If they have a TV set, you bet," I said, sounding like game show host Wink Martindale. "They're also set up to record and edit the wedding in real time. Everyone will get a finished DVD on their way out."

"I'll be damned," Ed nodded, really transfixed.

The third time was the charm. I could name my price. "Well, you folks can talk it over. Ed, I'll call you in the morning."

"Sure, but I can tell you now, this is a slam dunk," he said, pumping my hand.

"I'll have Reed give you a call to discuss the details," I said, excusing myself.

Instead of throwing rice, they'd throw beer cans.

Vic sat back down at the bar. "Isn't that something? Hey, Ed, got any more Bud?"

"Sure thing, buddy. Let me get that for you, now that we're in-laws! Ha-ha-ha!"

Vic joined in the laughter, and the two men were instant friends again. Meanwhile, Tina and Pearl converged on a full-size, cardboard standee of Jeff Gordon in the corner. A high-spirited conviviality was spreading through the room like petrochemical fumes, and the parents, having inhaled deeply of their high-octane fantasy, didn't seem to notice that Jackie and Lance had disappeared.

Going around the side of the house to where my offending Ford was parked, I saw the glow of a cigarette. The husband-and-wife-to-be were by themselves, having what looked like a serious discussion, so I decided to say a quick hello and good night and then get out of their way.

"Well, the big day is coming up," I offered.

"Yep," Jackie said, nodding, not really wanting to start a conversation.

"Well, we'll try and make it memorable for you."

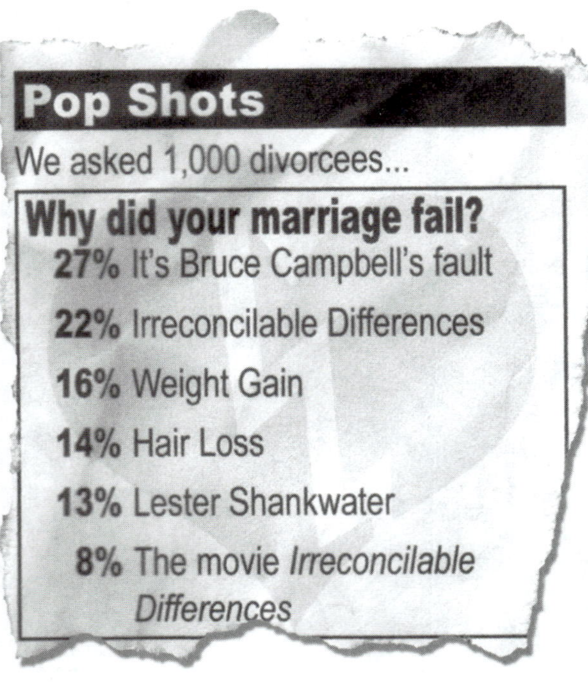

"Maybe too memorable," Lance said, dissenting for the first time.

"You think so?" I asked.

"I mean, whose wedding is this, anyway?" Jackie questioned, with uncharacteristic intensity.

"Yours, of course," I said.

"Did anyone once ask *us* what we wanted to do?"

"No," Lance said.

"Where *we* wanted to go?"

"No."

"Who *we* wanted to invite?"

"No."

"You two don't seem very happy," I said.

"We're not," Jackie sniffed.

"But don't tell them that," Lance backpedaled.

"We were afraid this would happen — that our parents would totally forget what the day is all about and force us into something we hate."

"Well, what do you really want to do?" I asked.

"What *can* we do? Nothing," Lance said.

"You have plenty of choices. You can go along with everything we talked about tonight, or you can bail on the whole thing."

"We don't want to bail," Jackie said. "We want to get married."

"Yeah, just not in this bullshit way."

"We'd rather just run away and tell everyone after we're married."

know that they want to share, but it's so personal. What do they know about us?"

"You could do that," I agreed, "but it would cause a big fuss."

"Well, what's more important?" Jackie wondered. "A wedding where everyone has fun, or a marriage that lasts?"

"The latter," I said, sliding two first-class tickets out of my pocket. Vegas okay?"

"Are you serious?" Lance asked, as if his cell door had just been lung open.

"Any wedding planner worth his salt has to have a contingency plan. My job, ultimately, is to plan a nuptial, not please the parents," I said, half-expecting Dick and Reed to appear from the shadows and deliver he much-discussed crippling.

"Oh my God, thank you so much," Jackie said, with tears welling up. What are you going to tell them?"

"I'm not going to tell them anything. Why spoil the fun? By the time hey realize you're gone, Jeff Gordon will be dancing on a table with our mother and it won't matter. And personally, I recommend the Elvis Chapel of Love. The guy does a great 'Hunka Burnin' Love.'"

"Okay, thanks, man," Lance said, whipping off his tie and taking ackie by the hand.

watched as they ran to his car and peeled away down Daddy's fresh sphalt driveway. As I hopped in my Ford, I wondered what the odds vere for Lance and Jackie in a world where half of all marriages fail. If he strength of a union is to be judged by early, key decisions, I'd give hem better than fifty-fifty.

I called Ida from the airport on my way back to New York City and we discussed the events in Columbus. We agreed that while we may not know what marriage is, Ida and I certainly know what it is not. There is no "fairy dust" sprinkled on your head when you wed, and happiness isn't guaranteed by symbols like a ring, a license, and certainly not by a prenuptial agreement. A decent union comes from both parties trying like hell for as long as they have the strength, and that's just the beginning. Marriage isn't fixed, it's a work in progress from the first vow, and anyone who tells you different is full of beans. At least, I decided, that's the opinion of one very wise New York City doorman.

10

A Fitting We Will Go

stuffed the last of a grilled corn muffin in my mouth, washed it down with lukewarm tea, and buzzed number twenty-two. I had arrived at Sandra Demming's costume shop in New York City's Greenwich Village.

"Can I help you?" squawked a voice from the little box.

"Yeah, Bruce Campbell here for a *Let's Make Love!* fitting."

The door buzzed and I was in.

Sandra's loft/sweatshop was mostly a huge open area with wall-to-wall windows and uneven wood floors. Assistants were scurrying about, making phone calls, hemming pants, and doing whatever else you need to do to win two Academy Awards.

An unflappable, supremely confident, four-foot-tall field marshal, Sandra had the energy of three people. "We're late, and you're early," she declared, "so you can have a seat and read a year-old fashion magazine, or you can see some of the things we're doing with Renée."

"I'll go for the fashion show," I said, and promptly followed Sandra through a maze of fabric, machinery, and testy gay men.

Turning a corner, we came upon a large fitting area with mirrors on three sides and flanked by comfortable chairs.

"Park it," Sandra said. "Renée will be out in a sec."

Before Sandra could finish her sentence, Renée emerged from a changing room, resplendent in a riding outfit that looked straight out of *Town & Country*, circa 1987.

"Hi, Brad," she said, seeing me.

"Bruce."

Renée made a face like she had stepped on a frog. "I'm so sorry. *Bruce.* I knew that — duh."

"It's fine. Brad Pitt and I get confused all the time."

"Well, now that you two have caught up," Sandra said, nodding, "I think the suit is marvelous."

"I do too," Renée said, turning around in front of a mirror. "It's fun, elegant, and very —"

"Baggy," I said, cutting her off.

Renée and Sandra looked at me in shock, but then back to her outfit.

"It's not baggy," Sandra said, defending the fit.

"Well, I'm not the Academy Award winner, but to a layman's eyes it is — particularly in the butt."

"Do I have a saggy butt?" Renée asked, turning her back to the mirror and looking over her shoulder.

"No, not you," I explained. "You have a very nice butt. You must work out a lot."

"I do," Renée said, frowning. "A *lot*."

"For my money, I'd like to see it a little more celebrated."

"Well, fortunately for us, this isn't your money, Mr. Campbell," Sandra scolded, "it's the money of Paramount Pictures, and we're going to —"

"Oh, but I beg to differ. It's the money of the guys who are coming to see Renée. They still have the image of her from *Chicago* swimming in their heads."

Sandra stepped toward me. "This movie is not for that type of person. This is a Mike Nichols film, and I know for a fact that his only concern is the story."

"Wrong, smarty-pants," I shot back. "I know for a fact, being a guy, that the only thing male audience members care about is the shape of Renée's booty. Sorry, Renée."

"Oh that's okay," she said, starting to doubt her outfit.

"This is a date flick, Bruce," Sandra argued. "Seventy-five percent of the viewers will be female."

"Well, whatever the percentage, if you want to get men in theater seats, you'd better dish up some serious eye candy."

Sandra shot me a "shut your mouth, or I'll shut it for you" look.

"What about the waist, Sandra?" Renée asked. "Do you think it needs to be tapered more?"

"It's fine, Renée — very flattering. You have to ride a horse, don't forget. It has to be practical. Don't listen to this blowhard."

"Okay, let me ask you both a fundamental question: When a woman gets dolled up for a night on the town, does she wear the sexy outfit for herself, or for the enjoyment of men?"

Renée bit her lip out of bewilderment. "Well, it depends on what the goal of the evening is, doesn't it?"

Sandra, eager to use almost any topic as a means of shutting me down, jumped right in. "For herself," she stated flatly. "If a woman feels sexy, the man will pick up on it."

"Okay, let's run with that scenario," I offered. "Renée, do you feel sexy in that outfit?"

"What kind of a question is that?" Sandra asked indignantly. "Of course she does."

"Why don't we let Renée answer for herself, Sandra?"

Renée looked at herself in the mirror and hesitated. "Well, it's certainly cute...."

"Cute? Yes. Sexy? No. Normally, I think you're sexy as hell, Renée but I'm not picking up any vibes from you." I turned to Sandra. "You want my honest opinion?"

Look, kids, it's the official Renée Zellweger magnetic dress up kit!

"No."

Ignoring her dismissal I appealed to Renée "Most of the guys I know who get the wood for you —"

"Excuse me?" Renée said.

"Well, you can't expect paying customers not to treat you like a commodity

They cough up the dough, they want to see the goods. I'll bet fan mail from men spiked when you did *Bridget Jones's Diary*."

"Well, it did, actually," Renée acknowledged. "But I assumed it was because they liked my acting."

"You were great in the movie, Renée," I assured her. "But guys liked you because there was *more of you to like*."

"I am *not* gaining thirty pounds ever again," Renée said, shaking her index finger at me. "Not counting sequels, of course."

"I'm not suggesting that at all, but there are plenty of ways to get more of the hourglass thing going."

"This I'd love to hear from the B movie expert," Sandra said, probably wishing that I had been run over by a bus on the way to the fitting.

"Well, we did this film called *Army of Darkness*, and Dino De Laurentiis, the producer, was used to actresses from the fifties, with curves that went on for days. The only way we could get a starlet approved by him was to make her look like she had a twelve-point rack, if you know what I mean."

"Renée has a beautiful bust," Sandra insisted.

"Could have fooled me," I said, casually sitting in one of the overstuffed chairs.

"And what would you have us do? Foam-inject her like a molding process?" Sandra wondered sarcastically.

"Nah, you stuff a few gel sacs into a larger bra and walk away."

"Okay, it's official — you disgust me," Sandra said, turning away.

"No, I hear what he's saying," Renée said, trying to bring Sandra back to the table. "You want to try it and see? Isn't that what these fittings are for — to experiment?"

Sandra paused for a second, then looped her measuring tape around her neck. "All right, you want boobs? I'll give you boobs."

Within ten minutes, Renée was virtually bursting out of her riding outfit in all the right ways. She walked back and forth in front of the mirror, taking in the new look.

"Tell me this isn't better, Sandra," I said, impressed at what they had pulled off in such a short time.

"Okay, it isn't —"

"I love it!" Renée said, cutting in. "It's provocative and pronounced."

"Well, honestly, neither of you count," Sandra said. "This is a case where an outside opinion is needed."

"But all the men who work here are gay," I protested.

"Sure, but they know a thing or two about sexy."

"Sorry, Sandra, not when it comes to women. I'll find a straight man for you."

I looked toward the entrance and saw a bicycle messenger getting a signature for a package.

"Excuse me, sir," I said, approaching him, "You're not gay, are you?"

"No," the messenger said, a little put off. "Why?"

"We could really use your help with something. Have you heard of Renée Zellweger, the actress?"

"Sure. She's a babe."

"Would you like to see what she's going to wear in her new film?"

"Shit yeah, dude, are you serious?"

I grabbed the messenger and walked him to the fitting area. As we rounded the corner, his jaw dropped. "Whoa" was all he could say.

Renée's face lit up.

"Tell us what you think," I prodded the messenger. "Be descriptive."

"Well, it's tight, and she's awesome. She looks like that chick from *Tomb Raider*."

"Very descriptive, thank you very much," I said.

The messenger started to fidget. He was wearing tight bicycle shorts and Renée's appearance was challenging his "comfort."

"Hey, well, if that's all you need me for, I'd better get going," he said, hurrying to the exit, messenger bag shielding his growing embarrassment.

"I rest my case," I said to Sandra, trying not to be smug.

"Hard to argue with that," Renée agreed, slightly uncomfortable. "I think we may have to take a second look at the other outfits."

Sandra looked at me with disdain. "Perhaps Mr. Campbell would like to stay and comment while we go through them all over again?"

"Oh, could you, Bruce?" Renée asked excitedly.

"Sure," I said, winking at Sandra. "How did these A-list productions ever get along without me?"

11

Midlife Miasma

When I was a kid, I had recurring "failure" dreams. If I were playing baseball, for example, I could smack the ball deep into the outfield, but I wouldn't be able to round the bases. Or, I'd be chopping wood, but just as the axe met its target, the blade would turn sideways. Prepping for *Let's Make Love!*, my failure dreams revolved around the telephone. The calls were always important, but the phone would ring and ring because I could only hear it faintly, like it was off in the distance, and by the time I got to it, the caller hung up.

I heard the phone ring again that morning and, as always, it was a thousand miles away. But the sound grew, and soon the phone was only a hundred miles away, then a hundred feet, then it was up on my nightstand…where it had been all along.

The early morning caller was Mike, my fearless — and relentless — leader. "Good morning, Bruce. It's Mike. I assume you're already up."

"Uh, yeah…of course," I said, trying to lubricate my dry mouth enough to form a sentence.

"Listen, I'm in the middle of a production meeting so I can't talk long. We're adding a car chase at the end of scene seventy-two, and we were about to pick a car, but it just occurred to me that Foyl is the one who chooses the car for Harry."

"You want me to choose the car for the chase?"

"No, I want your *character* to choose the car. We're playing for keeps here, Bruce, work with us."

"Yeah, sure, sure, how do you want me to go about it?"

"Quickly. I'm sending you to Dallas. Ever been there?"

"Uh, yeah, once — and why there?"

"It's home of the single largest car dealership in the nation. If you can't find Harry's car there, you can't find it. June, my secretary — you remember her — she'll meet you at the dealership to take notes, arrange payment, etcetera."

"Okay…when?"

"Today. People will call you about all that. Have fun. Get busy."

Click. Mike was done.

There were several things I noticed while shooting a film in Dallas a few years ago. First, the place was flat. Architects love it, because there are no mountains, rivers, or oceans to "distract" from their designs. That's why, architecturally speaking, you see so many weird buildings spread willy-nilly across the city.

Second, the world's largest car dealership made sense in Dallas because you've got your oil-drilling fat cats (still living off money they made two decades ago) and your general assortment of fortune seekers in a regulation-be-damned town.

I met June in the football-field-size, fry-an-egg-hot parking lot of Mid-Life Motors. I can't use their real name for legal reasons, so let's just stick with that. It wasn't hard to spot the sales manager, Duff Jenkins, Jr. His hair was perfect, his moustache was perfect, and his "I ain't got a care in the world" smile was perfect.

On this bright day, Duff wore a white cowboy hat that was impossible to view directly without protective eyewear. His suit was a hybrid of sorts — shit kicker meets city slicker: a silver sharkskin jacket and pants; a sky blue shirt with a string tie; an oversize longhorn buckle attached to a belt that was cinched tight around his expanding "shot and a beer" belly.

Duff was the number-one car salesman in Dallas, five years running. His hand was extended easily a dozen feet before we actually shook.

"Mr. Campbell?"

"Bruce'll do just fine."

"Duff Jenkins, Jr. Nice to meet you, sir. I sure loved *Cisco Kid*."

"*Brisco*. Uh, Duff, this is June — she works with the director."

Duff nodded politely. "Missy."

"June will be fine," she said curtly.

"Sure, okay. Now, you're doin' some research for a film, or whatnot?"

"Yes," I said. "I need to pick a car for an upper-middle-class, recently divorced man who wants to redefine himself."

Duff winked. "Got just the thing."

We walked to the "Import" section, where a canary yellow Subaru Baja sparkled in the sun. Duff went right into his thing: "Subaru Baja Sport — turbocharged, sixteen valve, single overhead camshaft, all-wheel drive."

"Okay, so what does this car say about the guy who buys it?" I asked.

"It depends," Duff pondered. "How old is he?"

I wasn't sure, and I glanced at June.

"Fifty-ish," she said.

Duff sucked air through his teeth like he just saw a dog get hit by a car. "In that case, it says 'I'm fifty trying to be eighteen again.'"

I shook my head. "Nope. Not quite right. He's having a midlife crisis, but he's not that desperate."

"I'll tell you a secret," Duff confided. "Thank God for men like him because he keeps men like me in business. I was just at a sales conference in St. Louis, and the keynote address was about the economics of a midlife crisis."

Duff walked us over to a small, stylish BMW. "The 2004 BMW MX9. The Bond car. Pierce Brosnan himself drives one."

"Yeah, because the car company gave him one for free."

Duff gestured to the rear of the car. "Notice that there is virtually no room for luggage of any kind. The man who drives this car doesn't want any more *baggage*."

"Interesting." I looked at June, and she was already jotting notes. "But the character we're buying for isn't that irrelevant."

Duff had obviously heard every reason ever given *not* to like (and therefore buy) a car. "This car gives you precision craftsmanship, ergonomics, and an on-board nav system. These features are not 'irrelevant,' Bruce, they are timeless."

"Duff, I can't blame you for trying. This car was cool for a couple years, but it's very 'then.' Let's move on to something new and different."

Duff steered us toward the cars closest to the main showroom — the high-end section. "The Lexus XL 5. Top of the line," he said with his trademark right-handed, palm-up presentation. "This car says CEO of a Fortune 500 company."

I hopped into the Lexus and had a look around. The interior was plush as hell, with heavenly seats and an instrument panel befitting a small airplane.

"You're right, I feel like a CEO."

Duff continued his pitch from outside the car. "I've sold this car not only to CEOs, but to politicians, athletes, movie stars —"

"Yeah, but it's not right. My guy isn't a CEO, and he isn't an asshole."

"Beg pardon?" Duff asked, taken aback.

June looked up from her notes.

"When I see them on the road," I explained, "they're driven by well-dressed, stern-looking guys, usually accompanied by some face-lifted, bottle blonde who looks miserable. This is also the kind of car you're most likely to see parked illegally in a handicap spot, or sideways, taking up three spaces. Close, but no cigar."

"Damn, this friend of yours is a picky sumbitch, ain't he," Duff said, suppressing his anger, "'cause we sell these like hotcakes."

Duff led me across the lot to the "muscle" section and gestured to a silver behemoth. "Here you go, Bruce. No man can resist the temptation of a Dodge Niagra 4X4 2500 XL GS 30 twin cab."

Huge is a word that is overused, but I'm going to use it — the truck was huge.

"This Dodge could fit that Baja in the back bed," Duff continued. "It's got three hundred and forty-five horsepower, with a Hemi Magnum V8 standard. By owning this car, you say to the world: Get out of my way."

"By owning this car, you say to the world: I have a needle dick," I countered.

June dug the tip of her No. 2 pencil into her legal pad.

Duff looked at me like he hadn't heard properly. "Come again?"

"The guys who drive these gigantic trucks are all little Napoleon bastards. They can't get it up, so they put a monster under their gonads. I'd be afraid that women would think my friend was impotent if he drove that truck. Christ, in a few years, he'd need a handicap ramp just to get up into it."

Duff invaded my personal eighteen-inch bubble to ask a question. "Bruce, does your friend suffer from erectile problems?"

"Actually, Duff, I have no damn idea. What kind of a question is that?"

"It's been clinically proven that the tire-to-frame vibrations from this truck stimulate blood flow to the extremities of the body, and I think you know what I'm talking about." Duff cracked a Texas-wide smile and rocked on the heels of his boots. "Not to mention what it does for the little lady. There's a reason why it's our number-one seller."

"I can think of cheaper ways to get a hard-on."

"C'mon, now," Duff said, holding up a puffy, ringed finger. "Don't make fun until you've tried it. Get up in there, take it for a spin around the parking lot, and then tell me I'm crazy."

I thought about declining, but my Motor City sensibilities made me weak. "Okay, Duff, sure — once around the parking lot."

Duff Jenkins Jr. modeling the megalithic Niagra 4x4.

Duff grinned and winked at June, who turned away, mildly horrified.

I climbed into the truck's elevated cab. Looking out, I could see the entire parking lot. Feeling like the king of my vehicular domain, I started the Dodge and revved the engine like a sixteen-year-old in a Wal-Mart parking lot.

Whoooaaaar!

Wow, that was smooth.

I did it again.

WHOOOOAAAAAAHHHHHRRRR!!!

June stepped back a couple feet, cringing at the loud noise and Duff, ever the gentleman, grabbed her by the elbow.

"Do you know what I think when I see this car?" Duff shouted over the heavy idling. "I think strength, I think rugged reliability."

I've got to drive this monster, I convinced myself.

I shifted into "D" and let my foot off the brake. The powerful engine propelled the truck forward. I pressed the gas, but the truck didn't lurch like my ranch junker — it was smooth, like a sports car. The tachometer bounced as I revved, braked, and turned my way around the parking lot.

It didn't take long for a tingle to work its way across me. The entire truck was vibrating like a coin-operated mattress. I swung around in front of June and Duff, but I couldn't bring myself to stop. His B.S. about what the truck does for the male species wasn't B.S. at all — I had a hard-on that would impress my dad. I turned beet red from embarrassment, but I found myself laughing at the same time. Soon, I was laughing so hard, I had to roll up my windows. The more I drove around the parking lot, the harder I laughed, and the harder I got. It was an insane scenario that caused a near miss with a Lamborghini.

"Ha-ha-ha!!!" I laughed. *I'm driving a real truck!*

Duff was laughing too. "I'll start the paperwork," he called.

I put the truck in park and wiped the tears of joy from my eyes. Towering above a row of brand-new Hummers in front of me, I felt like some sort of fuel-injected deity. Even the small, red pickup truck speeding along next to them amused me.

There is room for all vehicles, big and small, in my SUV kingdom.

Then I noticed that two masked men in the bed of the pickup were dumping liquid on the Hummers as they passed each one.

Holy ecoterrorist, something bad is about to —

KA-WHUMP! The entire row of Hummers became engulfed in ten-foot-high flames.

"Lord almighty!" Duff screamed, losing his hat from the concussion. He grabbed his cell phone and dabbed out 9-1-1.

June stumbled back and slammed into the side of a BMW. She

dropped to the ground, notes scattering.

The little red truck screeched out of the parking lot and down a residential side street. From my high vantage point, I could see exactly where the ecoterrorists were heading. Intent on cutting them off, I put the Dodge in gear and hit the gas.

The red truck was quick. More important, it wasn't as wide as my all-terrain oil tanker and fit neatly down a narrow alley. There was no way to follow, but I could blaze my own trail across a nearby backyard. I slipped the Dodge into low gear and roared across the freshly sodded yard, narrowly avoiding a kiddie pool and an angry pit bull.

I emerged out about ten lengths behind the red truck on a short straightaway and opened the monster up. The ensuing rush of speed was better than any truck commercial could possibly convey. Within seconds, I was poised to ram the destructive little fuckers off the road, but glancing down, I realized that I was also poised to embarrass myself.

Enough with the vibrations already! I thought.

Ecowarriors must prepare for various scenarios, in case their destroy-in-order-to-save-the-world plan goes awry, and these guys were on their game. Bags of nails and glass bottles hailed down on the road behind their truck. Consequently, I was too busy avoiding punctured tires to notice the Molotov cocktail sailing through the air, but I did perk up when it shattered on my front hood and erupted into a wall of flames.

I couldn't see through the inferno, but I knew I was reasonably close to their truck, so I opted for one last hurrah and jammed the gas pedal to the floor. The V8 propelled the Dodge forward, engaging the passing gear, and I hit something, *hard.*

The impact blew out the gasoline fire, revealing the crippled mass of the red truck, spinning out of control. My truck had nailed it square in the back and sent it careening down a steep grass embankment directly toward oncoming traffic.

I turned my attention toward my own vehicle, which was lurching irrevocably toward the same fate. The two front tires had blown from the collision, reducing navigation to a cruel joke. I jammed on the brakes as hard as I could, but from the lack of response, I knew right away that inertia was not to be overcome.

With no other choice, I kicked open the door and jumped out as the truck reached the lip of the hill. I tried to hit the ground running, but I misjudged the rate of travel and my legs were swept out from under me. I connected with Mother Earth at an awkward angle, and momentum kept me tumbling on the hardscrabble for what seemed like a hundred yards. Ahead of me, the Dodge rolled out of sight, and the rest could only be heard — the terrified screams, the twisting metal, the report of a huge explosion. Things didn't sound good for the ecoterrorists.

By the time I limped back to Mid-Life Motors, the gigantic fire was almost out. Duff and June had collected themselves and were giving interviews to the local police. The recent turn of events convinced me that I had found the right car.

"June, pay the man," I said. "I'm going to drive the Dodge back to New York."

Word traveled fast about the Hummer incident, so by the time I rolled the truck up to the loading dock behind Mike's brownstone, the production office was ready with an impromptu celebration. I revved the beefy engine to the delight of the assembled cast and crew, which included Mike, June (taking notes, now with a bandaged elbow), Richard, and even Renée.

I jumped out of the truck, stood on the hood, and raised my arms in victory. Instead of applause, there was a slight gasp from the crowd. In all the activity, I had forgotten the side effects of a long road trip in that particular vehicle.

Mid-Life Motors is now known as the dealership with the fewest eyebrows.

Renée blushed. "Well, at least you're happy to see us, Bruce," she said, staring unabashedly at my emboldened manliness. It was the first time she got my name right — and the last time she ever forgot it.

12

Testing, Testing, One, Two, Three...

The next morning, safely back in the land of *Let's Make Love!*, the next thing on our preproduction agenda was a camera test. Unlike low-budget movies, which tend to eliminate any procedure that costs money, big movies test everything before filming begins — cameras, lighting, even how the actors look in makeup and wardrobe.

I've always enjoyed the testing process, because it's more of a social event than a work day. The studio Mike used was big enough to accommodate plenty of film equipment, but it was small enough not to be intimidating. I took a sip of Earl Grey tea and walked to a designated mark on the floor, decked out in full doorman splendor.

The camera crew was led by the great cameraman Vilmos Sigmund. He is without a doubt one of the greatest living cinematographers. What I respect about Vilmos, apart from his distinctive, natural lighting style, is the fact that he got his start filming low-budget exploitation movies.

"You know, Vilmos, as much as I like your work on *The Deer Hunter* and *Close Encounters*, I also really liked what you did with *Echo of Terror*."

The title didn't immediately register with Vilmos.

"Also known as *Psycho a Go-Go*," I added.

"Oh, years ago, you mean," he said with a slight Hungarian accent. "Yes, yes, 1965."

"That's the one," I confirmed. "You had some wicked handheld sequences in that, and they were not the annoying kind — yours were focused and sharp."

"Yes, we did quite a bit of it," Vilmos said, lighting up at the fond memory. "That was hard on the shoulders, that one, carrying a goddamn Mitchell camera around all day. You know, we had seven days to shoot the whole thing."

"Get out of here. It looked way too good for that."

"Thank you. I developed something of a natural style because so many movies I worked on didn't have the time or money to light."

"Are you going to do any cool handheld shots in this production?" I asked.

Vilmos shook his head, somewhat resigned to his high-end movie fate. "No. Not this time around. This is a Hollywood movie. We're going for *pretty*."

"But scene seventy-seven, where Foyl chases Harry down the street dodging traffic, could play really well handheld, don't you think?"

"I know, believe me, I talked to Mike about this already."

"What's this?" Mike asked from across the room. He was known for caninelike hearing. "Is someone saying my name?"

Vilmos explained as Mike joined us. "Well, it's the sequence with the traffic. Bruce and I were just longing for some handheld in the middle of it."

"Really? You're not sold on the 'long-lens-keep-our-distance' approach?"

"Of course, that will still work," Vilmos reasoned, "but handheld might be a good way to put the audience in the middle of the chaos."

Vilmos took this film off his resume a long time ago.

I almost brought up Vilmos's applicable work in *Wild and Willing* (also '65), but I decided not to be the expert; I was happy just to have introduced the topic.

"Well, on the day, we might do a pass at that," Mike said, waffling a bit. "But let's keep the telephoto stuff on hand."

"Of course, sure," Vilmos assured Mike.

A peculiar feeling came over me as I watched these two legends interact. There was a mutual respect there, a reciprocity of esteem that momentarily raised the grubby business of moviemaking to an art. This, I realized, was why I was here. I wanted to be acknowledged by these men as a fellow artisan, a laborer in the machinery of the sublime. Desperate to make an impression, I used the tools I had. "You know, you could go shaky cam," I blurted.

There was a brief silence as both men took in this suggestion. I was certain that a "mind your own fucking business" speech was on its way, but I was pleasantly surprised:

"What is a shaky cam?" Vilmos asked, curious.

"It's just a camera mounted in the middle of a two-by-four with a bolt. You get a guy on either end of the board, and it becomes pretty stable. You can screw bicycle grips to the ends if you want, but the cool effect is that you can be chasing someone, like Foyl and Harry, through traffic, and the camera can rise up and glide over things, like taxicabs, garbage cans, people — whatever. A Steadicam operator can't do that. It also works great for demon P.O.V. shots."

"Ever work with one of these shaky cams, Vilmos?" Mike asked gamely, ignoring my last comment.

"No, but it sounds like it might give a great perspective above the traffic, so you can see the chase."

"I agree," Mike said. "Let's check it out. You're just full of good ideas today, aren't you, Foyl?"

What's the difference between an actor and a dummy? Residuals.

"Well, I just reread the script again last night, and I got curious about things. Like, uh, how were you going to do the scene where the concierge falls out the window?"

Mike and Vilmos looked at each other. "Same as we planned," Mike explained. "A high fall stunt that the second unit crew will shoot."

There was another silence as I considered his approach. "I was kind of hoping you were going to use a dummy."

Vilmos couldn't help but snicker, and I turned to him. "If you can use a dummy in *Deliverance*, Vilmos, you can use one on this film," I scolded.

"There was a dummy in *Deliverance*?" Mike asked Vilmos.

"There was," Vilmos admitted. "Just a quick shot. It was too dangerous of a stunt. This kid has a good eye."

"There was also a dummy used in *Bridge on the River Kwai*," I explained.

"Really?" Mike asked. "In a David Lean film? I always associated dummies with cheap and cheesy."

"They're cheap all right, Mike. They're one of the cheapest, most effective special effects around. A dummy can do what a stuntman will never attempt," I argued, basking in the director's attentive gaze. "I was thinking a dummy, because in the script it's described as 'a blur, happening out of the corner of Harry's eye.' It read funny to me, and nothing says comedy like a dummy, as long as the arms and legs don't bend backward."

Mike whirled to June, who always manages to stay nearby, yet never too close. "June, remind me to put in a call to Marty Sossin, the mechanical effects guy, about a dummy." Mike turned back, every bit the energized director. "Okay, Vilmos, Foyl, let's shoot this thing!"

As makeup, wardrobe, and hair did their final touches, Vilmos turned to Karen, his very butch camera assistant. "Take the camera off sticks. I want to shoot this test handheld."

When Mike heard that, he looked up from his monitor. "I like that, Vilmos. It's gritty. It's New York."

"I thought you might," Vilmos said, slipping a pad on his shoulder and hoisting the Arriflex camera up. "This is a lot lighter than a Mitchell, I can tell you."

Mike stood on his feet. He expected to see a bit of my character,

Foyl, come out today. "Foyl? You ready for this?" he asked. "Are you feeling handheld?"

"Any time, sir," I said, slipping into a southern gentleman drawl.

"Okay, let's have it. Let's have the back story — action!"

And I was happy to oblige, riffing for long periods about my character and the world according to him. Meanwhile, Vilmos was getting very creative in the handheld arena, dropping low at times, getting up close at others, all to Mike's great delight.

"And...cut!" he shouted. "Good, Bruce. You've been doing your homework!"

"Thanks Mike," I said, more relieved than I sounded.

Mike turned his attention to Vilmos, now sweaty from the camerawork. "You old dog, that was really effective. Let's talk about this shaky cam...."

Mike escorted Vilmos to the craft service table, chatting excitedly about camera techniques. I was filled with pride, knowing that in my own humble way, I had influenced their conversation.

People tend to make fun of low-budget movies, often because they lack the smooth sophistication of slick Hollywood fare. But what the average viewer fails to recognize is that low-budget movies, with almost nothing to lose, are far more likely to push the creative envelope. Granted, most of them fall flat on their face because of poor writing, choppy editing, and bad acting, but you have to love them for trying.

Before *Let's Make Love!*, I used to think that working on high-budget movies was boring, simply because they never tried anything new or daring. I also felt slightly out-of-touch working on blockbuster movies, mainly because the process of making them tends to be impersonal. But after a few weeks hacking around this interesting Mike Nichols movie, I hadn't had a boring day yet and, best of all, I was beginning to feel like I was part of something special.

13

Seven Brides for Seven Husbands

Richard Gere's character, Harry, gets divorced in the first scene of the film, and Foyl, the trusty doorman, is there to counsel him. Having been through the big D once myself, I wasn't willing to do it again in the name of research, but I could sure talk to an expert on the subject.

America is full of multidivorced people, but few can hold a candle to the queen of Splitsville, Elizabeth Taylor. As fate would have it, Ms. Taylor was slated to appear in *Let's Make Love!* as Richard Gere's mother, and she was staying in New York City at my old stomping grounds, the Waldorf.

I knew the chances of actually scoring an interview were pretty slim, so I hinged my plea on the fact that I was a costar doing research, not a reporter digging up dirt.

"Hey, everyone's gotta eat," were the first words out of Elizabeth Taylor's mouth over the phone. "What are you doing tonight?"

"Having dinner with you, Ms. Taylor," I said, sounding cool, yet pumping my fist in the air silently.

Elizabeth Taylor is about as close to royalty as you can get in the States, so she feels comfortable in really nice places, like the newly restored Visaro restaurant in the Waldorf. We agreed to meet for dinner at seven o'clock. I wore the best suit I could find, but I still felt like a homeless person as I stepped out of my cab in front of the famed hotel.

Waiting dutifully was Vinnie, a fellow doorman during my single day of work. "Well, well, well," he said, with a wry smile. "If it isn't John Hinckley, Jr. What brings you back here?"

"I'll have you know, Vinnie, I'm here as a guest."

"Okay, well, try not to start another incident, 'cause a certain you-know-who is coming here again tonight."

"No shit, Colin Pow —?"

"Ix-nay, Owell-pay," Vinnie said, hushed.

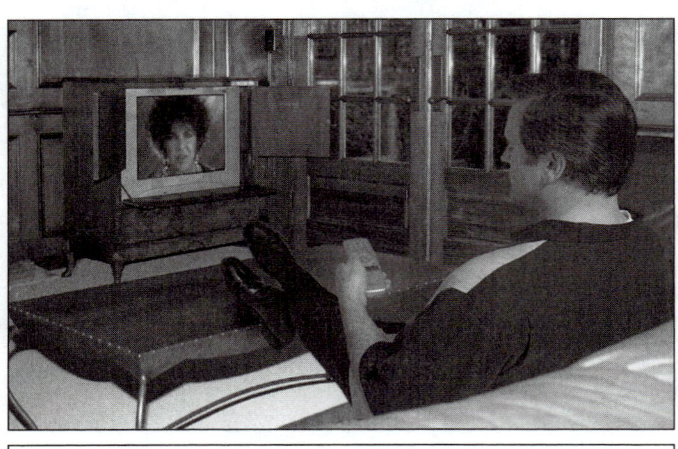

Acting for Dummies: boning up on Elizabeth Taylor.

I nodded silently then looked at him expectantly. "Aren't you forgetting something?"

Vinnie looked around then realized he hadn't opened the hotel door. "Oh, sorry, man," he said, swinging it open wide.

I tipped him a buck and stepped inside. The Visaro restaurant, which was across the lobby, looked like a movie set: well-dressed extras eating fine cuisine in low light. I approached a stuffy-looking fellow about locating my date.

"Good evening, my good man."

"Good evening, sir," he said in a thick English accent. "May I help you?"

I have a theory about why there are so many English chaps working as hosts and receptionists in New York and Los Angeles: It's because there are truckloads of unemployed British actors in both cities, many from the Royal Shakespeare Company, and what else are they going to do to pay the rent? Rich enclaves tend to max out on the pretension thing, and nothing fits that image better than a snooty English fellow who isn't particularly interested in helping.

"You sure can, slick," I said casually. "I'm here to sup with Ms. Elizabeth Taylor — you know, the movie star?"

"Of course I do. You must be Mr. Campbell. Right this way. Ms. Taylor is already here."

Yikes, I thought to myself. *I thought only people from Michigan showed up early.*

The maitre d' led me to a quiet, corner booth. Seated alone was Elizabeth Taylor. My knees buckled a bit when I saw her for the first time, just thinking about all the movies she's been in, from the epic bomb *Cleopatra* to one of my all time favorites, *Who's Afraid of Virginia Woolf?* Even in her golden years, Liz was still pretty and elegant. She held out her hand as I approached the table.

"Hello, dear, you must be Bruce."

"Yes, ma'am. It's a real pleasure to meet you."

"I'd get up, but my hips aren't what they used to be."

"Oh, that's quite all right, uh, how should I address you? Ms. Taylor? Dame Taylor?"

"Liz is fine," she said with a smile. "Dame makes me sound like an old battle-axe."

"Although you must have enjoyed being crowned."

"Oh, it was marvelous — so opulent, deeply opulent," Liz said.

"When I heard you were crowned, I thought to myself, well, from one Queen Elizabeth to another."

"Oh, you dear man, sit down right next to me," Liz said, patting the chair nearby. "Jules, let's get some iced tea for this charmer."

Jules, the snooty English fellow, didn't quibble with Liz. He nodded and was gone in two seconds.

"I gather from your note that you're playing Foyl, the doorman," Liz said.

"Right, and since he's full of relationship advice, I thought I could round out my research by talking to you, a woman who's, uh —"

"Been around the block?" Liz offered.

"Well, you have had quite the life."

"With quite the men, yes." Liz nodded. "I'm sure I'm the perfect subject. Where do you want to start?"

"Well, let's see, you've been married seven times."

"Have I? I lost count," Liz said, obviously numb from the amount of times she's talked about this.

"I just want to know what it is about marriage you enjoy so much, seeing as how you went through the process so many times. Most people would have stopped riding that horse after the third or fourth time."

"Well, if you fall off a horse, you have to get right back on, don't you, or you might never want to ride again — I learned that from *National Velvet*. I like the company of men, I don't hide that. I find them to be fascinating creatures."

Liz finished her last words while looking directly at me. I'd like to flatter myself in thinking that her burning, violet-eyed stare, the one that went right through me, was the result of my wit and obvious charms. Sadly, Liz is just a dynamic woman — when she looks at you, you know

t. I guess that's why she's a movie star. My trance was broken by Jules, eturning Liz's iced tea.

"And Jules, could you fetch me some Sweet 'n Low?" Liz asked sweetly.

"Of course, ma'am. I'll *fetch* it right away," he said, turning on a heel, briskly.

Liz watched him go approvingly, then turned to me. "I don't even use Sweet 'n Low, I just love to watch him walk."

I cleared my throat and continued. "I applaud your attraction to men, being one of them myself, but that doesn't mean you have to get married in each case."

"No, but I was married for the first time in 1950. In those days, if you dated a man for any length of time, you were more than likely to end up married. I was eighteen, but that wasn't unusual then, except for the fact that I was a movie star. Movie stars were expected to make a little whoopee before they tied the knot. You're married, aren't you?"

"Yes ma'am, second time around."

Liz held her hand up to her mouth in shock. "Oh, you've been divorced?"

"Yeah, I'm afraid I have," I said, enjoying her antics.

"And how long did you know her before you got married?"

"Whose interview is this, Liz?" I asked.

"Shush, answer the question."

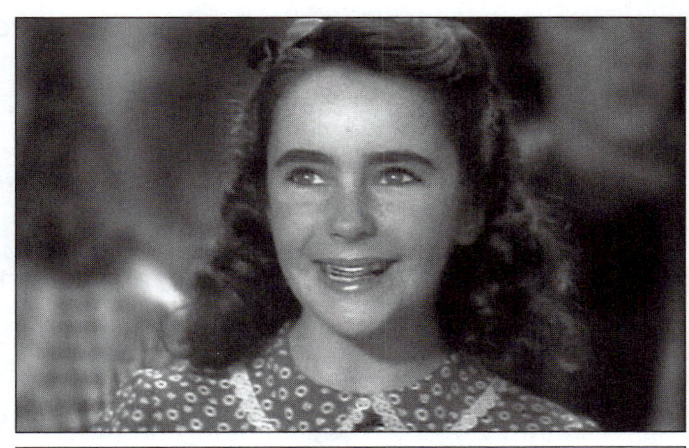

"I'd like another husband, please."

"A year — she was married when we met."

Liz held up her hand again in horror. "Oh, the scandal!"

"Wait, it wasn't like that," I explained. "For the first six months I jus worked with her."

"Hold that goddamned cue card closer, moron!"

"Okay, so yo broke up a marriag and got hitched si months later. I don feel so bad now."

I opened my mout to explain the situatio but Jules arrived wit her Sweet 'n Low.

"Here you are ma'am."

"Thank you, darling."

Jules walked away and Liz watched him go, a faint smile across he classic lips.

"Liz, I ran the numbers the other day. You've been married seve times, encompassing about thirty-three or so years. That's an averag of almost five years per marriage."

"Yes, but my goodness, if I wasn't an actress, I wouldn't have bee married nearly as many times. Every party I went to — and in thos days you couldn't say no because it was all arranged by the studios – I'd meet rich men, and famous men, and powerful men. It was all too ir resistible. Hollywood, in its day, was just one big playground."

"Yes, you have had your share of each of those types. First tim around, it seems like you went for the money."

"You're referring to Nicky Hilton — Conrad, Jr."

"Son of the hotel magnate, yeah."

"Nicky was a combination of things," Liz said. "He was very cool, a classic playboy. He would do crazy things like get his father's jet and take us to Miami for the weekend. As an eighteen-year-old, what did I know? It was all marvelous. The studio fought it at first, but they relented and, of course, I got married in a studio wedding dress."

"Membership has its privileges."

Liz smiled, but it was slightly sad. "And then, of course, it all turned to custard."

"Out of eight months with Nicky, how many were good?"

"Was that all it was? You've done your research?"

"I have, and yeah, it was. If it's any consolation, my wife has a friend who stayed married only four months."

"Some marriages just burn hot, then burn out."

"Then you married an actor, for God's sake."

"Yes, Michael Wilding. I thought he was gorgeous."

"There must have been more than that — you had several children with him."

"Well, because we were in the same profession, we just had so much in common. And he was so charming with his British accent. Jules reminds me a bit of Michael."

"That marriage was about four and a half years," I elaborated. "Just about the average. I love the fact that Michael was, at one time, a stand-in for Douglas Fairbanks, Jr."

"Well, you have to start somewhere, Mr. *Evil Death*."

"*Evil Dead*. You've heard of those films?"

"I've heard about them but I haven't seen them. It's a chainsaw film, isn't it, lots of gore?"

"Yeah, that's the one," I said, sipping some tea to wet my dry throat.

"But next time out of the gate, you went higher up the food chain. You went for a producer."

"Yes, and that was the beginning of what I call the scandal years. All the hoopla hid the fact that I was still marrying these people, it wasn't like I was just shacking up. Have you ever lived with a woman, Bruce?"

"Uh, well, yes, I have."

This time, when Liz put her hand up to her mouth in shock, I joined in and we performed it in sync.

"Now, Mike Todd was a big thinker, a pioneer of sorts. His company Todd-AO, developed the 65-millimeter film frame thingamajig. It was the best big-screen system in its day."

"You know, women are attracted to men for all kinds of reasons," Liz explained. "But I always liked men who had a plan. Besides, that marriage doesn't really count, because Mike was taken away from me," she said, dabbing her brilliant blue eyes with a tissue.

"You obviously loved the guy."

"I sure did. He was loud and bombastic, but he got things done. He was one guy who never crapped around."

"I guess things got sticky later with Eddie Fisher."

"Well, sure, because Eddie was Mike Todd's best man, and he was married to Debbie Reynolds, a national treasure. You couldn't have planned a more ludicrous scandal, but it all happened pretty organically."

"What was the appeal of Eddie Fisher at that time?"

"You can't be serious. Eddie was bigger than Elvis Presley in his day. He had one of the largest endorsement contracts ever. People always talk about me getting a million bucks for *Cleopatra*. Granted, that was a lot of money in the sixties, but it was a lot more when Eddie got that much from Coca-Cola in the *fifties*! I didn't know the world drank that much Coke. I went for Eddie because the rest of America was after him too."

"But he had a lot to lose at that point. You at least were coming from a sympathetic situation."

"Sure. Eddie had a lot to lose, and he lost it all. Love is a gamble. Eddie knew that to divorce his terrific wife in the fifties, he would face repercussions, and he sure did, bless him."

"Of course, he wasn't jumping ship for chopped liver exactly," I corrected. "There are a lot of men who would take a leap for you, Liz."

"Oh, you delightful man, you," she said, playfully pinching my cheek.

"But by your own calculations, that marriage actually *exceeded* the average. You were married to Eddie for five years."

"I guess I was," Liz said with a nod. "Not bad for a tabloid marriage. Eddie and I had been around the block even before this blew up. You learn to develop a stomach for the scrutiny, the pressure. I'd love to see what would happen to the average marriage if they were photographed and written about twenty-four hours a day."

"They have a TV show like that now."

"Oh that's dreadful," Liz said, truly horrified. "You know, Richard and I put up with a lot of scrutiny, both professionally and as a couple."

"I'm assuming you're referring to Richard Burton."

"Of course, silly."

"He seemed like a pretty dynamic guy, enough so to marry him twice."

"Dynamic, that's a fun choice of words. Yes, Richard was bigger than life. Our marriage was bigger than life. Our work during that time was bigger than life. I guess we were looking for a bigger than life experience and we found it. We fought loudly, we loved loudly, we laughed loudly, we cried loudest of all."

"It sounds very theatrical."

Liz's own rogues' gallery of ex-husbands.

"Yes, it was as if we were both 'on' the whole time. It was very memorable, though. I don't regret either marriage to Richard, because he was so extraordinary. And I didn't worry about the scandal because by then everything was a scandal. I was even rebuked by the Vatican, you know."

"You got me beat there," I said. "Of course, I'm guessing the Pope hasn't seen *Evil Dead* yet."

"They published a statement denouncing my 'erotic vagrancy,'" she said proudly.

"Well, lewd behavior aside, I thought you and Richard worked really well together and that you did some great stuff during that time."

"In between the chaos, yes, I think so too," she agreed.

"Now, while I won't use the term 'love of your life,' Richard was certainly the most long-term marriage. Counting both times, you were together eleven years."

"Yes, that's the equivalent of sixty-seven years in Hollywood," Liz giggled. "It lasted that long because we were working a lot and we were working together — it kept us out of trouble. We kept the trouble between us."

"Okay, I have to ask: John Warner, husband number six. What was the deal with that?"

"What do you mean 'what's the deal?' When I was with him, he was a statesman, a powerful man, a true gentleman."

"But he doesn't seem very exciting."

"You're not up on current events," Liz countered. "John has done it all: Secretary of the Navy; work with the Defense Department; a five-term senator. You don't have to be snapping your fingers all the time to be a type-A go-getter. He had a strong will and genuine drive. I couldn't help but admire that."

"I understand he called you his 'little heifer.'"

Liz smiled. "John called me that because of how often I had a cow," and then she lifted her head, roaring with laughter. "It suited me well, I guess. I think Richard Burton would agree."

"So, there's only one husband left," I said, glancing at my crumpled list with six names crossed off.

"Now, be nice. I've heard a lot of jokes about Larry, who is a really sweet man."

"I have to say, with Larry, you really shook the pattern up. You'd been married to famous actors, singers, politicians, business moguls, but that was the first time you ever landed a teamster. You have to understand the public's fascination with that one."

"Of course — the newspapers jumped all over it," Liz said, still angry, framing the imaginary headlines with her delicate hand: QUEEN ELIZABETH MARRIES A PAUPER, LIZ FINALLY GETS HER DREAM HOME — BUILT

By Larry! My God, it was absurd. And then there was the 'age' issue."

"I didn't want to bring it up."

"There's no way to avoid the topic. That was the second part of the scandal. It wasn't bad enough that he was 'just' a construction worker, he was also twenty years younger than me."

"Yeah, the year Larry was born, you married your second husband, Michael Wilding."

I raised my hand to my mouth, and Liz brought hers up as well — another shared, shocked moment.

"But I'll tell you what," Liz explained, "by the time Larry came along, I was ready for a man like that. The downside of a whirlwind life is that it's a whirlwind life — you can't keep playing can-you-top-this forever. Very successful men can also be very unpleasant to be around, and Larry was just...Larry."

"Was it really that simple?"

"Yes, it was. When we met in group therapy, I wasn't there hoping to find a younger man, I was there to get sober."

"Well, something must have clicked, because you stayed married for five years."

"Aside from making his lunch every day, being married to Larry wasn't bad at all. It was the closest I've ever had to a 'normal' life."

"Okay, so the obvious question after all this is: what makes a marriage go bad?"

"I think people either oversimplify or overanalyze that concept. Divorce is different for each person. For me, marriages ended for a variety of reasons, usually a combination of growing apart, *being* apart too much, the occasional abusive situation, boredom — the same reasons anyone else gets divorced."

"What makes one work?"

They say there's no such thing as bad publicity.

"Oh, honey, I don't have any idea. I think the entire institution is something of a flawed notion."

"All right, so last question. You've had a lot of divorces. I only had one, and I barely walked away from it. How did you manage those dark days, after a divorce?"

Liz was about to answer when an incredibly fit blond man arrived at our table. Liz looked at me knowingly. "Oh, you get by," she said, gesturing to the beautiful man. "He's my head of security, aren't you, Lars?"

"Ya," he said simply.

Liz held out her hand for Lars and he helped her up. "You know, I've had a lot of heartache in my life: failed marriages, movies that bombed, health problems, I've been in and out of rehab," she said, snuggling up to Lars. "But the rest of the time, it's great to be Elizabeth Taylor. I mean, what do you expect me to do, sleep alone?"

This ageless beauty winked at me and escorted Lars back to her Waldorf penthouse. I glanced at the check ($147.40 for iced tea, a mint julep, and a fruit plate) and gasped. *Thank God for the Screen Actors Guild*. Being on location, I had a week's worth of per diem burning a hole in my pocket, so I paid the bill in cash and walked out.

On my way across the very familiar lobby, I noticed a lot of activity. Men in dark suits were prowling about the entrance, excusing their way though the usual Waldorf clientele, while keeping one finger on the communication device in their ear.

Secret Service agents are trained to notice body language. They look at hands and eyes, and take note of erratic ticks. I made eye contact with a familiar, clean-cut Agent Grunow, looked away too quickly, knew I'd made a mistake, and bolted for the exit.

"Halt!" Grunow shouted, and began running after me.

I just wanted to get the hell out of there so I decided to ignore him, and by the time we converged at the revolving doors, we were both in a full-out sprint. Grunow dove at me from behind, and our combined inertia took us through the doors and out the other side — directly into Colin Powell, who had just reached the entrance himself.

The three of us did a painful group hug down the broad steps of the Waldorf. Secret Service agents, doormen, taxi drivers, and guests all watched in horror as we rolled past the first landing and kept going down the second set of stairs.

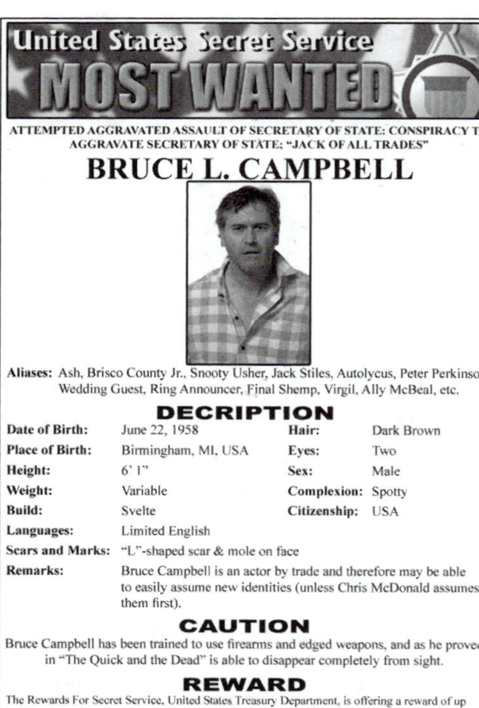

United States Secret Service
MOST WANTED

ATTEMPTED AGGRAVATED ASSAULT OF SECRETARY OF STATE: CONSPIRACY TO AGGRAVATE SECRETARY OF STATE; "JACK OF ALL TRADES"

BRUCE L. CAMPBELL

Aliases: Ash, Brisco County Jr., Snooty Usher, Jack Stiles, Autolycus, Peter Perkinson, Wedding Guest, Ring Announcer, Final Shemp, Virgil, Ally McBeal, etc.

DECRIPTION

Date of Birth:	June 22, 1958	**Hair:**	Dark Brown
Place of Birth:	Birmingham, MI, USA	**Eyes:**	Two
Height:	6' 1"	**Sex:**	Male
Weight:	Variable	**Complexion:**	Spotty
Build:	Svelte	**Citizenship:**	USA
Languages:	Limited English		
Scars and Marks:	"L"-shaped scar & mole on face		
Remarks:	Bruce Campbell is an actor by trade and therefore may be able to easily assume new identities (unless Chris McDonald assumes them first).		

CAUTION

Bruce Campbell has been trained to use firearms and edged weapons, and as he proved in "The Quick and the Dead" is able to disappear completely from sight.

REWARD

The Rewards For Secret Service, United States Treasury Department, is offering a reward of up to $25 million for information leading directly to the apprehension or conviction of Bruce L. Campbell.

At this point, Secret Service agents began doing what I would describe as a World Series pile on, hurling themselves at our tumbling group until we became a human mass, undulating down the steps and finally crashing to a halt by the horse-drawn carriages waiting out front.

At the bottom of the pile, I was pressed face-to-face with Colin Powell.

"Mr. Secretary, it's not what you think," I explained through lips that were pressed against the bottom of someone's dress shoe.

Before he could respond, I was hoisted to my feet by a baker's dozen Secret Service agents and shoved into a waiting town car. Colin Powell got the "human shield" treatment back inside the hotel, and aside from a few bumps and bruises, he was no worse off.

I couldn't talk my way out of this "incident," and it necessitated a call to Dale, my dutiful lawyer. Unfortunately, because of my new status on the ISL (Internal Security List), no amount of legal wrangling or corroboration (and Liz Taylor wasn't happy about being interrupted that night for questioning, let me tell you) could spring me before they ran a more detailed Security Threat Analysis, or STA. The fancy title meant that they were going to take a deeper look into the ways I had irritated the U.S. government in the past.

As I lay in the holding cell, numerous past infractions flashed before my eyes, any one of which could land me on an ESTL (Elevated Security Threat List): parking violations, late library books, failing to renew my Jefferson County Sheriff's Association membership.

It was a long, cold, sleepless night.

14

Lights, Camera, Mayhem!

I must have checked out clean enough to avoid "Enemy Combatant" status, because I was discharged from my "undisclosed holding cell" at 6:15 A.M. — forty-five minutes shy of call time for my first shooting day on *Let's Make Love!*

My cab screeched to a halt outside New York's Astoria studios at 7:05, exactly five minutes late — a miracle, considering the fact that I had no idea where I was coming *from*. I paid the driver, but didn't get very far before a harried woman with a walkie-talkie and a name badge swooped down on me.

"Good morning, Bruce, I'm De-BOR-ah, the DGA trainee," she said, already grabbing my arm.

"You don't have to grab me, Deborah, we'll make it," I assured her. "And please refer to me as Foyl from now on."

Deborah sighed and let go of me. "Sorry…Foyl. And, my name looks like Deborah, but it's pronounced de-BOR-ah."

"Okay, sure."

"Base Camp is this way," she said, leading us through the Astoria complex.

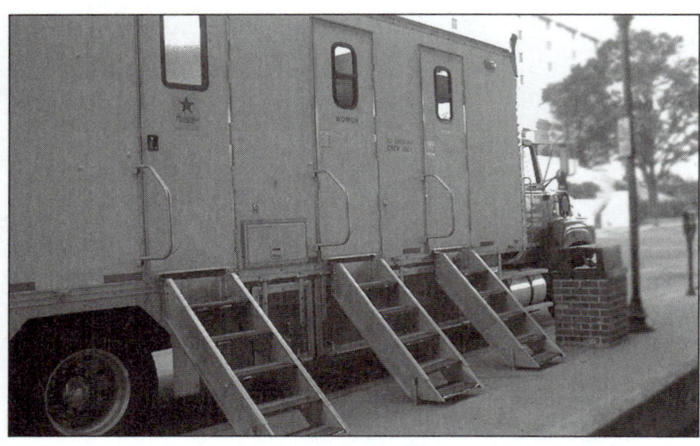

Base camp: an actor's home away from home.

"So, how's the shoot going?" I asked. "You've been at it for what, a week now?"

"God, it seems so much longer than that," Deborah exhaled.

"That didn't sound very optimistic — this is a Mike Nichols film!"

No sooner had the words come out of my mouth than we had to pause to let a half-dozen grips move a twenty-foot-square portable green screen — an indispensable special-effects tool, used for compositing layers of motion-picture images.

"Well, because of things like that," Deborah said, "this film is two weeks behind after only one week of shooting."

"Wow," I said, surprised. "Is that typical for Mike? I know he likes to improvise."

"Improvise? We should be so lucky. No, this is about rewriting, rethinking, reinventing."

Just as she said this, Deborah and I steered clear of a group of puppeteers, each dressed in ninjalike black clothing and wearing harnesses with rods attached to surreal human figures.

"Is Cirque du Soleil shooting on the lot?" I asked, looking back after we had extricated ourselves from the puppeteers.

"Script changes started coming so fast, the crew never had a chance to read them before a new batch would come in. Now, we're all just swinging it one shot at a time."

We had to sidestep a stake bed truck that was backing up to unload what could best be called a shaky cam on steroids. Some ambitious young go-getters in the mechanical effects department had since gotten their hands on the same primitive camera rig I told Mike about. For a device usually comprising a two-by-four, bicycle grips, and a bolt, it was far more tricked out now, with leveling capability, safety devices, a gyroscope, and even a drink holder. Either way, I was intensely pleased to see it was now part of this massive operation.

Deborah and I got to the edge of Base Camp, a loose configuration of vehicles, generators, catering equipment, and trailers. My trailer was the type affectionately known as a "double banger." I'm not sure which snide teamster named it that, but a double banger is the duplex of actor housing, meaning that I shared a wall with some other unsuspecting thespian.

I unloaded my stuff and had a look around. Every so often, an actor gets lucky and the trailer is brand-new, with the latest perks. Mine was hot off the assembly line, and that meant the lights worked, the toilet flushed, and there was even hot water.

In the corner, I noticed a climbing harness draped over my padded swivel chair, with a note pinned to it:

BRUCE,
HAVE A LOOK AT THIS HARNESS AND
FEEL FREE TO MAKE ANY ADJUSTMENTS.
I'LL DROP BY AND HELP YOU INTO IT
— JOHNNY.

The note was from my buddy, Johnny Casino, the stunt coordinator. *Harness? What the hell is the harness for?* I wondered. My wardrobe was laid out, and as I sifted through the clothes, I noticed a pair of pants that had been prepped for interfacing with stunt rigging.

Knock-knock-knock

I opened the door to a tall, thin man with a cigarette in his hand.

"Hi, Randall Klein, wardrobe supervisor. Is it true we should only refer to you as Foyl?"

"That's right."

"Are you finding everything okay?"

"I think so," I said, "but I wonder if I'm in the right trailer. What's with the harness, and the rigged clothes?"

"We're doing the harness first up. I left a note pinned to your jacket."

"For what scene?" I asked, growing concerned.

"Well, it's not a scene, per se, it's...an *enhancement* — yes, that's the word we're using now — an enhancement to scene seventy-six where you fight with Richard, or should I say Harry? Let me know if you and Johnny need any help putting that thing on."

"Sure."

Randall sucked on his cigarette and scampered off. I shut the door, locked it, and rifled through the script to scene seventy-six, where Foyl confronts Richard's character. We grappled and wrestled, but why did we need wire work?

Knock-knock-knock

I opened the door to a tall, muscular fellow.

"Bruce, how are you, buddy?" Johnny asked, flashing his trademark rodeo grin.

"Confused," I said, "but come on in and let's chat about this harness."

Johnny followed me in. I shut the door, and we exchanged a hearty handshake.

"Been a while," Johnny said, hooking a thumb into his belt. "Not since the *Death* movies, right?"

"Yeah, pretty much. Hey, so, what's with the harness? What part of the scene is it for?"

"It's during the fight. You get Richard in a bear hug and he throws you off. And Mike, well, he wants to add some 'mish-mash.'"

Evil Dead 2: Some of my best harness work.

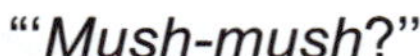

"'*Mush-mush*?'"

"Yeah, that's the term. I gotta tell you, it's a little weird. I've worked with him for twenty years and I've never seen him like this. I gaffed *Wolf*, and he left all the stunt stuff up to me because he hated it. Now, it's like he's John Woo or some shit, but, hey, we aim to please — and cash the check!" Johnny slapped his hands together. "So, we're almost ready out there. You just slip it on and cinch it up. We'll tighten it on the set."

"Okay, Johnny, thanks," I said, somewhat resigned to my fate.

I locked the door again and changed out of my street clothes. I wriggled into the harness, which is similar to the type of rig worn by rock climbers, and a terrible wave of dread swept over me. The last time I wore a similar harness was for the film *Army of Darkness*, and my memories of the experience were anything but fond — the toll on my extremities, the nausea, the strap rash on my inner thighs. To this day, I walk with a slight limp because a nylon strap did a number on my left hamstring.

Knock-knock-knock

De-BOR-ah was back with an update. “Makeup and hair are ready to see you, Foyl.”

“Thanks.”

I slipped into the flannel robe they provided, and found my way to the brightly lit makeup and hair trailer.

“Good morning,” I said, shielding my eyes from the white fluorescent light. “I’m Foyl, reporting for duty.”

“Hold that goddamned cue card closer, moron!”

“Hi, Foyl — we got the memo about your name — please have a seat. I’m Anne Herono, and I’ll be doing your makeup.”

Anne put on a pair of small, round glasses and leaned toward my face, inspecting it.

“Just get rid of the bags under my eyes, and we’re gonna get along great,” I said, winking.

“I’m going to do a lot more than that, Foyl. Scene seventy-six is the middle of a fight scene. You’re not allergic to anything, are you?”

“Just fake blood.”

Anne was only mildly amused. “I’m going to apply two bruises, a cut on your forehead, and pavement rash on your nose.”

“Don’t you think that’s excessive for just a scuffle?”

Anne shrugged. “This came directly from Mike. He’s the director, right?”

The one nice thing about enduring long makeup applications is that I can get a forty-minute catnap out of an hour-long procedure.

Drooling has been an issue in the past, and I'm told that I snore on occasion.

My last stop on the glamour train was Jeri Feldman, hair stylist. She was a little too full of good ideas so early in the morning.

"Foyl, as you know, we're in the middle of the fight. Mike wants the hair to be really active and adaptable."

"What does that mean?"

"I'm not sure exactly, but that's what he said. Mike's been saying a lot of things, lately. We're all tap dancing as fast as we can."

"Sure, well, take your best shot," I said, thumbing through a fashion magazine.

Between makeup and hair, two and a half hours had elapsed. I emerged from the trailer looking like a man who had been on the losing side of a soccer riot.

Deborah led me to stage eleven, where an entire facade of the Park Avenue Arms had been built. Under these conditions, Mike would have complete control over the atmosphere. It was an impressive scene, with extras and cabs bustling everywhere, their movement coordinated by a squad of assistant directors, and the Shaky Cam Deluxe, standing by for use.

"Where's Mike, De-BOR-ah?" I asked.

"He's by the camera," she said, pointing. "They're setting up."

I waddled to the set, since that's all you can do when a harness is wrapped around your gonads, and caught Mike's eye.

"Good morning, Foyl, you ready for a little fun today?" Mike asked jovially.

"Yeah, the harness gag is an interesting touch."

"I'm just driving the truck down the highway that you and Richard have been paving. I'm running with this and having a ball."

"Okay, I hear you," I said, smiling. "But where does this piece fit in the scheme of things?"

"I'll show you," Mike said, walking over to his multimonitor video setup. "June, have you got the boards for this scene?"

"Right here," she said, handing Mike an immense binder with easily three hundred pages of storyboards. "I've marked the page with this shot."

"Thanks, hon," Mike said, opening the binder to storyboard number 785-A7.

"Since when did you start using storyboards?" I asked, surprised.

"Well, there are so many gags in this scene now, I had to lay it out shot for shot. Okay, in this one, you and Richard are here in the foreground. On action, he'll throw you back. I'll be shooting handheld —"

"You actually shoot too?"

"Well, I haven't before, but this film has cracked wide open for me. I'm going to Shaky Cam away from you, as you go away from us."

"Uh-huh...."

Mike grabbed me by the arm. "You're over here." He led me to a neon yellow, T-shaped mark on the sidewalk. "You'll be ratcheted back from here."

"To where?"

Mike turned to a group of fit, T-shirted guys and whistled. "Terry, let's get Johnny." He turned his attention back to me. "Up there, to the second story. Just get as far as you can. You don't actually have to reach the windowsill, because when you're halfway up, we'll paint you out and fill in the rest of your movements with a digital rendering. Okay, good luck!"

Mike patted me on the shoulder and headed back to the camera as Johnny arrived.

Mike tells me that Foyl will ultimately be replaced by a CGI character nicknamed "Door-Manimal."

"Sorry, just setting a pick point for another gag," he said, slightly out of breath.

"It's fine, I'm in no hurry to lose my breakfast. Now, Johnny, give it to me straight — is this going to be ugly?" I asked.

Johnny looked at me with an expression that lacked his usual cocksure smirk. "Yeah, coyote ugly. They're gonna jerk you into next week, so I better cinch you up like a son of a bitch."

"Do what you must," I said, wincing at the thought.

Johnny performed a series of painful strap checks, then turned to Steve "Overtime" Krasner, the first assistant director. "All set here, Steve!"

Richard Gere arrived on set, looking refreshed and happy. "Hey, Foyl!"

"Vegas high five," I said, smiling and offering up a hand.

Richard slapped me loud and proud. "Hey, I did my first stunt today, a high fall, about twenty feet, into boxes. It was awesome, like ballet. I wish I had gotten more into this physical stuff a long time ago. I have you to thank for that. And listen, that Dodge is absolutely crazy. I used to have a thing about gas-guzzlers, but in this day and age, I'm willing to be more open-minded. Thanks."

I had myself to thank for what I was about to endure as well, but I wasn't as giddy as Richard.

"First positions!" Steve called out.

I stood behind Richard and wrapped my arms around his shoulders, assuming the "bear hug" stance.

"Be glad of two things, Richard: one, that you're wearing a hat, and two, that I had a light breakfast."

"Okay, here we go — roll sound!" Steve shouted, and the crew went through its usual pretake gyrations.

"Speed!" the sound man shouted from afar.

"All right — three, two, one, *action*!"

Before I could say Mary Poppins, I was yanked off of Richard's back and catapulted forty feet into the air. The sudden, violent movement knocked the wind out of me, and when I finally came to a stop, high above the soundstage, I found myself suspended, upside down.

The crew whooped in delight, the "cut" bell rang, but I remained in place.

"We're gonna release you in a second, Bruce," Johnny called from below. "How you doing?"

"Just...keep...doing your thing," I said, turning red in the face.

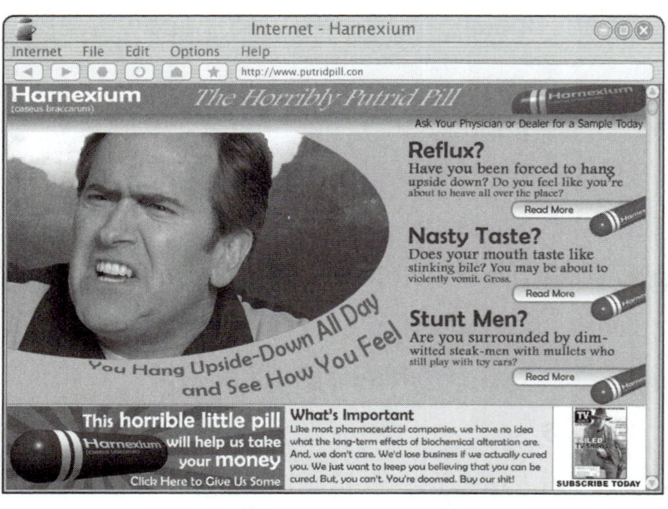

In my unbridled youth, I used to enjoy the freedom of being suspended and heights never bothered me. In my maturing years, however, the antigravity thing doesn't sit well at all. Then I got a nasty taste in my mouth.

Is this triggering some kind of heinous acid reflux? I feared. "How you doing, guys?" I asked, trying to sound unworried.

But the previous night's incarceration, plus the nervousness of the day, combined with the height, the motion, and that second goddamn Sausage McMuffin with Egg were all just too much.

"Hey, folks, sorry, better watch it down there, I think I'm gonna —"

And I blew — the fast food, the hot tea, the "curiously strong" Altoids — I blew it all. Several lucky crew members were able to heed the warning and dive to safety, but a group of four stunt guys, responsible for keeping me aloft, were not able to abandon ship and took the brunt of my acidic offering.

Let me go on record by saying that the stunt guys took their sweet damn time lowering me to the ground. By the time I got down, I was more dizzy than ashamed, and the only crew remaining was a hazardous materials team, brought in to sanitize the set.

The barfed-on stunt guys were getting towels from wardrobe as I waddled past.

"Really sorry, guys."

"That's okay, Mel Gibson blew chocolate cake into my face during *Braveheart*," one stuntman offered.

"That's good to know."

I looked over to where Mike was stationed; he was getting ready for the next shot. I could only walk as fast as a person who needed a hip replacement, but I caught up with him eventually. "Hey, Mike, that shot go okay for you?"

"Yeah, pretty good," he said, already on the move. "I think between the four cameras we should have it. Got a hell of a barf shot on B camera — extreme closeup."

"Yeah, good, hey Mike, can I ask you a couple of questions about some upcoming scenes?"

"Sure, as long as they're quick. I have to look at a dummy the effects guys made, for when you land from that last gag. It's wild, we just did an expensive digital shot, and now we're just going to throw a dummy out a window. I love it — I love that grab-bag thing you were talking about."

"Oh, good, good — but beyond this scene, I had a quick question for you about tomorrow's monologue in scene seventeen."

"Seventeen — the one in the foyer?"

"Yeah, I was hoping you'll let me really work the room in that scene — you know, get some movement going."

"Room? There is no room. We're shooting the whole foyer on green screen."

The look on my face must have urged Mike to continue.

"We're playing a much more fanciful look, Foyl," he explained. "This is a romantic comedy. We're injecting helium into this whole thing, so the foyer is going to look huge, very big, like Grand Central Station, and it won't be real, it'll be computer generated, so I'm not sure what there will be to work, but you're welcome to have some fun with it on the day."

"I see," I said, not hiding my dismay.

"But that's been pushed on the schedule anyway, so we can kick some ideas around as we get closer."

Mike and I arrived at the rear end of the mechanical effects trailer, where Marty Sossin, a bear of a man, was inside, putting the finishing touches on his latest work of art.

"What do you think, boss?" Marty asked, displaying the dummy from the back of his effects trailer.

Mike shrugged. "Looks pretty spiffy, but what can it do?"

Marty lifted the dummy high over his head. "Well, it's a titanium frame for starters, so it's really light."

He tossed the dummy down a set of metal steps where it bounced

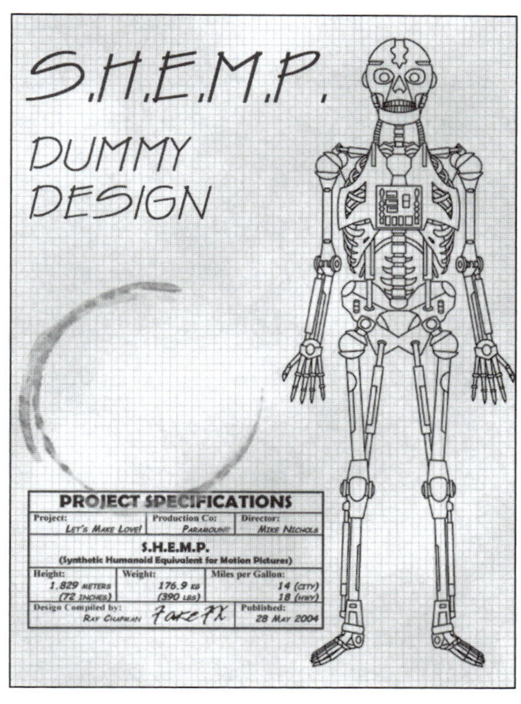

and shuddered before slumping to the pavement below. The movements of this inanimate object were eerily accurate, and I felt suddenly overwhelmed by a strange fondness for it. What that thing could have done for us in the Super-8 filmmaking days. Without having to restuff it with newspapers, or reattaching the head after every take, we could have thrown this Robo-dummy off the highest parking lot in the land with nary a scratch.

"That's the most beautiful dummy I've ever seen," I said, enviously.

"Not a bad endorsement," Mike said to Marty, walloping me on the back again. "Consider it approved. Another triumph, Mart-o."

Mike winked at me and turned to go. "Great first day, Foyl. Big one coming up with Renée in about a week."

I waddled back toward Base Camp, wondering what the hell Mike was talking about. The only big anything on my schedule was a simple bump and "excuse me" with Renée — just an eighth of a page of material. But I had more pressing issues, like returning the flow of blood to my loins.

Back in the comfort of my double banger, I wiggled out of the Harness of Death and threw it against the shared wall. I felt nauseous and sweaty, like I was coming down with a fever. I grabbed a bottle of jojoba oil, plopped into the recliner, and slathered the healing salve on my raw, rashy inner thighs.

Ruminating about the day, I wondered if Mike Nichols was just having a renaissance in his directing career, or if this classy production was being infected by my B-movie sensibility? The changing schedules, frantic rewrites, lack of communication, and unpredictable director made my first day on *Let's Make Love!* feel exactly like a B movie.

Dear God, I've spent twenty-five years climbing up the food chain in this business, and it all culminates in this, another goddamn B movie? Maybe all that "evil" stuff is real after all and I'm diseased — cursed!

I stood up to get a bottle of water and suddenly felt very light-headed. I steadied myself on the linoleum counter and tried to get centered but it was impossible — images of the past weeks flashed forward and rewound backward in my head:

The nerve-wracking audition process; Rob Stern busting my chops; dummies falling through the air; Mike lecturing me; shaky cams floating by; handheld cameras moving up to my face; crew members laughing at me, always laughing....

I looked around the trailer and the walls began to move in, ever so slightly. The place was shrinking. I became short of breath, tearing at my collar to let more air in, like the Wolf Man under a full moon.

Wracked with guilt and horror, I ran outside to my appointed Lincoln town car and dove inside.

My driver, Julio, was startled awake. "Ready to go, Mr. Campbell?" he asked politely.

"I'm ready all right, Julio. This worthless, B-grade nobody is ready to go nowhere, so hurry up and take me there."

Julio shrugged and put the car in gear. "Whatever you say, man."

He interpreted my ramblings as a request to take me back to the hotel, but upon arrival, I knew I couldn't stay there either. I couldn't go from one box to another; I had to roam, like the free-range actor I was.

and sort out my confusions.

My belligerent meanderings led me into nearby SoHo and past a familiar theater, the Angelika, which specializes in revivals, off-beat stuff, and lots of independents.

Bleary-eyed from sensory overload, I looked up at their marquee. Showing, through special arrangements, was a "Troubled Child" film series, featuring filmmakers who fought the studios. The films currently in exhibition were *Apocalypse Now*, *Brazil*, and *Bonfire of the Vanities*.

Yeah, fought the studios, I thought. *And lost.*

Each of the three films had great potential, but were hamstrung by a volatile mix of auteur excess and studio meddling. *Let's Make Love!* had all the warning signs of a troubled movie, but Mike Nichols was never prone to such excess in the past. Something stunk in La-La-Land. I began to suspect that Mike was being manipulated by that movie geek of an executive, Rob Stern, but the only way to know for sure was to puncture the corporate world of Paramount Studios and sniff around. I had a week off, and I had connections — they weren't A-list, but they were connections nonetheless.

15

Last Supper

Lanny Sticks, my costar from *Death of the Dead,* was a fine actor. I met him in Detroit, years prior, on a training film for Chrysler where Lanny played a mechanic and I was a disgruntled customer. During the three-day shoot, we shared dreams of acting in films that would be seen outside of car dealership conference rooms, and became fast friends. In the late '80s, we both relocated to Los Angeles, and our professional association continued for the next decade.

But work slowed for Lanny and, like many actors, he took a job to make ends meet, as a security guard at Paramount Studios. "At least I'm still in the movie business," he used to joke, trying to keep a brave face on his economic situation. Over the next decade, big-city distances and faraway locations diminished our contact until we lost touch entirely. It was time to change all that — I needed Lanny to get me in.

"Hey, Lanny —"

"Who is this?"

"Bruce."

"Bruce who?"

I rolled my eyes. Surely, my costar of big and small screen hadn't forgotten so quickly. "Bruce Campbell, your only true friend."

"Oh...."

This was followed by a pause that made me think the line had gone dead, but Lanny broke the silence.

"It's been awhile."

"Yeah, when was the last time I saw you, two, three years ago?" asked.

"Seven."

"No way."

"I haven't heard from you in seven years," Lanny confirmed. "Does my pal Bruce call me just to shoot the breeze? Nah. Does he call me when he's doing the special-edition DVD for *Death of the Dead*? No too much trouble. Why are you calling me now? Did someone die?"

"No, no, everyone's all right. Hey, Lanny boy, easy. I know I was lame at keeping in touch, but it's a two-way street, my friend. I haven't heard boo from you either."

"You moved once a year, on average, for a decade," Lanny said, with building anger, "and never forwarded — well, not to me, anyway — your contact information. Great way to maintain friendships, amigo."

"Okay, Lanny, I'm guilty. It's all my fault. Can we move on now?"

"What do you want?" he asked tersely.

"I need your help."

"You're right, Mr. B-Movie Man. You do need help. I saw your film *Icebreaker* the other day on cable, and I got two words for you: 'acting lessons.'"

There was a distinct hang-up click on the other end of the line.

stared at the phone as my mind veered toward self-doubt.

Had I been cruel to him? Had I been insensitive? Had I really been that bad in Icebreaker?

Well, okay, he had me there, but Lanny's role of a backwater hick in *Death of the Dead* was a lot of fun for him. And while maybe I had been a disappointment in the friendship department, I didn't recall Lanny reaching out over the years. My thoughts shifted to anger: *That bastard! Here I am, calling to see how he was, and he bites the hand that has fed him in several films.* But then I thought, *Okay, let's give it one more shot. If he blows me off after this, at least I can say that I tried.*

I let Lanny's phone ring long enough to get his answering machine: "This is Lanny, and *this* is the beep —"

Beep

"Lanny, this is Bruce. Hey, I'm just looking for some help, for old times' sake. If you won't do it for me, I understand. All a guy can do is —"

Click — "What do you need?"

The shock of Lanny picking up the phone made me jump. "Well, 'm working on *Let's Make Love!*"

"The Nichols flick, sure. I hear t's in trouble."

"Yeah, same here. So here's the deal: I need to be a fly on the wall — get on to the lot, catch some dailies, and nose around the executive offices a little bit."

"Let me get this straight. After gnoring me for seven years, you want me to risk getting fired to

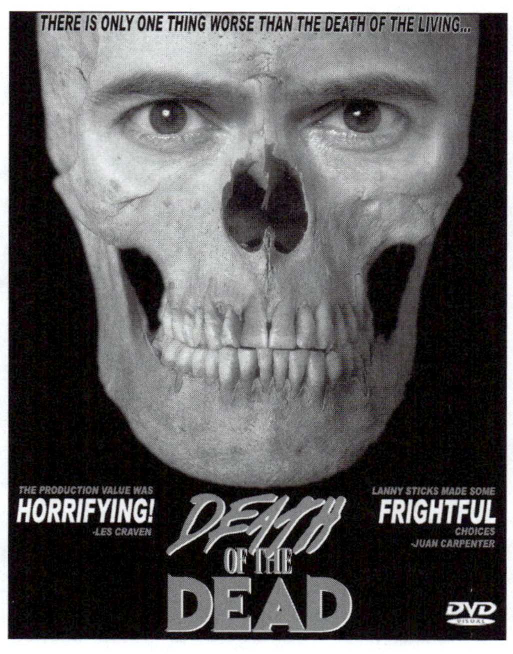

sneak you into a place I'm paid to protect?"

"Yes."

"Okay, I'll do it."

"Really?"

"Yeah. Long story. Come on over tomorrow night for dinner and we'll talk."

Lanny lived in Canyon Country, California, where I bought my first house west of the Rockies. In the mid-80s, this area was just beginning to experience a building boom. Almost twenty years later, it was completely out of control.

I took the Soledad Canyon exit off the Antelope Valley Highway, made my way past brand-new, homogenous, "American Beauty"–style developments, and pushed into the Los Angeles backcountry.

Lanny had a modest trailer on a small piece of desert. He lived alone these days, mostly because he wanted to and, frankly, because he was so cantankerous. His four dogs surrounded my car as I drove up. Two rottweilers, one pit bull, and a German shepherd — not the friendliest dogs on earth.

Sticksville, USA.

Lanny stepped out, grinning that trouble-making grin of his. He was weathered and unshaven, and seemed comfortable with both.

"Aren't you gonna come and say hi?"

"Hell no. I have a wife and kids and these dogs look hungry."

Lanny shouted something guttural and unintelligible, and his dogs mmediately sat on the ground, eyes still on me, tongues wagging in the ιot air.

"They only understand German," he explained. "It's a strong lanjuage."

"And so romantic."

"You can get out now."

I stepped around the dogs gingerly and greeted Lanny on his porch. offered a shake, he went for a hug, and it was all a little awkward, nainly because he had a double-barreled shotgun in his right hand. .anny squeezed me hard, like he was pissed off.

"Hey, man, great to see you. Welcome to my humble abode."

"Thanks," I said, getting the air back in my lungs. "You've got yourelf some place here."

"I make do. I bought this with *Death of the Dead* money, you know."

"Did you? That was smart. I pissed my money up a rope."

"It's a blessing and a curse."

"How do you mean?"

Lanny began to walk around his expansive rock-and-garbage-strewn ɔt.

"Well, some days I look out at this forty acres and I think, *my God, I wn this*, and other days I look out, and I think about…the injury."

"The injury?"

"You say that like you don't remember," Lanny said, with hurt in his yes. But before I could respond, he slapped me on the shoulder. Great to see you, Bruce — let's get some grub!"

The moon was full over Canyon Country that night. In the desert, an xposed moon makes everything look like a 1950s western — fully illuninated and washed in a blue tint.

Inside the trailer, Lanny was acting as short-order cook, and he had a greasy mixture of fried eggs, onions, and hamburger spread out on his oft-used grill.

"Lanny's hash — served twenty-four hours a day."

I was at his dining table, looking at an overhead schematic of Paramount studios, map grid number 593-G6. Latitude: 34.08365; Longitude: -118.32219 — otherwise known as Hollywood, U.S.A.

"I borrowed that from the maintenance department," he said proudly

"So, Lanny, any ideas how we pull this off so there's no paper trail or 'drive-on pass' hassles?"

"Easy. Look north to the cemetery."

According to the map, the Hollywood Memorial Park Cemetery, resting place of Marilyn Monroe and other Hollywood heavyweights, was due north of the studio. The second I saw the configuration, a story told to me fifteen years ago suddenly made sense.

"Wait a minute. I know this place. My makeup man on *Maniac Cop* — another film where you beat me up — was a young makeup apprentice on *The Ten Commandments*."

"I think I know this story," Lanny said, squinting at the memory, "but I thought it was just Hollywood B.S."

"No. This guy was there. His job was to spray dark body makeup on the extras in a special ventilated shed on the Paramount lot. But, as the wind blew, so did the makeup residue —"

"Directly on the tombstones in the cemetery," Lanny said, finishing my thought.

"Cecil B. DeMille was so horrified when he heard the news that he dispatched a small army of U.S.C. students with brushes and buckets to scrub the tombstones."

Lanny laughed at the image. "That's how close together they are

There's a hidden gate back there that connects them. I know the groundskeeper. We used to hook up and raise hell — gave 'graveyard shift' a whole new meaning. Now, look, if you want to sneak into the Paramount lot, here's what I would do: I'd go to the cemetery, pretending I was visiting the grave of some big star. Who do you like?"

"The old-fashioned guys, like Tyrone Power — is he there?"

"Sure as shit — right next to Harry Cohn, the prick who ran Columbia."

"Hey, don't say that — Columbia is responsible for *The Three Stooges*."

"He was still a prick. The point is, you stop by to pay your respects to Ty or whoever, and then make your way back to Rosemary Avenue, the road behind the pond, until it dead-ends. The gate is back there. I'll meet you."

"Sounds like a plan," I said, smiling. "But Lanny, tell me your reason for doing this. On the phone, you said something about a long story."

Lanny was about to answer, but dinner was fried up and ready. "Grab your plate, cowboy — grub's on!"

I held out the mismatched plates to my bachelor friend, and he heaped on the food like it was our last meal together. Sitting down at his Formica-topped table, I couldn't help notice Lanny's pressed guard uniform hanging on the back of a chair.

"Pretty snappy duds, Lanny."

"I tailor mine," Lanny said, digging out two Coronas from his small refrigerator. "I picked that up from the film *The Border*, with Nicholson. He tailored his uniform. At first I thought it was just an ego thing, but then I realized that it makes a lot of sense. When you're put together, you look together, and when you *look* together, folks assume that you *are* together. It's all smoke and mirrors, but hey, we *are* in Hollywood, right?" Lanny said, dropping a beer in front of me. "If you were being squeezed out, you'd do the same thing."

Variety Reporter

Trouble at Paramount. Upstart Sticks makes waves, egg salad

By Mike Avalon

Hollywood and the entertainment industry can be stubborn sometimes, and a certain major film studio off of Melrose is no exception.

Yet, seems this fact is not common knowledge to all of the studio's employees. Recently a relatively young and new Security and Studio Wellness Associate Officer had the audacity to approach his ob visously superiors with a ist of ways the studio's security forces and valet parking could ...energized and retrofitted ... paradigms ... on his the

"You're being forced out by the studio?" I asked, wiping my greasy lips.

"Yeah, it's been a long time coming. I made a name for myself right away there, see? I started as a pass checker at Gate Two. That's where they break you in, see how you do under pressure. My failure rate was 4 percent the first year of my guard career — 4 percent. Most guys are 13, 14 percent."

"You were a climber."

"It wasn't that," Lanny continued, "I was just a natural. So they moved me up to the Gower shipping gate. I did check-ins there and turned a few heads. I caught five loads of stolen shit going *out* the door in the first month. In thirty days, I saved the studio my entire year's salary. That's when the squeeze began," he said through a clenched jaw.

"For doing a good job?"

"Yep," Lanny said, taking a slug of beer. His quiet, understated reserve fell away, and a hidden anguish played out like Marlon Brando in *On the Waterfront*.

"I was too good, Bruce — that was the problem. I started to shake up a good-ol'-boy guard system that had been in place since the Great Depression. Some of these guys used to drink with John Barrymore, for Chrissakes, you know what I'm saying? Suddenly, here comes a guy who ain't makin' mistakes, and he's payin' attention, and he starts to see that the security infrastructure in place here isn't any good. And what did they do to reward me?"

"It doesn't sound good, whatever it is."

"They gave me 'the watch.'"

"I hope it was a Rolex."

"No," Lanny said impatiently. "They put me back in what we call the DMZ, no-man's-land. They did it to break my will. Because of the isolation, most guys would crack within three months. I did it for *five years,* Bruce."

There was a clunky pause, as I tried to think of something to say that wasn't stupid, rude, or insensitive. How do you say, "Yeah, that must have sucked," without saying that exactly? The best I could do was, "Yeah, freaky shit. Why not just quit and work at Universal, or Sony?"

Lanny turned his hash over and over, defiantly. "That's just what they would want me to do."

After a second helping of everything, Lanny and I watched the sun set from the porch of his trailer. Across his small patch of desert, a cacophony of barking dogs serenaded us. We shared a beer and talked about the good old days, before *Death of the Dead* and "the accident," whatever that was.

16

Dailies from Hell

Parking in Hollywood is a nightmare: NO PARKING WITHOUT A SPECIAL PERMIT; NO PARKING BETWEEN THE HOURS OF TEN AND TWO ON TUESDAYS FOR STREET CLEANING; NO OVERNIGHT PARKING. Why not just put up a concrete riot barrier around the entire city?

That's why I took a cab to 6000 Santa Monica Boulevard, the address of the Hollywood Memorial Park Cemetery.

"You know, Mary Mon-roe is buried here," my Pakistani driver informed me, counting out the change from my twenty.

"Do you mean Marilyn Monroe?"

The driver looked at me like I was a fool. "Tha's wha I say — Mary Mon-roe."

I stuffed the change in my pocket and stepped out of his gypsy cab. There it was before me, the cemetery that housed the tombs of Hollywood's greatest old-timers: Rudolph Valentino, Douglas Fairbanks, John Huston. It was a classic cemetery, built in 1899, with

Gothic tombstones, and giant mausoleums for the long-forgotten elite. The only time I saw it before this was on an episode of *Charmed*.

I glanced at my watch. The time read 5:30 P.M. — half hour until closing. I was to meet Lanny at 5:45, so I paid ten bucks to get in, and consulted the free map they included. From the main entrance, I turned left and headed toward the pond. Lanny's secret gate was on the far side. As I walked along Lakeview Avenue, I began to pass the final resting places of well-known showbiz people. Cecil B. DeMille, the Steven Spielberg of his day, was housed in a giant tomb.

And it probably went over budget, I reasoned.

Around the corner was Jayne Mansfield, a blonde bombshell made prominent as a studio threat to Marilyn Monroe. Marion Davies, a forgettable actress from the 1920s and '30s, had a massive tomb as well — but then again, her sugar daddy was William Randolph Hearst, the newspaper magnate.

Raimi favorite Tyrone.

Just beyond Marion, my man Tyrone Power was laid out in a fine memorial. Ty was a man's man from the old school, with dark, penetrating eyes, and a cigarette-enhanced voice. This dashing leading man had a permanent place in my friend Sam Raimi's household. His mother, Lu-Lu, was so crazy about him, she hung framed portraits everywhere. Sam even faked his autograph on one picture, convincing Lu-Lu to this day that it was real.

Tyrone's hypnotic powers were still in evidence. A woman in her sixties was standing silently by his grave, cradling an old black-and-white glossy of the handsome star, and dabbing her glistening eyes. As I got closer, the fan spotted me, but she didn't try and hide her sorrow — or rage, for that matter.

"Damn you. We could have had such a life together. Why did you have to leave me so young, so virile? You bastard!"

Assuming she was talking to Tyrone Power, I offered my condolences. "Rumor has it, ma'am, he died of a heart attack while in the act of bedding a much younger woman. At least he went with a smile on his face."

"That's not true," the fan shot back defiantly. "We made beautiful love in the afternoon. Ty told me he was tired, so I let him drift off to sleep. I tried to wake him several hours later, but he…he was gone…."

The grief etched on the woman's face seemed real, not some delusional story.

"You're the woman?" I asked incredulously.

"Not everyone in this town is a phony, mister," she said bitterly.

I decided against baiting her further, and headed north to Rosemary Avenue. Near the end of the poorly maintained street, I spotted an overgrown, rusted gate with a simple lock. There were no others like it in this part of the park, but Lanny was nowhere in sight.

Then, through the thick foliage, I heard the secret call: "Where do you think you're goin'?"

It was one of Lanny's favorite lines from *Death of the Dead*, when his redneck character takes control of a group of people in an isolated cabin and forces them outside to certain death. I walked over to the gate as Lanny was unleashing the padlock. With a quick look around, I ducked into an obscure, overgrown section of the Paramount back lot.

"This is it — the outback," Lanny said, gesturing around.

"It's creepy as hell."

"And this is during the *day*," he added, leading us along a footpath through this overgrown area. "Try being here at three o'clock in the morning, when the freaks have Marilyn Monroe parties in the cemetery. My job was to keep fans of dead actors from getting into the studio that once employed many of those same actors. How sick is that shit?"

Lanny and I arrived at the edge of the "New York City" portion of the back lot. One particular brownstone seemed oddly familiar.

"Was that Ally McBeal's apartment?"

"Sure was. Hell of a nice gal."

We walked past Ally's place in silence, mainly because Lanny was still stewing about his situation. "See, the payback is to stay, Bruce," he said, rubbing his hands slightly, "and to stick their noses in it by excelling."

We got to the end of the "block." To our right, administration buildings began.

"We cut through Eddie Murphy Plaza," Lanny said, indicating the route with his hand as he walked. "Turn left at the Gene Kelly Building, and the DeMille Building is all the way down on the right — that's where the screening room is."

The Eddie Murphy Plaza was very tidy, and the early evening light, refracted through the Los Angeles smog, bathed the area in a warm glow, which I'm sure is exactly how Eddie would have wanted it. As we approached the Gene Kelly Building, the plaza narrowed to a two-person pathway. Just ahead, a sunny courtyard revealed the immaculately maintained Cecil B. DeMille Building, a vintage complex from the '40s.

"This is it," Lanny said, gesturing to the building. "When DeMille was working, he insisted on his own private screening room, so they put one in the basement. Now, it's an execs-only situation. We, of course, will go in the service door."

Lanny rifled through his ring of keys and opened the door. Inside, typical of all the old office buildings on the lot, the décor was faded plaster, rounded edges, and a myriad of hallways.

"Just keep heading down," Lanny said, pointing to a stairwell on our left.

A dark doorway at the bottom posted a cheery sign: AUTHORIZED PERSONNEL ONLY. Lanny selected a new key, and the door opened easily.

"Angelo's the projectionist. He's been on the lot since time began — a little crabby, but a great old geezer."

Lanny arrived at a nondescript metal door. He knocked lightly.

A gruff voice came from behind the door: "Just a fuckin' minute!"

Lanny smiled at me, as if to say, "See?"

The door swung open, and we were greeted by a bald, cigar-chomping, cardigan-wearing curmudgeon.

"Angelo, this is that fellow I wanted to bring by — Bruce Campbell, one of the actors in *Let's Make Love!*"

Angelo looked at me, rolled his eyes, and shooed us inside. "Okay, hurry up, the execs don't like the smell of my cigar, and we're ready to roll."

Inside, Angelo led us toward his projection booth. "*The smell of my cigar*," he repeated derisively. "Let me tell you something, the executives who used to sit in this screening room smoked nothing *but* cigars. I couldn't get two feet out the door before Zukor, or one of the top brass, would shove a Del Fuego in my hand the size of a ham sandwich. You could tell how much work a picture needed by the amount of cigar smoke in the room. Now, these little pricks are playing Nintendo during reel changes — sheesh."

We rounded the corner to Angelo's "lair." The large room was encrusted with fifty years of movie-projection-booth stuff — some of it work-related, like strips of film hanging above an editing bench, and some of it just items that piled up over time, like posters, clippings, and notes pinned to an overflowing bulletin board.

Anchoring the room were twin Peerless movie projectors. I had seen a few over the years, hanging out in projection booths during theater appearances, but never this pristine.

The first dailies shown through the Peerless.

"Holy cow," I exclaimed, "Peerless."

"The originals," Angelo said with pride. "Carbon arc. You gotta adjust 'em every fifteen minutes as they burn, and replace 'em every two hours. You got sixteen different lube spots to keep oiled, so you can't just walk away like they do in the multiplexes. These should be in a museum. A hundred and two thousand hours projecting dailies, rough cuts, final cuts, first trials, trailers, recuts — you name it — without a major problem, and that's only since '52, when I got here."

I was enjoying Angelo's crusty ranting, but I was more interested in saving my movie from the scheming of the man I had begun to think of as my nemesis.

"Dailies are when?"

"Right now," Angelo huffed. "Back off while I crank this sucker up."

The Peerless came to life and it purred smoothly as the film fed through its sprockets. I walked over to one of several viewing windows. A small speaker, held up by a coat hanger, broadcast the accompanying sound.

"Turn it up if you want," Angelo said, jamming his stub of a cigar out in an overflowing ashtray. "Don't know why you would bother. No offense, but this picture is a stinker."

I looked back to Angelo in horror. "Really? Why do you say that?"

Angelo cracked a wizened, jaded smile. "Kid, I can tell a stinker from the first take of the first reel of dailies. It's not about the star, or the writer, or the director, it's the whole ball of wax. You make a picture, and it's a collision of elements — sometimes it's magic, and sometimes it, well, it's this," he said, jerking a thumb at the dailies, now playing.

I turned up the volume and watched. Stylewise, Mike Nichols was indeed going ape shit. His footage, while gorgeous to look at, was frenetic, choppy, and full of gags. Something comic and ingenious might emerge once assembled, but currently, the dailies had the feel of a Roger Corman movie with a bloated budget.

"A 75-million-dollar movie, and they're throwin' fuckin' dummies around. That never would have happened when Zukor ran this place.

The execs now, they're more worried about stock options, golden parachutes, and production deals than making pictures. The punk screening these dailies is a classic example," Angelo said, pointing to Rob Stern, lounging in one and a half seats, with his feet draped over the back of the leather chair in front of him. Looking at him was the visual equivalent of chewing on tin foil.

"He's on the cell phone half the time, or he's dictating some B.S. to his big-tittied secretary. Listen to this...."

Angelo turned up an ambient speaker. "We use this to check the sound in the room itself. We also use it to listen in on the schmucks. The things I've heard, kid."

Through the speaker, we could hear Rob spouting off: "You know what, Kari? Move my detailing to tomorrow morning. I'm sorry, Johnny, go ahead."

"He's watching dailies, dictating, and talking on his cell phone — all at the same time," Angelo said with disgust.

"When you're good you're good," Lanny interjected.

Angelo tended to the Peerless as the last of the dailies threaded through. "Thank God they're over."

Rob Stern could be heard swinging into postdailies, high-gear executive mode:

"Okay, memo to Mike: 'Mike — saw Tuesday's dailies. While I enjoyed the handheld stuff, I think it's too confining. Suggest more crane use and wide-angle lenses to give us more of a sense of scope. General note: more extras, the streets look too empty — maybe we could add digital people in post? In addition, please talk with Bruce Campbell re: his first day of shooting. Loved the barf — a great DVD extra, but suggest reshooting the shot — too stilted. He looked like he was waiting to get pulled back. Not organic. More notes later. Yours in making a classic, Rob.' Okay, memo to Kevin Jarre, re: dialogue...."

I turned the volume down and glanced into the screening room below. Rob was dictating, and punctuating his long sentences with frenetic hand gestures. His legs, as if working an invisible Thigh-Master in fast motion, never stopped wobbling open and closed.

"The worst part," Angelo complained, "is that the punk leaves the biggest mess you've ever seen — candy wrappers, memos, Doritos. What am I, his mother? And let me ask you: how the fuck can anyone drink sixty-four ounces of anything? In two reels of dailies, he can go through an entire Big Gulp. Go figure."

Rob Stern multitasking.

Down below, Rob gathered his things and headed toward the exit, still blabbing on the cell phone. "Hey, Kari, is the conference call still on with Mike and Terry?"

I glanced at Lanny. "I'm assuming 'Mike' is our Mike. Who's Terry?"

"Executive vice-president of production at Paramount," Lanny explained matter-of-factly.

"Could be interesting. Think we can tail him?" I asked.

"Who do you think you're dealing with, amigo?" Lanny asked in return, a little put off.

We said our good-byes to Angelo (I even got a free cigar, though Ida doesn't abide them) and slipped out the side door. The difference between Angelo's dungeon and the afterburner brilliance of the late-day California sun was something like a thousand percent, and I stumbled about blindly, trying to spot Rob Stern before my eyes adjusted.

Lanny, smart enough to slip his shades on before exiting the building, kept the fledgling executive in his sights. "He's on the move — let's take a short-cut."

Terry Feingold
Head Meathead

Paramound Studios
Suite 297
Los Angeles, California

(323) 555.9565, ext. 19
FAX: (323) 555-9560
e-mail: penny_pincher@paramound.con

"Where is Rob's office?" I asked.

"On the third floor of the Sturges building," Lanny said. "His boss, Terry Feingold, is on the fourth — dead ahead."

Lanny and I headed toward the southeastern corner of the lot, taking a shortcut through every building we encountered.

"See, the heavy, dark keys are part of the original lot. Those will get you into the older buildings on the older parts of the lot. The next generation, between '37 and '79, used these silver jobbies. Brand-new buildings have swipe cards that can be reprogrammed. Either way, there isn't a door I can't get into."

"So, Lanny, Rob is about to have a conference call with this guy Terry. Any way to listen in?"

"As long as you're not claustrophobic there is," Lanny acknowledged, using his second-generation key to open a loading door of the Sturges building, then a smaller key to activate a service elevator inside.

We arrived on the fourth floor and Lanny led us hurriedly to an unmarked door almost vibrating from the hum of machinery behind it.

"The old air duct routine," Lanny said, smiling as he produced yet another odd-shaped key.

"Really, that's possible?"

"You bet," Lanny said, throwing open the door, revealing a metal stairway. "You can have a bird's-eye view of any office built after '43."

"How do you know all this?" I asked, sizing up the ladder and the network of metal ducts looming above.

"Sunday nights are usually pretty slow on the lot," Lanny said. "Me and a buddy used to play Dungeons and Dragons. This is the one place he could never find me. Now look, you'll see a vent at each office. Terry's is three vents down. Good luck."

"Wait, you're not going with me?"

"Hell no. Last time I was up there, I drank a can of Coke and my belly swelled up enough to trap me for an hour. That's why now I carry Tums wherever I go."

Lanny unclipped a small, rubber-coated flashlight, and flipped it on. "You'll need this."

"Okay, see you soon," I said, ascending the rusty ladder.

The duct system was very tight indeed. I cursed every bacon cheeseburger ever consumed as I dragged my carcass thirty horizontal feet to the first grate. I peered into what looked like a casting office. The walls were lined with actor headshots, and a heated negotiation was under way.

"Look, I could give a shit if Corey got a pinball machine in his trailer on *Trancers III*. After the third failed drug test, he'll be lucky to get per diem!"

I didn't need to hear the rest of that tragic conversation, and dragged myself to the next grating. Down below, a money guy of some kind was deep in the middle of a convoluted explanation:

"It's very simple, actually," the man continued. "The first eight hours are straight time. The next four are time and a half, and every remaining hour after that is double time. No, that doesn't include night premiums, meal penalties or forced calls...."

Before I fell asleep, I hauled myself forward, to what would hopefully be the office of Terry Feingold, who was one of about ten executive VPs at Paramount. When I arrived, Terry was on the phone:

"No way. Look, you blew a big deal for me because of it, and I'm not going to let it happen again...."

This Feingold is a tough cookie, I thought. But his conversation continued:

"No, next time, *you're* taking him to soccer practice. Yeah, well, whatever — talk to the lawyer."

Terry slammed the phone down and stared at it in silence. The downward tilt of his head revealed a substantial bald spot that was in the process of being "restored." Pressing my face against the metal slats in the vent, I could see that his office was typical of a midlevel executive, decorated in a Southwestern theme, with a faux stucco fireplace and generic tapestries.

Bzzzzzz! Terry's intercom came to life, and the slightly bored voice of his secretary came across the speaker phone. "Terry? Rob's here for the conference call. Should I send him in?"

"Do me a favor, wait five minutes, then let him in."

"Sure," his secretary responded.

With that, Terry leaned in his relax-the-back executive chair and put his feet up on the desk. Was he finishing an important call before Rob came in? Freshening up? No, he was simply making his subordinate wait because he could.

After wasting exactly five minutes, lying on the cold metal duct, I watched as Rob entered Terry's office. The dynamic between studio executives was usually cautious, to say the least, but even accounting for the usual Hollywood paranoia and ambient venom, "warm" is not a word I would use to characterize their relationship.

Unlike Terry, Rob was hired as a "creative" guy at the studio. He'd be *making* movies instead of "overseeing" them if he had a creative bone in his supersize body. Rob was all about "development." I was told by a writer I knew that the kid had many failings, but was nonetheless regarded as a sort of wunderkind who could "develop the hell out of a script." I wasn't sure if that was a compliment or not, since far too many decent scripts have been shanghaied in "development."

The subject of the day, of course, was *Let's Make Love!*, the film assigned to the two execs. Mike Nichols was about to call in for a status conversation, and they wanted to get their stories in sync.

"Well, financially, he's going 'Kurtz' on us," Terry said, rifling through a stack of paperwork on his desk. "He's projected to go over by 25 percent, and that's *after* burning through a 10 percent contingency already."

Where's Lester Shankwater when I need him?

Even from my ridiculous vantage point, I could see Rob's eyes suddenly ignite. "Listen, Terry," Rob spat, "Mike is attempting to do something really special here, and I think we should all be cheering him on rather than...than...."

For just a moment, Rob had appeared to be in danger of stating an actual opinion, but his deeply ingrained sense of self-preservation returned just in time, assisted by Terry's withering stare. *Interesting,* thought to myself. *Stern seems to have an awful lot invested in Mike's new "vision."*

"This is a romantic comedy, asshole, not Arma-frickin'-geddon," Terry barked. "Can't you creative guys rein him in?"

"Hey, whoa, whoa, there," Rob said, putting his hands up, trying to erase any hint of his previous backbone. "You bean counters say the same thing every time a creative force — and this is Mike Nichols, mind you — changes his mind or enhances a script."

"LET'S MAKE LOVE!"

Producer: Robert Evans Shoot: 32 Days
Director: Mike Nichols

Budget Date: 02/11

Acct#	Category Title	Page	Total
11-00	STORY, RIGHTS & SCREENPLAY	1	$1,192,040
12-00	PRODUCERS	2	$1,820,750
13-00	DIRECTION & SUPERVISION	3	$2,314,300
14-00	CAST	4	$18,130,762
15-00	ESPRESSOS	5	$514,204
16-00	TRAVEL & LODGING	7	$2,828,703
	TOTAL ABOVE THE LINE		**$26,800,759**
21-00	PRODUCTION STAFF	9	$644,739
22-00	CAMERA	11	$537,438
23-00	ART DEPT	12	$293,420
24-00	SET CONSTRUCTION	14	$1,193,194
25-00	SPECIAL FX	14	$1,226
26-00	SET OPERAT	15	$453,237
27-00	ELECTRIC	16	$338,041
28-00	SET DRE	17	$331,991
29-00	PROPS	18	$348,404
30-00	FILM	18	$428,834
31-00	EXTR	19	$220,386
32-00	WARI	19	$431,691
33-00	MAKE	20	$215,178
34-00	MEAL	20	$160,701
35-00	SOUN	21	$222,923
42-00	LOCATI	21	$568,516
43-00	TRANSPO	23	$530,951
	PRODUCTI		**$6,920,870**
61-00	EDITING	25	$422,150
62-00	MUSIC	26	$734,126
63-00	SOUND	26	$232,376
64-00	FILM & STOCK SHOTS	26	$152,502
65-00	TITLES	[illegible]7	$77,126
66-00	OPTICALS	[illegible]	$51,126
67-00	POST PRODUCTION ESPRESSOS	[illegible]	$278,234
	TOTAL POST PRODUCTION		**$1,947,640**
	TOTAL ABOVE THE LINE		**$26,800,759**
	PRODUCTION PERIOD TOTAL		**$6,920,870**
	TOTAL POST PRODUCTION		**$1,947,640**
	GRAND TOTAL		**$35,669,269**

$1,947,640
$35,669,269

Before...

"Shooting entire sequences green screen isn't enhancing, Robbie, it's reinventing the wheel."

"I was brought here to breathe some life into these old Paramount walls, Terry. Personally, I have enjoyed watching *Let's Make Love!* blossom into a higher-concept, albeit slightly more expensive, story. It's gonna appeal to a much younger, and *broader* audience than Mike Nichols ever had before, and marketing will back me up."

"We already got our slate of high-tech action flicks, Rob, we don't need another one to kneecap us when we're down."

"Wow, that's a real hard line," Rob said, dabbing the sweat along his hairline.

"It's my ass, is what it is," Terry said, poking his own chest. "Glick gave me the max I can spend under the new cap — remember the one we all agreed on in writing? I can't let this, or any picture, go over it, and I'm putting the onus on *you*, to bring your genius director around."

"But the new stuff is really cool," Rob protested, weakly.

"No, the new stuff is really expensive. Can't we have cool stuff that isn't expensive? When I first read this script, it was three people in a room talking, 95 percent of the time. Who's been taking growth hormones here? How did this one get away?"

A buzzing sound prevented Rob's answer. "Mike's on the line, Terry."

"Okay, tell him to hold just a sec," he said, turning his attention back to Rob. "I'm always bad cop. Can you be bad cop for once?"

"I'm no good at being bad cop," Rob said, shaking his head no. "And as the creative exec, it isn't really my job."

"But you always complain that when I'm bad cop, I'm too bad," Terry reasoned. "Maybe if I play good cop, and you're bad cop, we might get somewhere."

"Okay, I'll try it, but no guarantees," Rob warned.

The two wary allies nodded, and Terry stabbed at a blinking phone button.

"Hello, Mike," Terry said, warmly. "Rob Stern is also here on speaker."

"Hey, Mike," Rob feigned cheerfully, "how's everything going?"

"Not bad, but I'd like another week of shooting," Mike said flatly.

Terry and Rob exchanged a panicked look, then broke into laughter. "Hey, Mike, you're a funny guy!" Rob said, smiling, as a fresh drop of sweat rolled along his sideburn.

"Is that a no, then?" Mike asked, not joking.

As the reality of the request sank in, Terry signaled to Rob to be quiet, and a stony silence followed.

"You still there?" Mike asked over the speakerphone.

"Oh, we're here, Mike," Terry said, now pacing in front of his desk.

"That's a pretty tall order, particularly after all the new expenses, like a storyboard artist, helicopter shots, forty new digital effects, and a special armature dummy. I could go on."

Rob shot Terry an "I thought you were going to be *good* cop" look. "But, Mike, make no mistake," he urged. "It's all terrific stuff, it's just starting to add up, heh-heh."

Rob tried to continue, but Mike interrupted him.

"You know, fellas, I haven't exactly been making this movie in a bubble," Mike said, as politely as he could under the circumstances. "I've got enough memos from Rob alone to fill a book — and not one of them was to tone it down, they've all been about making this movie bigger and bigger. Now, I haven't heard a bad word from corporate on any of this, so, until I do, I'm going to continue to make a great movie for this studio. I'm sure you bright young men have it in yourselves to help instead of hurt. Good day."

And with a faint click, the three-way conference suddenly dropped to two. Terry immediately turned his wrath on Rob.

"You call yourself 'bad cop'?!"

"Hey," Rob countered, having sweated through an undershirt, a dress shirt, a tie, and an outer jacket, "your 'good cop' shouldn't have been worse than my 'bad cop'!"

"I had to do that, numb nuts," Terry hissed, "because your 'bad cop' was such a pussy!"

The two fell into silence, Terry slumping into his chair behind the desk, and Rob blotting his shiny forehead with a hankie.

"Now what?" Rob asked forlornly.

Terry leaned back, plopped his feet on the desk, and shrugged. "It's up to you, Rob. As I recall, you brought this project to the studio, not me."

“What?” Rob protested. “We did it together, don’t you remember, Terry?”

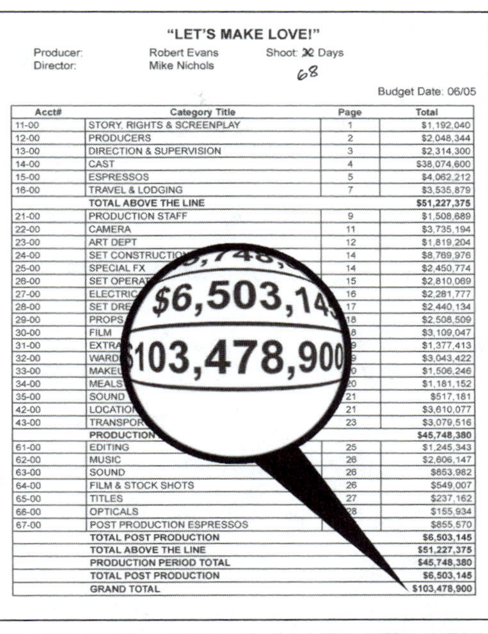

“LET’S MAKE LOVE!”

Producer: Robert Evans
Director: Mike Nichols
Shoot: ~~32~~ Days 68

Budget Date: 06/05

Acct#	Category Title	Page	Total
11-00	STORY, RIGHTS & SCREENPLAY	1	$1,192,040
12-00	PRODUCERS	2	$2,048,344
13-00	DIRECTION & SUPERVISION	3	$2,314,300
14-00	CAST	4	$38,074,600
15-00	ESPRESSOS	5	$4,062,212
16-00	TRAVEL & LODGING	7	$3,535,879
	TOTAL ABOVE THE LINE		**$51,227,375**
21-00	PRODUCTION STAFF	9	$1,508,689
22-00	CAMERA	11	$3,735,194
23-00	ART DEPT	12	$1,819,204
24-00	SET CONSTRUCTIO	14	$8,769,976
25-00	SPECIAL FX	14	$2,450,774
26-00	SET OPERA	15	$2,810,069
27-00	ELECTRIC	16	$2,281,777
28-00	SET DRE	17	$2,440,134
29-00	PROPS	18	$2,508,509
30-00	FILM	8	$3,109,047
31-00	EXTRA	9	$1,377,413
32-00	WARD	9	$3,043,422
33-00	MAKEU	0	$1,506,246
34-00	MEALS	20	$1,181,152
35-00	SOUND	21	$517,181
42-00	LOCATIO	21	$3,610,077
43-00	TRANSPOR	23	$3,079,516
	PRODUCTION		**$45,748,380**
61-00	EDITING	25	$1,245,343
62-00	MUSIC	26	$2,606,147
63-00	SOUND	26	$853,982
64-00	FILM & STOCK SHOTS	26	$549,007
65-00	TITLES	27	$237,162
66-00	OPTICALS	28	$155,934
67-00	POST PRODUCTION ESPRESSOS		$855,570
	TOTAL POST PRODUCTION		**$6,503,145**
	TOTAL ABOVE THE LINE		**$51,227,375**
	PRODUCTION PERIOD TOTAL		**$45,748,380**
	TOTAL POST PRODUCTION		**$6,503,145**
	GRAND TOTAL		**$103,478,900**

...and, after.

“As my e-mails and interoffice memorandums will prove, I fought against this project, yet you continued to champion it.”

Rob flinched at the mention of a paper trail. “Are you saying you’re not going to cover my back on this?” Rob asked, incredulous.

“Not this one, amigo,” Terry confirmed. “If *Let’s Make Love!* tanks, you’re taking the fall. Life’s too short. I’m going to fiddle while the whole thing burns.”

Rob’s eyes turned arid and reptilian. “Terry, I couldn’t agree more with your assessment of this project. It’s flatlining. But that’s no more my fault than it is yours, or even Mike’s. No, I think that once everyone has had a chance to review the facts they’ll see that this entire fiasco can be laid at the feet of one man: Bruce Campbell. Just check out the Internet Movie Database — everything he touches turns to straight-to-video crap. He’s like a carrier for a B-movie Ebola virus. I heard he almost brought down *Spider-Man 2* and he was only in that for five minutes. He’s in *Let’s Make Love!* for, what, almost thirty? We gotta make him disappear,” Stern said definitively.

“Well, do what you gotta do,” Terry said in a dismissive tone. “This baby is yours now.”

I began to shiver, not only because of the chilling scene I had just witnessed, but because the cold metal duct was lowering my body temperature to a dangerous level.

Shimmying backward to the access ladder, which was much harder than forward, my mind reeled.

So, I wasn't going crazy — that little prick Stern was the evil puppet master after all! First he tries to keep me out of the movie, now he's trying to blame all of his dumbass decisions on me. I should have guessed he was a troublemaker from the first time I saw him smelling his puffy fingers.

Lanny and I rode back across the lot in silence. He had upgraded our means of travel to a golf cart, mainly because he felt sorry for me. At the vine-riddled back gate we shook hands.

"Well, Lanny, I almost wish I hadn't seen that," I said, finally.

"Yeah, kids today," Lanny said, jingling his ring of keys. "He came over from New Line. He was their 'franchise' guy. He has a lot to prove I guess."

"He's proven a lot to me already," I said.

"Well, watch your back," Lanny urged grimly, closing the gate between us. "Say hi to Ty for me."

With a wink, I vanished into the cemetery, en route to the Los Angeles Airport. I was due back in New York in two days.

17

Bad Day at Black Rock — The Sequel

Stuntmen, as a rule, are funny. But the stuntmen working on *Let's Make Love!* were downright hilarious. Waiting in my trailer the next day was a gift basket of Egg McMuffins, Earl Grey tea, and a can of Altoid mints, nicely laid out like haute cuisine.

The attached note read:

Before I could say "har-dee-frickin'-har-har," there was a knock on the door.

"Hang on!" I said, in a tone reserved exclusively for annoying assistant directors.

"It's Mike," he said, through the door.

"Holy shit." I stumbled to unlock the door. "Hey, good morning —

come on in."

Mike stepped into the trailer and smiled politely, looking around. "You actors have it pretty rough, don't you?"

"We make do."

"Hey, listen, Foyl, I have to talk to you about the dailies. May I sit down?"

"Sure," I said, gesturing to my "lounge" chair.

"It's like this," Mike began. "What we're making here is a film that wants to break out, do you know what I mean?"

"I'm not sure I do, Mike. No."

"Maybe that's the problem," he said in that irrefutable director tone. "I need to know that you're going to be on board."

"On board? I'm not sure what you mean. What do you need from me specifically?"

"I need you to start rounding out your performance."

"Mike, I've only been in one shot," I protested.

"And it was flat."

"Flat? You could tell that from me being flung forty feet into the air?"

Mike nodded. "Foyl, a shot is a scene and a scene is a shot. I need you, for lack of a better expression, to camp it up a little."

I let out a bitter, ironic laugh. "Well, this is the first time I've been asked to do *that*!"

"Are you with me?" he asked, in his no-nonsense manner. "You're either in or out, bucko. I need to know."

And it appeared that Mike was happy to wait for my answer. Blushing at the embarrassment and confusion of the situation, I shook my head yes. "Sure, of course. Anything you want, Mike."

"Thanks, Foyl," he said, rising. "See you out there — big scene coming up."

And he closed the door behind him.

Stern probably put this in his head, I fumed, looking at the flimsy wall n front of me and wondering if I could put my fist through it like countess other actors had in the past. But before such wicked thoughts could get the best of me, someone began pounding on the door.

"Damn them to hell," I growled. "What?"

I whipped open the door to reveal Kevin Jarre, the screenwriter, smiling awkwardly. "Good morning, Foyl. Is this a bad time?"

"Oh, hello, Kevin. No, I got nothin' but time. Come on in."

We assumed the same seating arrangement, and Kevin looked around the trailer as all visitors do.

"These things are getting much better."

"Yeah, they sure are," I said, not wanting to get drawn into an inane trailer discussion. "What's on your mind?"

"Well, Mike and I were kicking around today's scene last night, and these are the new ideas. I just wanted to sit down with you, to see f you had any questions."

Ground zero.

"Okay," I said, glancing at the single page. "I thought this was just a bump-and-go with Renée."

"It was, Foyl, sure, but Mike is having quite an *evolution* as a filmmaker. I'm sure you can appreciate that."

"Sure," I said, scanning the new page, "I'm just trying to keep up." As read on, the new action sequence seemed not only extensive, but exhaustive. “Wow, this is pretty, uh….”

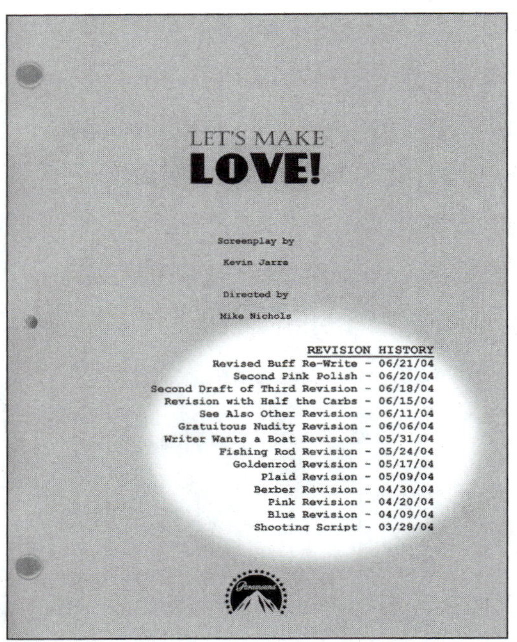
LET'S MAKE
LOVE!

Screenplay by

Kevin Jarre

Directed by

Mike Nichols

REVISION HISTORY
Revised Buff Re-Write - 06/21/04
Second Pink Polish - 06/20/04
Second Draft of Third Revision - 06/18/04
Revision with Half the Carbs - 06/15/04
See Also Other Revision - 06/11/04
Gratuitous Nudity Revision - 06/06/04
Writer Wants a Boat Revision - 05/31/04
Fishing Rod Revision - 05/24/04
Goldenrod Revision - 05/17/04
Plaid Revision - 05/09/04
Berber Revision - 04/30/04
Pink Revision - 04/20/04
Blue Revision - 04/09/04
Shooting Script - 03/28/04

“Fun?” Kevin offered.

“If you’re a triathlete, yeah,” wheezed, getting tired just fron reading. “And what’s with my las line?”

Kevin smiled at his own handi work. “We thought that would put a nice button on the scene.”

“But that line is from the *Ev Dead* films.”

“‘Groovy’?” Kevin said. “That’s not even a line, that’s a single word.”

“I know, but in context, it’s too weird. I’ve already said it in movies twice, and I’m afraid of the cliché association.”

“So, what, you can’t say ‘groovy’?”

“Did Stern make you write that?”

“Stern? Are you insane? No. Nobody tells me what to write.”

“Well, either way, I’m not sure if I want to go there,” I said, shrugging helplessly.

Kevin paused to gather his thoughts. Not all writers roll over and play dead when an actor has script issues — particularly playwrights. “Look neither you nor I nor your pal Sam Raimi made up, or owns the rights to, the word *groovy*. I’m comfortable with it. The word is appropriate fo your character and the situation, and if you’d like to change it, you’l have to take it up with Mike.”

Without a further word, Kevin stood up and left my trailer. I watched him go in silence, then grabbed a cold Sausage McMuffin with Egg from ny "gift basket" and wolfed it down angrily.

Out in front of the Park Avenue Arms set two hours later, the cast was assembled to block the new scene. Mike was laying it out for us all, helping us to see the big picture.

"Okay, gang, now we begin with Harry and Debbie exiting the building. Foyl, you tip your hat as she passes, but you didn't know that they were in the middle of a real knock-down-drag-out-fight. Debbie turns to clock Harry, but he ducks, and Foyl gets smacked in the face. Meanwhile, Harry gets around in front of Debbie and stops her from leaving. Foyl is shaking off the hit, and he steps forward to see what's going on. That's right when Debbie winds up with her purse to hit Harry, and she whacks Foyl on the backswing, sending him backwards into the revolving doors — which are rigged to spin around — and they throw him back out, right into Debbie who clotheslines him with another backswing, and Foyl drops to the ground. Debbie and Harry then make up, and jump into the back of a waiting cab. End of scene."

"Sounds like a 'oner' to me," Johnny Casino joked from the sidelines, and the entire crew let out a raucous laugh.

"That's exactly right," Mike said matter-of-factly. "I want it as one continuous shot."

The residual laughter subsided almost immediately, because the crew knew that Mike never joked about what he wanted to do. Renée and Richard Gere exchanged a slightly worried, albeit excited look.

"You really want to do this in one, chief?" Johnny asked, shifting his weight uncomfortably from boot to boot.

"Yes," Mike nodded. "The scene requires a single, uncut piece that plays out in real time. The pacing has to be exact."

To accomplish this, we began a grueling trial-and-error period where the scene was paced out slowly, methodically, then performed with increasing speed, and for longer periods without stopping. Tragically advancements were not without collateral damage. During a three-hour period, I managed to bash my knee on the side of the building, get an ankle caught in the revolving doors, and take a full-on punch in the face from Renée Zellweger.

"Oh, my God!" Renée exclaimed, as I tumbled to the pavement clutching the bridge of my nose. "I am so sorry."

"I'm okay, I'm okay," I assured her, going the stalwart route. "I'm good to go."

"Good to go, my ass," Johnny said, not fooled by my false bravado. "You're bleeding like a pig. Let's get the medic over here!"

Steve, the first assistant director, looked at his watch and rolled his eyes. "Okay, that's lunch, one hour!"

As the crew stampeded away from us, Mike walked over to offer his condolences. "Hey, Foyl, for what it's worth, that last go-around was finally leaning in the right direction."

I weakly gave Mike the thumbs-up as the medic shoved cotton in each of my nostrils.

De-BOR-ah approached. There was a grim look about her. "Mike you have some visitors who need to see you."

"I don't have any visitors today," Mike said, dismissing it as unimportant. "June handles all that business anyway."

Deborah took Mike aside. Her words were lost to me, but from Mike's reaction, I could tell that she was relaying serious news. Mike glanced at an idling black Cadillac Escalade, and took a deep breath.

My stomach bested any further curiosity, and I joined the lunch line. The prime rib was looking really good. Lunch is always a great time to people watch, but as I looked around, I noticed that crew members were socializing in small groups, and the mood wasn't as happy-go-lucky as usual.

Must be middle-of-the-shoot doldrums, I assumed.

Digging into a cold beet salad, I tried to make peace with what Mike said in my trailer. Deep down, I knew that my job as an actor was to be a good soldier and to carry out the vision of the man in charge, regardless of whether I'd do things the same way. I finished a massive piece of cherry pie, washed it down with a cup of hot tea, and worked my way back to the trailer.

When acting, my post-lunch regimen is very specific: I brush the lunch out of my teeth, take a fistful of vitamins, and grab a catnap. But after the physicality of our run-throughs, I decided to skip parts one and two and proceed directly to the catnap.

The calm before the storm.

Two hours later, I awoke in a panic, haunted by recurring dreams about forgetting lines — an actor's worst nightmare. I got up slowly and shuffled to the bathroom. The mirror revealed a serious case of Pillow Face, and a glance at my watch confirmed the elapsed time.

I opened the trailer door and squinted into the late-afternoon sun. Across the base camp, Deborah spotted me and hurried over. "Hello, Bruce. Sorry you haven't heard from us."

"What the hell is going on?" I muttered, feeling the pull of dried drool on my face. "Why haven't I worked?"

Deborah looked around nervously. "Well, it looks like you've been...*released*. I can sign you out."

"Oh, wow," I said, confused. "What about the scene we were rehearsing?"

Deborah struggled to find the right words. "It's being retooled, they say, but I'm always the last to know. Sorry."

"That's fine. What's my call time for tomorrow?"

Deborah fixed her eyes on the pavement between us. "There isn't one right now. You're a 'will notify.'"

18

Quest for Liar

Will notify” in movie lingo means that the production doesn’t have a rm idea of when an actor will be needed. I was in my executive suite vatching the Home Shopping Network at eleven o’clock at night when received official “notification.” It came in the form of an emotional hone call from my agent, Barry.

“This is huge,” he said, choking back tears. “This is fucking awful.”

For an agent to cry, I knew it was bad. “Okay, Barry, let me have it.”

“Paramount wants to…get out of the Bruce Campbell business,” he aid, sniffling.

“Wow. He did it. He really did it,” I said, chewing on my lower lip.

“Who did what?”

“Who else? Rob ‘Big Gulp’ Stern. He had it in for me from the start.”

“Look, they admit that it was their mistake,” Barry said, trying to reasure me. “Mike Nichols himself told me that he loved working with you, nd that he would keep you in mind in the future.”

"That and a buck fifty will get me a cup of coffee."

"Hey, you're pay-or-play, so don't worry, you won't be out an money."

"Good thing, because I smell a drought of biblical proportions com ing on."

"Please don't do anything stupid, Bruce. I have a call int Paramount."

"Don't do anything stupid, he says," I repeated with venom. "Let m tell you, Barry, I already did something stupid — I agreed to audition fc this goddamn role!"

I expected Barry to come back with some sort of plastic bromide ca culated to calm me down. But there was nothing but dead air.

"What?" I asked.

"There's more," said Barry, hesitantly. "Have you ever heard c something called a 'B movie virus'?"

My own little lost weekend.

I slammed the phon down so hard I cracke the base and split a fir gernail. I quickly decic ed to vacate the prem ises before I coul inflict any more damag to the hotel room c myself, and proceede to tear up the "city th never sleeps" with a all-night bender.

The long flight back to the West Coast gave me plenty of time to d three things: recover, rethink, and regroup. I have a very healthy eg but I wasn't concerned about my own well-being — I was concerned about my bank account. Potential employers in this fickle industry could easily get the wrong impression and run for the hills. Abominable behavior has long been tolerated from big-name stars, but the average thespian gets no such slack.

An actor who has a blowout with a director might be labeled "difficult," regardless of the circumstances. If he or she shows up late for call enough times, or forgets their lines often enough, they'll become "unreliable," and the label will stick like residue from a Band-Aid. But no one, to my knowledge, had ever been stricken with a "disease carrier" tag. If word got out that I was not only fired from a supporting role in an important film, but that I had infected that film — and possibly the director, cinematographer, and other actors — with some sort of career-killing pathogen, the ripple effect could be staggering.

Back home in Oregon, I typed the name of a certain Big Gulp–sucking executive: R-o-b S-t-e-r-n, into a movie database website. The information that popped up both surprised and horrified me. *Army of Darkness* was listed as one of his credits — an acting credit.

Army of Darkness*? That was back in 1991. How old was he, fourteen?*

I rifled through storage boxes in my attic that contained research from my last book, *If Chins Could Kill: Confessions of a B Movie Actor*. In it, I included snippets from production reports showcasing what a perilous shoot *Army of Darkness* was.

Production reports, depending on your point of view, can be a beautiful or horrible thing. Each day, at the end of shooting, the Unit Production Manager, in conjunction with the First Assistant Director, fills out this form, detailing exactly what happened that day, down to who worked, how many lunches were served, how many feet of film were exposed, etc. A production report is often cited in legal and insurance matters, so the information included is usually corroborated and almost always exhaustive.

One particular part of the form, from which I got the best material, was the "comments" section, where the assistant director would include delays, accidents, and anything else of interest to the production. One such comment section indicated the hiring and subsequent firing of an underage extra. My jaw dropped as I read:

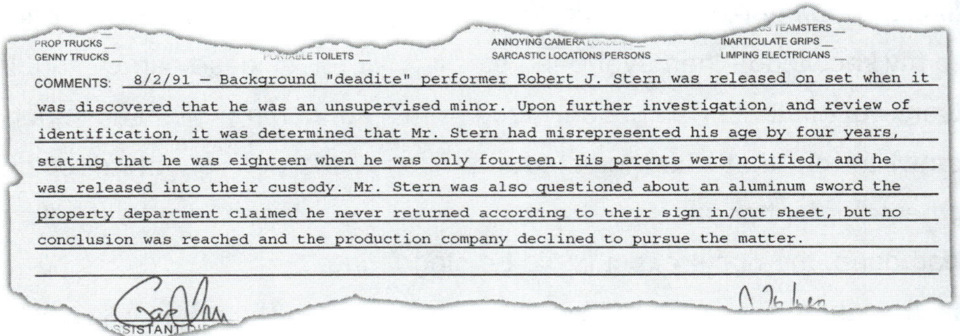

PROP TRUCKS __
GENNY TRUCKS __
PORTABLE TOILETS __
ANNOYING CAMERA LOADERS __
SARCASTIC LOCATIONS PERSONS __
TEAMSTERS __
INARTICULATE GRIPS __
LIMPING ELECTRICIANS __

COMMENTS: 8/2/91 – Background "deadite" performer Robert J. Stern was released on set when it was discovered that he was an unsupervised minor. Upon further investigation, and review of identification, it was determined that Mr. Stern had misrepresented his age by four years, stating that he was eighteen when he was only fourteen. His parents were notified, and he was released into their custody. Mr. Stern was also questioned about an aluminum sword the property department claimed he never returned according to their sign in/out sheet, but no conclusion was reached and the production company declined to pursue the matter.

Rob frickin' Stern, I said to myself. *The bitter little liar.*

I decide to consult with my Paramount insider, Lanny Sticks, and gave him a call. He sounded groggy and unfocused at eight-thirty that night.

"Hey, Lanno — BC here. How are ya?"

"Uh...hi. Better than you, I guess. I still have a job."

"Yeah, funny. It's that little know-nothing, Stern. He may have gotten a few cheap shots in, but if I go down, I'm takin' him with me. Are you in, Lanny? Can you help me?"

There was an unusually long pause as Lanny considered this.

"Hey, look, man, I'm just a security guard. What can I do?"

"You can help me get back in there and kick some major executive ass, that's what," I urged. "All I need are your keys, Lanny."

"Sorry, buddy, but I gotta think about my future. I didn't make a zillion ›llars like you on all your failed TV shows. They have a good retire- ent package here at the big P, and I want to take advantage of it."

"But you said yourself they were forcing you out," I countered.

"Let's just say things have changed."

I knew there was no talking him into it. On top of it all, his subtle per- ›nality shift made me suspicious, so I didn't want to tip my hand any rther.

"Okay, Lanny, I understand. Be well."

I hung up the phone and walked ıtside to enjoy a brilliant Oregon ınset. The image of refracted ght beaming through the clouds as hauntingly surreal, and it eminded me of the esoteric end- g of *The Incredible Shrinking 'an*. The lead character was ırinking uncontrollably, and ecame so ineffectual that normal- ze adults were no longer aware his existence. I felt that way right ›w — so small and helpless that I as virtually invisible.

But I wasn't going to go out like that. I was going to crawl back from planned obsolescence and clear my name in Hollywood. The infor- ation age leaves a vast, digital footprint and I knew a doofus like Rob tern would leave a slimy trail everywhere he went. I could link his jig- y ass to this whole disaster, but to do it I needed those e-mails.

19

Belly of the Beast

Why would you want to be Robert Evans?" makeup queen Mel Tooker sked.

"He's the producer of *Let's Make Love!*, and I want to pull a gag on im. It has to work, Mel. I have to be able to pass as him for a couple ours."

Mel smiled and shrugged. "Don't ask, don't tell. . . ."

Together, we sorted through a stack of miscellaneous Robert Evans hotos she had assembled, taken over the years at numerous Hollywood functions. Robert got his start as an actor back in the studio ra, so there was a plethora of reference material on his distinctive ace.

"This should be no problem at all," Mel said, in her usual chipper oice. "Let's get busy."

The procedure was very similar to the transformation I underwent in rder to play Elvis Presley at seventy. Guessing that Robert Evans was hovering around that age, we salvaged the jowl moulds from *Bubba* and even adapted a hand-stitched Elvis wig to suit the desired look.

Two and a half hours later, I emerged from Mel's warehouse an squinted into the L.A. haze. I was a new man: a powerful producer wh could throw his weight around where he needed to. Robert Evans ha been a fixture at Paramount since the 1970s, and I was going to mil every bit of deference and privilege he had coming.

Lincoln town cars in Los Angeles are a dime a dozen. With plate like Snoop, FilmCo, and Star21, they roam the hills and valleys of Lo Angeles in search of dark-shaded famous types to ferry about. In m New Zealand TV days, Executive Class Limousine Service was th appointed carrier, and I got to know the drivers on my way to and fror the LAX airport.

I still had a card from George, a wannabe actor who drove for them We always got along well because he hated Los Angeles as much, not more, than I did, and he was always up for shortcuts and funk routes. On top of that, he owned his own town car, and that would su my nefarious scheme better.

"George, Bruce Campbell here, how are you doing?"

"Hey, dude, what' up?"

"I need you fc another adventure."

"Sure thing — I' call dispatch and we' schedule it."

"No, George, thi one has to be unde the radar. I want t

ire you separately from the limo service."

"I see," George said, getting more interested. "What's the deal?"

"The deal is this: On Sunday, I play Robert Evans, and you play his river. Together, we crash the Paramount gate. Think you can do that?"

"In my sleep, daddy-o. Can we do it after the Rams game — about hree-thirty?"

"Sure."

"Cash?"

"Of course."

"You got yourself a deal, Mr. Robert Evans."

t turned out that George had also driven for the real Robert Evans, and ccording to him, he always entered Paramount at the Van Ness gate, a lesser-used shipping entrance on the east side of the lot.

The basic drill at studios is that the only way you can get on the lot s to possess a coveted "drive-on" pass, usually called in by some uthorized person affiliated with a current production. I was sure that Robert Evans, once head of the entire studio, wouldn't put up with any of that, so George and I had nothing to display but sheer bravado as ve neared Gate Four.

"Okay, George, I'm thinking we pull up, I'll do the 'I do this every day' wave to the guard — you do the same — and odds are we're in the door."

"Sounds good, boss," George said, nodding dutifully.

The town car swung in front of the guard shack, and my heart sank or two reasons: the attending guard was very young, and *Lanny Sticks was training him*.

"Fuck," I spat, under my breath. "Okay, George, stay sharp."

The twenty-two-year-old guard, Luis Rodriguez, stepped forward, clipboard in hand. "Can I help you?"

"Robert Evans," George said simply, with just the right amount of boredom in his voice to sound convincing.

"Do you have a pass?" Luis asked politely.

Lanny Sticks took note of the name, and stepped toward the town car. Instinctively I rolled my window down and nodded to him.

"New guy?" I asked, delivering my first line as Robert Evans.

"Yes, sir, Mr. Evans, thanks for your patience. How are you today?"

"Just fine, Lanny," I said, smug in knowing that I didn't even have to look at his tag. That reading *must* have sounded convincing.

Lanny held my look for a beat, then glanced at Luis. "This is Mr. Robert Evans, Luis. He's one of the most famous movie producers in the world. He comes here all the time. He's one of the few people who doesn't need a drive-on pass. You might want to put his name in that special column on the right — see it there?"

"Yes, sir, okay — I got it," Luis said, jotting the name down.

Lanny looked back at George, who was waiting in a wonderfully passive mode. "Mr. Evans, where's Keith?"

Before I could answer, George jumped in. "He's sick as a dog," he said. "He showed up this morning at the dispatch office, and barfed in his own car while he was cleaning it. Naturally, we swapped it out for Mr. Evans."

"Naturally," Lanny repeated, giving George the once-over.

We had complied with the basic needs of the gate guards, so I wanted to avoid further interaction. I thanked Lanny and rolled the window back up.

George let his foot off the brake, and the town car groaned forward in another subtle indication that we wanted to leave.

"How's that new office working for you, Mr. Evans?" Lanny asked.

Bruce the Robert.

That bastard. Could he kick ack on a Sunday afternoon and 'ave a few cars through? No, my al, Lanny Sticks, had to be a fas-dious prick.

"Just fine," I said, rolling the win-ow down two inches. "It smells ke a new house in there."

As I was saying this, my hands fled through the latest *Hollywood* *reative Directory*, an exhaustive uarterly listing of where to find vir-ally anyone in Hollywood, and ocated the production office of Robert Evans.

"Of course, the Adolph Zukor Building is worth all that effort, wouldn't ou say?"

Lanny rocked back on his heels. "Sure is, Mr. Evans."

He signaled to Luis, and the arm rose up. We were free to enter. anny and his new recruit watched in silence as we drove past.

Around the corner, in a reserved parking lot, George and I caught ur breath.

"Well, that was a first good test," I said, slumping back in the plush eat.

"Can I change my shorts now?" George asked. "That was close."

"Too close. But George, I have to say, you were at the top of your ame. That might go down as one of your finest unseen performances."

"Well, thanks," he said, modestly, pointing to his head. "I'll always

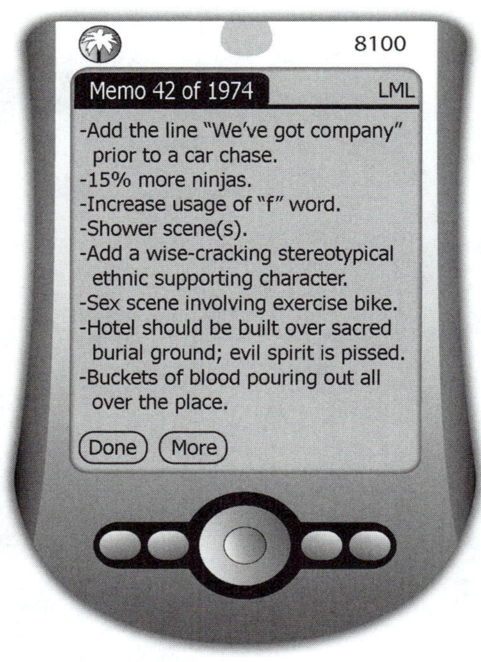

Rob's latest brilliant ideas.

have it up here."

Trying to reference the locatio of Rob Stern on the map Lanr Sticks pilfered was almost imposs ble. The Paramount back lo became what it is in 1926, an grew in fits and starts. An overhea schematic is like looking at th maze of a secret garden designe to confuse and disorient.

"I know the studio pretty well, if means anything," George offere "What are you looking for?"

"The Sturges Building."

"What's your plan?"

"For your own sake, I shouldn't tell you any more than I already have

George rolled his eyes and took the map from my hands. He pulle out a yellow highlighter from his glove box and traced the route for me

"There you go, mystery man. Enjoy."

"Thanks, pal. It's for your own good."

"Whatever."

"Now, do me a favor and just hang right here. I'm going to nee between fifteen minutes and a half hour."

"You got it," George said, sliding his chauffeur cap over his eyes.

I walked with confidence down the colonnade in front of the admir istration building, glancing at George's markings occasionally.

So far so good, I thought. My getup was working, even though I fe like a Disney character at a theme park.

I cut behind the Lubitsch Building, across an open plaza, and slippe around the Dressing Room building, hoping to duck into the rear of the Preston Sturges Building. As I approached the door, a frumpy young man stepped out — Rob Stern! Holy hell, I was hoping to find his office, not the man himself.

Why are you here on a Sunday? I cursed secretly. *Shouldn't you be home, mowing your mother's lawn or playing Nintendo?*

"Hello, sir," Rob said, reverently. "What brings the great Robert Evans to my little building on a Sunday?"

I suddenly realized that the actor in me was relishing the encounter. I was Robert Evans, the producer of *Let's Make Love!* and Rob was just a little pissant junior executive from East Nowhere. It didn't make up for being fired, but it soothed my ego somewhat.

"I know you put in a lot of time on this project," I explained. "I mean, you're the one who brought it to the studio, kid. You're responsible for its development, responsible for its *current state*," I added, with an edge in my voice. "So, I knew you'd be here working today. I wanted to get your notes on the latest *Love* draft."

"It's funny you should ask that, Mr. Evans," Rob said, inflating himself. "I just e-mailed them out to everyone."

"Great, I look forward to reading them," I said, with genuine sincerity.

"Cool. Well, I'm off to the Buddha Bar to meet some friends about a new project."

"Hey, kid, before you go — quick question about the Campbell situation."

Rob bristled at the subject matter. "Uh-huh?"

"What really went down there? I don't see what the problem was. I never heard anything negative about him from Mike."

"It was an internal situation," Rob said, hesitantly.

"Who authorized it?"

"The decision was made on upper levels."

"Don't bullshit me, kid. I used to run this place. Give me a name."

Rob pursed his lips. "I say this with due respect, Mr. Evans — the Campbell case is a Red file. You've been there before, so you know I can't talk about it."

"Well that's fine, kiddo," I said, blowing him off as Robert Evans would have. "Red, blue, green — pick whatever color you want, but I'm going to get to the bottom of this Campbell thing. You studio chumps can't muscle me. I know where the bodies are buried around here — literally."

"Sure, I understand, Mr. Evans," Rob said, his face flushing from the threat. "I wonder how these things happen myself."

You're going to wonder all right. You're going to wonder how my right shoe got so far up your ass.

"Well, I'll let you get back to your nice, new office," Rob said, unable to hide his resentment.

"Yeah, got some big deals coming down — better get to it."

I stepped toward the Sturges Building, but Rob stopped me.

"I thought your office was *that* way," he said, jerking a thumb behind him.

I turned to see a low-profile building, with a facade like something from the set of *Chinatown*, the classic film produced by Robert Evans. Then I noticed a sign above the door: ROBERT EVANS INTERNATIONAL.

"Of course, kid. I've had so many offices here over the years, I get turned around. Ciao."

"Have a good one," Rob said, pausing to see if "Robert Evans" actually entered "his" office.

I waved back and ducked into the plush lobby.

HOLLYWOOD LEAST WANTED

RED FILE!

BRUCE L. CAMPBELL

Aliases: Ash, Coach Boomer, Joe Fasulo, William Cole, Jack, Ray, Wrestling Announcer, Roland the Intrepid Explorer, Barney the Dinosaur, etc.

DECRIPTION

Date of Birth:	June 22, 1958	**Hair:**	Dark Brown
Place of Birth:	Birmingham, MI, USA	**Eyes:**	Pretty
Height:	6' 1"	**Sex:**	Male
Weight:	175 pounds	**Complexion:**	Brazen
Build:	Slight	**Citizenship:**	USA
Languages:	Spanglish		
Scars and Marks:	"L"-shaped scar & mole on face		
Remarks:	Who the hell is Bruce Campbell?		

CAUTION

Bruce L. Campbell has proven that he doesn't have what the networks want for renewing a television series.

RESIDUALS

The Screen Actors Guilt is attempting to remove all residual benefits for Bruce L. Campbell.

That brief encounter accomplished two things on my mission: 1. though risky, I was able to glean useful information and get under the weasel's skin, if only a little bit; 2. I now knew definitively that he was not going to be in his office for the rest of the day.

"Bob, there you are."

I turned to the bored, supermodel-type receptionist.

"Jack's waiting to see you," she said.

"Jack?" I asked, trying to hide my utter confusion.

"How many Jacks do you know, silly?"

"Ha — right!"

"I put the usual on your desk."

"Thanks…kiddo," I said, not knowing her name, and I walked out of the lobby.

At the end of a dimly lit hall was an enormous oak door, the kind you'd see in an old library. Some people in Hollywood earn a lot of money making movies. Some people in Hollywood earn so much money they spend more time decorating their offices than actually making movies.

I swung the heavy door open to see a man with his back to me, dressed in golf attire, putting at the far end of what was my enormous, seventies-era office. Large enough to host a full-scale party, but sprinkled with enough cozy nooks to accommodate intimate business dealings, this was a Hollywood mogul's wet dream.

I almost tripped over the shag carpeting as I entered, and my guest *Jack Nicholson*, turned around with that characteristic Cheshire grin.

"Hey, Bobby," he said simply.

It was *that* Jack, after all. *Christ, I'm dead*. Jack Nicholson and Robert Evans went back thirty years, and surely knew each other's ticks and tastes.

"Jack you old dog," I said, initiating a hug, but Jack pulled back, surprised by my intimacy.

"All touchy-feely again, Bob?" he asked, a little confused.

Jack and Bob.

"I'm just happy to see you again, Jack."

"What, you missed me since playin' poker last night?"

My blank stare didn't help the awkward situation, so I shifted topics. "What can I get for you, Jack-a-roo?"

"The usual, thanks."

Of course he would say that.

I gestured to the expansive wet bar, trying to get more information. "Pick your poison."

Jack looked at me like I was off my nut. "Tomato juice, same as always." He went to the mini fridge and got it himself.

On top of a slightly agitated Jack Nicholson, I had yet another conundrum to deal with: I had no idea why we were meeting, or who initiated it.

Taking a deep breath and exhaling loudly, Jack pulled the tab on his can of low-sodium tomato juice and sat down on a plush sofa. "So...."

"So..." I echoed, nodding my head, as if we shared a secret.

"Wanna hear it?" Jack asked.

I was a nanosecond away from saying "hear what?" but I caught myself and sat down in an adjacent chair. "Sure do."

Jack took a swig of juice and stood right back up. "All right, here it is: the other day, I was makin' some salad dressing in the kitchen. I had a little water, I had a little oil, but I was out of vinegar. And then it hit me — we need to make another *Chinatown.* The first one was about water, the second was about oil, and the third should be about *vinegar*!"

"Vinegar," I said, looking confused, but still nodding yes.

"Work it backwards in your head, Bob — vinegar, wine, grapes — the land they're grown on. *The Two Jakes* was set in '48. You set this one a few years later in the Napa Valley, when Jake is retired, see, and it turns out the land he owns is tied up in this whole scheme to pave the way for a vineyard."

I kept nodding yes. Having already jeopardized the fate of one film, what else could I do?

"I'm calling it *Grapevine*."

You didn't have to be an executive to know that *Grapevine* stunk as a title, but that never stopped movies like *Ishtar* and *Gigli* from getting made, and who was I to judge?

Jack interpreted my continued lack of response as a sign of disinterest. "Townsend is in, what more do you want, Bob?"

"Well, Jack, uh, you know how I feel about these movies —"

"Is it the deal? Is that's what's buggin' you?"

I had to stay neutral; I couldn't intimate that my deal was any better or worse than Nicholson's, since I didn't have a whisper of inside information. "No Jack, not specifically...."

"Look, I talked to Townsend. He'll give you five gross points and I'll give you five gross points."

He was referring to Robert Townsend, one of the luminaries of seventies screenwriting, and he was also referring to gross profit participation, money from dollar one at the box office.

"Will that do it, Bob?" Jack implored, getting impatient. "Can we make the deal?"

Considering the fact that I just got Robert Evans 10 percent of gross revenues for a *Chinatown* sequel starring Jack Nicholson, I felt pretty good. It was the most productive ten minutes I'd ever spent in Hollywood. "Jack, if you feel that strongly about it, sure — let's do it."

Jack's Cheshire smile came back in full force. "Good thing — my tee-time is in twenty minutes."

Jack initiated the hug this time, but I was the one who pulled away. Our verbal exchange was sweat-inducing, and I smelled like a rubber glove simmering on low heat. Jack got a good whiff.

"Whoa, Bob, you're sweatin' up a storm there, amigo. Everything okay? You don't look so good."

I realized that a dreaded "edge" of my makeup appliance began to show. On a film set, hiding makeup lines is a never-ending battle, requiring constant attention between shots. In a live context, it meant that my time as Robert Evans was limited, even under the best of conditions.

"I just had a little work done," I whispered to Jack in a knowing, sotto voce, "and the results were not exactly what I had hoped for."

Jack gave me a say-no-more wink and excused himself from the office. "I'll be in touch, Bob."

I decided to remove myself from Robert Evans International before I could green-light another project.

"Hold all my calls," I said over my shoulder as I dashed outside.

Rob Stern's office was on the third floor of the Sturges Building. I knew for a fact that there was a generic bathroom on the second floor where I could take the makeup off, wash up, and continue my quest without incident.

Bathrooms on back lots aren't what you might think. Far from opulent, the average biffy-in-a-bungalow was closer to the Navy than Hollywood. Color schemes were either drab brown and creme, or dark gray with a light gray trim. But it didn't really matter how many coats of paint had been added since the days of Adolph Zukor, because all I was gonna do was rip my face off and get out of there.

I pushed the door open, expecting to see exactly nobody on a Sunday evening. I was wrong. Chris McDonald, a very busy actor, was washing his hands in front of the mirror. Chris kept busy as an actor, mainly by stealing roles from me. At last infuriating count, he was up to seventeen. He and I play the same "type" a lot — the smarmy, snotty, or obnoxious guy, only he lands most of the roles I'm trying to get.

I met Chris once at a function in Century City, and unfortunately he turned out to be a very nice guy — I say unfortunately, because it made it more difficult to hate him. I knew exactly why the bastard was here — for an *audition* — and he was killing time in the bathroom.

If I didn't take action, I knew what was going to happen: Chris was going to tell me, Robert Evans, about his latest gigs, and how nice it was to meet me, how he'd love to work with me some day, and blah blah, blah, and then he'd notice that something was wrong. With makeup that was about to take itself off, it didn't take long to devise a plan.

"There's that actor I see everywhere," I said, going the gregarious route. "Bob Evans."

"I know who you are, Mr. Legendary Producer," he said, offering his hand. "Chris McDonald. Great to meet you."

I shook Chris's hand all right. I shook it long and hard, enough to get a worried look out of him.

"You here auditioning for something, kid?"

"Uh, yeah, the new Zemeckis film, *Double Down*."

"Oh, that picture. What role are you reading for?" I asked, curious.

"The lieutenant who gets killed at the end — Ryan."

"Ahhh, it's funny, Bob Zemeckis is a good friend of mine. He used to shine my shoes on Sundays. All I ever hear him talk about is this Campbell kid."

"Bill Campbell? That bastard always gets my stuff!" Chris said, shaking his head.

"No, no, the other one," I corrected.

"Glen? He's a singer."

"No, *Bruce* Campbell."

"The *Evil Death* guy? Why would Bob want him?" Chris asked, puzzled.

"Something about a certain quality," I said, shaking my head. "Look, I don't know, kid, I'm not directing the picture."

Chris became utterly befuddled, wringing his audition sides in his hands. "But if Campbell is already a lock — and you would know, Bob — then why should I even bother to read? You were an actor once, what would you do?"

"Well if it was me, I'd go home, check the mail for residual checks, and make a sour apple martini. But, it's Hollywood, kid, anything can happen."

"Yeah, I guess you're right, Bob, I —"

That's when I started to tear my face off. Sticking a thumb into the foam crevasse that had opened up earlier, I began to pull the prosthetics away from my face.

"Oh, my God, I'm melting!" I whimpered, in my best horror film reading.

Chris reeled back. The blue-green fluorescent light and the gray-on-lighter-gray bathroom lent itself perfectly to a ghoulish atmosphere.

My right hand was able to separate a huge chunk of my cheek, and I threw it into the sink. Chris almost vomited on the spot.

"Don't just stand there, Chris, get help!" I wailed, tearing my lips clean off.

Chris ran out of the bathroom, cupping a hand over his mouth, presumably to either barf or spread the word that something horrible had just happened to Robert Evans.

"Try and audition with *that* on your mind, Chris McDonald," I said, nodding ruefully.

Three hours of sweat had loosened the makeup substantially, so I finished tearing off what was left of Robert Evans and dumped him in the trash.

I emerged from the bathroom as a pasty-faced Bruce Campbell, and walked up to the third floor. I worked my way toward Suite 3350, passing a night cleaning crew that was going from office to office. *Had they passed Rob's office, or were they working their way toward it?* I wondered.

As I rounded the corner, I realized that Suite 3350 was being cleaning at that very moment. Acting is bluffing, so I took a deep breath and plunged into Rob Stern's office suite. A Latina woman was vacuuming, and another was spraying every surface with a horrid pink cleaning solution. As I entered Rob's world, I didn't hide the fact that I hated the smell.

"Whooh," I said, waving my hand in front of my nose. "Hey, it's okay. No more."

The spraying woman looked at me. "No?"

"No, thank you." I turned to the woman who was vacuuming. "Hello. It's okay. No need to do that."

The vacuuming woman finally noticed me. "No?"

"That's okay, really. Don't empty anything, no vacuum, no spray. Thank you. Good night. I have to work. *Mucho trabajo*."

The women were happy to shave ten minutes off their work schedule. I ushered them out, threw the deadbolt behind them, and then turned to face Rob's world. Strewn around the office were posters of *Star Wars* and *American Pie*, *Evil Dead* action figures, signed photos from miscellaneous celebrities, and — I actually did a double take — the sword from *Army of Darkness*!

Rob had it mounted above his desk on a plaque, the way you display a beautiful elk rack.

"That little thief," I muttered, as I worked my way behind his desk through stacks of unread scripts. I yanked the sword off its display and twirled it in my hand. I knew immediately that it was authentic. The aluminum swords used on *Army of Darkness* were very sturdy and mercifully light — they felt like no other.

Hating him even more, I put the sword aside and scanned the surface of Rob's black, wood composite desk. It was littered with memos and candy wrappers, neither of which applied to my case. I turned my attention to his computer terminal. Rob had mentioned to "Robert Evans" that he had recently e-mailed his notes on the latest draft, so the challenge was to hack into his e-mail system.

His *Lord of the Rings* welcome screen displayed an access window, waiting for the correct password. If this were all a movie, I'd be a computer wiz and I'd hack in, get what I needed, and change the timing of the stoplights in Beverly Hills just for kicks.

The transition from soul-swallowing ghoul to film producer was an easy one for Stern.

But this was reality, and I had no such computer skills. I stared at the blinking cursor for a solid minute, until a shiny glint on the monitor led my eye over to the aluminum sword, which gleamed under Rob's bright halogen lamp.

I looked from the sword to the sign-in screen and typed "deadite." No response. I typed "Ash," and got nothing. Breaking into a cold sweat, knowing that many computer systems give you three attempts at the password, then shut you out, I bit my lip and typed the third and last try: "groovy."

Instantly, Rob's welcome screen changed, the *Army of Darkness* theme came up, and the character Ash said "Groovy." I was inside!

The inner workings of network computer systems have always been daunting, but I managed to navigate his e-mail system enough to call up a search mechanism. I typed in two words sure to get matches: *Campbell* and *Love.*

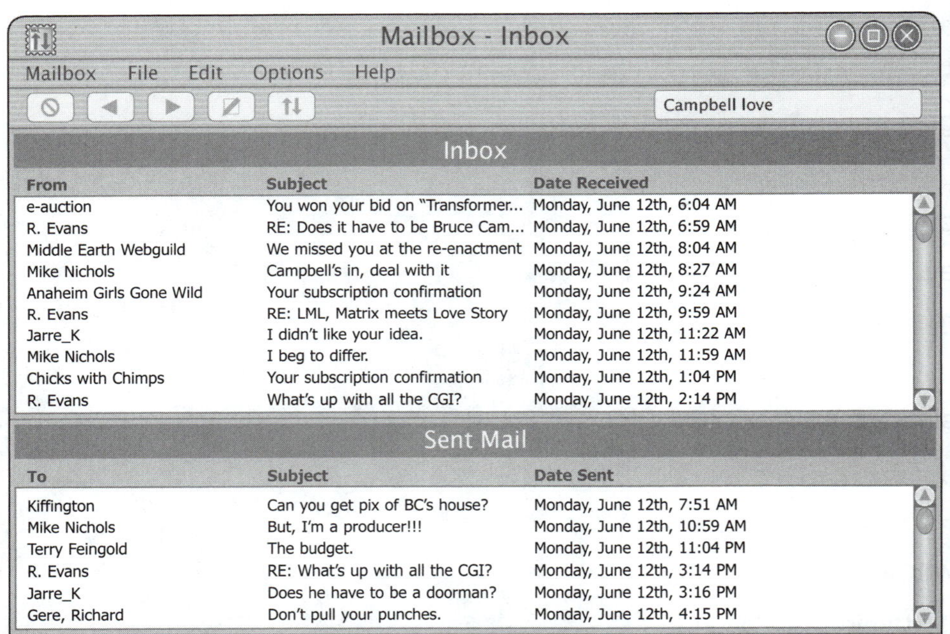

Probably a hundred e-mails, dating back almost a year, sprang up on a list. As a studio executive, I knew he wouldn't have deleted them — and what, erase his legacy? Randomly, I opened enough of them to learn that Stern had slowly, methodically masterminded the "*Army of Darkness*-ization" of the *Let's Make Love!* script, ignored budget implications, and when things began to go horribly wrong, blamed it all on an enthusiastic but undeserving actor (that would be me). I now had enough to take this kid down.

As fast as my mediocre computer skills would allow, I downloaded the damning e-mails to Rob's desktop and copied them to a blank CD-ROM.

"Ha! I'll show that punk —"

I headed for the door but before I could exit, a mixture of Paramount security guards and plain-suited men poured in, all led by Lanny Sticks.

"That's him," Lanny said, pointing at me. "That's Bruce Campbell. He's the perpetrator."

I froze.

"Robert Evans, my ass," Lanny said, approaching me with a mangled chunk of my Robert Evans appliance in his clenched fist.

"How did you find out?" I asked, my mind racing, churning through one B-movie-inspired escape after another. Suddenly I noticed that the aluminum sword that had helped me a decade before was within easy reach. I began inching toward it.

"In all the years I would say hello to Robert Evans," Lanny explained simply, "he never once called me Lanny."

"So it all boiled down to a name," I mused.

"The call about Robert Evans's face melting off helped too. That's when I —"

That's when I grabbed the sword. In a neat two-step move I learned on the failed TV show *Jack of All Trades*, I deftly stepped behind Lanny and placed the jagged aluminum blade tight across his neck.

The other security guys freaked and backed away, one falling over a chair.

"Get away from the door," I barked.

Using Lanny as a human shield, I made my way toward the exit.

"Let him do it," Lanny urged, feeling the discomfort from my blade. "I'm good, don't worry about me."

I backed out the door with Lanny in tow and we worked our way to the edge of the nearest stairway.

"You're gonna take a big fall, Bruce," Lanny warned. "If you let me go right now, I can clear this up. You keep going with this, it's gonna get serious. Studios have heavy-duty backup when they need it."

Caught on tape: "Bob Evans" lurking around the lot.

"I'm innocent, Lanny," I explained, grabbing the enormous ring of keys from his belt. I clipped his walkie-talkie to my pants and shoved him to the floor. "From one actor to another, I'm telling the truth."

"I don't care," Lanny scowled, massaging an elbow.

I ran down the stairs and past the "meltdown" bathroom, sidestepping the Haz Mat team that was hosing the place out.

Out on the relative expanse of the back lot, I picked up speed and made my way past the administrative offices, where George and the town car were parked. But as the Lincoln came into view, I discovered George spread-eagled across the hood. He was being rousted by four serious-looking men.

Poor bastard. To serve the greater good, one must be prepared to sacrifice a few innocent chauffeurs.

I took off in the opposite direction at a dead run, checking in on walkie-talkie broadcasts as I went. Between four channels, I did the best I could to monitor what Lanny and his men knew — or *didn't* know.

Channel 1: =SQUAWK= "I'm heading south on Ave E...."

Channel 2: =SQUAWK= "I'm gonna be here awhile, Stu, the police want the melted face stuff as evidence...."

Channel 3: =SQUAWK= "on 5th Street, westbound...."

Channel 4: =SQUAWK= "no, no, it was liverwurst with mustard — in a bag under the desk. Can you check again?"

My only logical escape route was due north, through the cemetery. I knew Paramount well enough to know that avenues ran north and south, and streets were east and west. The guards were obviously covering the main drags. As long as I stayed on the streets, I wasn't safe, but a man with keys could head north, to freedom.

The Crosby Building was right in front of me. I tested the keys methodically, just as Lanny had explained, and within a minute I was inside.

I quickly realized that I was on a scoring stage — one that was actually scoring a film. Fortunately, I had come in through the rear and was facing the backs of some forty musicians. They, in turn, faced a large digital screen, which played a climactic chase scene from some unnamed Adam Sandler movie. I scoped a door on the opposite side of the paneled room and predicted an easy walk around.

All actors love props, so I used the walkie-talkie to engage in a very important, silent conversation as I eased past the woodwinds. But just beyond the percussion section I became distracted by some good sight gags in the film. I became the guy at baseball games who walks back to his section, a beer in each hand, looking up at the scoreboard rather than straight ahead. You don't want to be behind the idiot, because he walks about one mile an hour, and you don't want to be in front of him, or seated in his row, because half of his beer is emptying in all directions.

My version of that guy was walking into a drum set, sending the cymbals crashing to the ground at exactly the wrong time. The music stopped, lights came up, and all heads turned to me. I fumbled with the cymbals before resorting to the walkie-talkie gag.

"Yeah, ten-four, good buddy — just checking out some strange noises in the Crosby stage, but it's nothing unusual, over."

Before anyone could penetrate my cunning ruse, I slipped out the north door and found myself in a hallway lined with other doors, all leading to rooms seemingly related to postproduction sound.

I chose a door toward my end of the hall and promptly stumbled into an active Foley stage. These recording studios are almost always dark and are floored with a number of surfaces that simulate anything from a concrete walkway to a grassy knoll. Before my eyes could adjust, I stumbled noisily across every surface except the one the engineers were trying to match — Meg Ryan walking barefoot in the sand, for some soon-to-be-released romantic comedy.

Don't these guys ever take a day off?

I pushed through a side door and realized that I was now interrupting an ADR session, the process where dialogue is replaced in a controlled environment, after-the-fact. "Controlled" became more of an abstract concept as I plowed my way into George Clooney's session.

"Hey, hey, what the...?" George wondered as he spun away from the microphone to see who was behind him.

"Sorry, Mr. Clooney, just a routine security check," I said, hiding my face, never really stopping.

"That was good, George," the technician said over the studio speaker, "but the line is: 'Hey, hey, *where* the ...?' Let's try one more."

Before the big-shot star could explain, I snatched a seedless grape from his complementary fruit basket and snuck out. George gave an incredulous look to nobody in particular, and put his headphones back on.

The exit led to an alley adjacent to Studio 15. No sooner had the loor closed behind me than a familiar, angry voice echoed down the alley.

"Well, I guess it's just you and me."

I turned to see Lanny Sticks blocking my exit. He wasn't carrying a un, just a big riot stick.

"Mano a mano," he said, twirling the baton like he had paid attention luring training.

I was bigger than Lanny, and ad a sword, but I didn't feel like isking a rubber-coated bash to the neecap if I could avoid it. The only vay out was a door to Stage 15, nmediately to my right, but unlike ne other ones, it was older, funki-r, and harder to key. It would be a ace between my door-opening kills (mediocre) and Lanny's olice brutality training (unknown ut possibly extensive).

I decided to risk it. I took off toward the door and whipped out the key ng. Lanny charged, baton in attack position. I tried the first key, but it vas no good. I spun around and — *whannnng!* — parried Lanny's pproaching baton with my sword, then kicked him in the chest and ied a second key — still no good!

I spun back and head blocked the next swipe from Lanny, but I new aluminum was no match for steel, and that this type of contact vouldn't last long. Based on a move a stuntman taught me during *Aindwarp*, I dropped to the ground and swept my legs under Lanny, knocking him on his ass. He fell hard, losing both his breath and the baton.

I tried a third key, and it worked! I pulled open the insulated doors and walked right into a full-fledged barbarian fight scene, staged courtesy of American Express. There must have been a hundred leather-and-fur-clad warriors, hacking away at each other with crude weapons. I promised myself it would be the last time I infiltrated Paramount on a Sunday, and fought my way north, through the smelly Angelinos.

Lanny was soon on my heels, blocking blows from wooden swords and shoving unsuspecting extras out of his way. As we neared the exit he inadvertently walked into the middle of two stuntmen diving at each other and got sandwiched in the middle.

Across the stage, in "video village," a goatee-sporting, baseball-cap-wearing director leaped from his low director's chair.

"What the *fuck* was that? Cut, cut!"

I pushed open the doors to 12th Street, one of the most northerly of the lot. The outback was close. The last building standing in the way of victory was a storage facility. Inside the musty, damp place, unused sets from movies and TV shows were stored. I hustled past saloon sets, bank facades, and...*Captain Kirk's chair?!*

The original *Star Trek* had been one of my favorite shows as a kid and I would imitate William Shatner for days on end. I wiped some residual dust off the wide vinyl arms and sat down. The chair wasn't nearly as comfortable as I had assumed, and it didn't swivel or do anything cool, but it didn't matter. I leaned back and assumed command of the starship *Enterprise.*

"Gentlemen, I suggest you get my ship out-of-there," I bellowed to an empty warehouse, in perfect Shatner staccato.

"Aye-a-eye, sir," came the reply from across the large room (though not, I might add, in a particularly convincing Sulu).

It was Lanny, with a big lump on his head, back for more. I bolted out of Kirk's chair and kicked open the side door.

Blessed wilderness awaited at the fringe of the back lot — my way out. I ran through the dense underbrush. Shrubs and pickers tore at my clothes and skin, but nothing could affect the elation I felt now that freedom was within my grasp.

But at the overgrown gate to the cemetery, Lanny was there, waiting.

"I knew you'd go out this way," he said, tapping the baton in his palm. "A word of advice: never try to out-shortcut a security guard. They'll beat you every time."

Before a standoff could occur, I reached down and threw a fistful of dirt at Lanny's face and then rushed him. It was a surprise move, and it gave me a momentary edge, but Lanny hadn't slept through that 20-minute self-defense video. Using his baton as a barrier, he made sure the butt of it impacted with my chin when we landed on the ground.

A split second of white-hot pain exploded in my head and I released my grip. Lanny rolled over and readied his baton for a crippling blow, but not before I backhanded him across the face. You see it in movies all the time, but in reality it hurts like hell, and is absolutely no good for your knuckles.

Either way, it was enough to get this little bulldog off me and we squared off again. The similarity of this scenario triggered a vivid flashback from *Army of Darkness*. I was rehearsing swordplay in the gravel parking lot of the Polsa Rosa Ranch with our sword master, Dan, and he taught me a slick, disarming maneuver where you attack and evade at the same time.

Before you could say "action," I ducked, swiped, rolled, and knocked his heavy baton high into the air. The cool move ended with me placing the tip of my sword against Lanny's jugular vein.

"Ow, shit, that hurt!" Lanny complained.

"Sorry, man, it never worked on the first take before."

Lanny and I faced each other, breathing heavily. I could hear the rustle of footsteps and shouting near the edge of the outback — trouble was closing in.

"If I didn't know better, Lanny, I'd say you were pissed about something. What the hell did I ever do to you?"

Lanny shot a hard look at me. "Think about it, Bruce. Do you ever see me with women? Did you ever notice that I don't have any children?"

"Wow, I never knew you were gay, Lanny."

"I'm not gay, dumbass!" he barked. "Did you ever wonder that maybe it's because ol' Lann-o is shootin' blanks?"

"You're...*sterile*?"

"Why don't you just come out and say it?" he said, looking around nervously. "You know the scene. *Death of the Dead* — I'm Snake you're Nash. I'm takin' you outside the cabin at night and I knock you in the back of the head with the butt of my shotgun."

"And Nash flies off the porch to the ground below," I finished. "Yeah I remember — it hurt like hell."

Lanny turned back to me, eyes glistening at the tragic memory. "You ıave no idea. When you fell off the porch, you kicked a back leg in the ıir, didn't you?"

"To balance myself, yeah," I said defensively. "I always do that with alls."

"You put the heel of your boot right into my dingleberries."

"I did?" I asked, puzzled. But then I remembered Lanny approaching ne after the take that night, sweaty and pale, mentioning that he was ı some kind of pain. "I did. I did kick you in the nuts, Lanny," I admit-ed. "That made you sterile?"

"It was a hell of a shot," he said, avoiding eye contact.

"But why didn't you say something before?"

Lanny wiped his eyes and smiled, but it was forced and tragic. "Hey, 's not something you talk about while shootin' pool with the guys on a riday night, you know?"

The advancing footfalls grew louder. A flashlight swept the woods, nd we began to hear the tinny, "blah, blah, blah" of walkie-talkie hatter.

"Then it won't mat-er if I do it again," I aid, kicking Lanny ead center in the lanters. He buckled ıstantly, an indescrib-ble look of pain arved onto his face.

The exact moment the term "Brucectomy" was coined.

I turned my atten-on to the lock on the ate and pulled out

the prodigious collection of keys. *Too long*, I reasoned, and swung th fake sword with all my might. The aluminum blade pinched the meta chain against the stone wall and severed it. The lock fell off and th gate swung wide open. I raced into the cemetery just as officers of a jurisdictions swarmed upon the scene. It was now an old-fashioned foo chase.

20

Run, Bruce, Run!

I retraced my steps backward through the maze of the large cemetery, praying I wouldn't get lost. With a couple of Paramount security guards setting time trials behind me, my decision-making process became very spontaneous.

I rounded a corner near Tyrone Power's tombstone, and his devoted lover was there again, placing fresh flowers on his grave. I grabbed the middle-aged, frumpy woman and looked deep into her eyes.

"Kiss me once — for old Ty's sake?" I implored, as sincerely as I could for being completely out of breath.

"Anything for Ty!" the woman said, throwing her arms around me.

Our kiss was convincing enough for the security team to run right past without stopping. After an uncomfortable moment of trying to disengage from this surprisingly strong woman, I thanked her profusely and headed on my way.

Out by the main cemetery entrance, the security guys were chatting with the groundskeeper and I slipped out undetected. But as I approached Santa Monica Boulevard in search of a cab, I was amazed to see that the entire street seemed to have been closed off. A few blocks away, an official-looking motorcade approached, while a group of men in suits milled around, fingers to their ears.

Behind me, an agitated voice rang out: “It's him — it's the guy!”

When you're on the lam, you don't always have time to examine a situation as carefully as you'd like. So it wasn't until after I had hurdled the concrete security barrier lining Santa Monica Boulevard and collided with a strangely familiar man wearing an unseasonably warm dark wool suit that I realized harassing a world figure for the third time wasn't the best way to make a clean getaway.

“You?!” Agent Grunow hissed accusingly as I struggled to extricate myself from our impromptu embrace.

“Are you following me?” I asked suspiciously, buying time while I unhooked my pant cuff from his gun belt.

“I'm here on official business,” he explained. “Secretary Powell has been invited to a screening of *The SpongeBob Squarepants Movie*. Hey! Come back here!”

As with so many things in life, zigzagging between screeching black government SUVs was fun for the first thirty seconds, but got old fast. As I ducked and weaved my way across the boulevard, my new Sprint PCS phone kept thumping around in my breast pocket. I trapped it against my chest and fished it out. I'm not a gadget freak, but this sucker had it all — photo/video capability, wireless access, text messaging, even video games, which is why I had it in the first place, because the phone was given to me to approve an *Evil Dead* game (buy yours today!).

It occurred to me, between huffing and puffing, that although I didn't ve in Los Angeles anymore, I still had plenty of close friends in pseudo high places. Any one of them would help me at a moment's notice; ll I had to do was call.

The first person I dialed was good buddy Sam Raimi. Since the *Spider-Man* movies kicked major box-office ass, Sam's stature as a lirector had grown considerably. Now he was an A-list director, and I new he could pull some strings.

As expected, I got Sam's assistant, J.R.

"J.R., Bruce here, how are ya, buddy?"

"Fine, thanks. What can I do or you?" he asked.

"Well, I'll tell it to you straight ecause I don't have much time – I'm in trouble, and I need Sam's help desperately."

"Okay, I'll give him the message."

"The hell you will, J.R.," I said, starting to wheeze, "I need to talk to him *now*."

"Sorry, man, Sam's writing *Spider-Man 3*. He's not returning nyone's calls until the end of the day."

"Even if I said I was being chased by dark forces of evil?"

"He was pretty adamant."

"Okay, no sweat. Tell Sam it was nice knowing him."

"Okay, will do," J.R. noted, as if he were taking a message to pick up loaf of bread.

I hung up the phone and cursed *Spider-Man*. How dare those films do so well! I shouldn't have given such great performances! *The he[...] with him*, I rationalized, *I'll call my pal Rob Tapert.*

Rob was a successful producer and he would no doubt have major connections, legal or otherwise that could help. I dialed Rob and of course, got his assistant, Sue.

"Sue…Bruce here. How are you…doing?"

"You sound like you're running a marathon," she said.

"Something like that. Listen, I need to get hold of Rob — it's really important."

"Rob's not here right now, but I can give him a message."

"Sue, you don't understand — I really need to talk to him."

"That might be a little difficult. He's on a flight to New Zealand right now to prep a film. He won't touch down for about five more hours."

"All right, forget it. I'll be making national headlines by then."

I flipped the phone closed and cursed New Zealand. Goddamn global economy — why the hell can't Americans make movies in *America*

I ducked up an alley on the north side of Santa Monica Boulevard and glanced back at my pursuers. Fortunately, they were making phone calls too, and it kept them at a corresponding distance.

Okay, L.A. sucks for friends. I needed someone who would support me unconditionally. Who would be there when the chips were down? Who would be there even when I wasn't at the top of my game? That' when I realized that the help I sought couldn't be found in my Rolodex – what I needed was a fan!

Even with a squad of angry, trained men after me, the notion of calling a fan to ask for help made me laugh. I laughed so hard I dialed up the Internet and connected to my website. Or rather, that's what I attempted to do. The buttons on my PCS phone were tiny, which made it impractical to surf the web while jumping fences and eluding rottweilers. Nonetheless, after slowing to a dead run, I was able to download a fan database.

The next challenge was finding the nearest fan. I cleared another fence and thumbed through the addresses that popped up on the nice color screen ("visible even in low-light conditions," the rep had assured me). The names Jan and Ryan Gritton were easy to find, because they were the only listing for Hollywood, U.S.A.

I maneuvered around a line of fresh laundry, blowing lazily in the breeze, and pasted Jan's address into MapQuest. While the operating system's tiny hourglass symbol taunted me, I sprinted across Huckleberry Lane and jumped over a cinderblock retaining wall.

The directions eventually popped up, and I made my way to 509 Beech Lane, a small bungalow, tucked off the street.

Bam-bam-bam! I pounded on Jan's door like a cop.

An exhausted-looking woman in her late thirties opened the door and looked me over. "Not interested," she said, slamming the door in my face.

Bam-bam-bam! I pounded on the door again, even harder.

The door was opened the second time by sixteen-year-old freak Ryan Gritton. With a classic *Evil Dead* fan look of dyed black hair, an ashen face framed by black horn-rimmed glasses, tattoos, and multiple piercings, he was clearly trying to intimidate me.

"Look, dude, what do you want?" he demanded.

I took a wild guess. "Ryan Gritton?"

"Yeah?"

"Don't you recognize your only true friend, Bruce Campbell?"

It took a moment for Ryan to alter his posture from defensive t unbelieving, but the transformation was fun to watch.

"I don't believe it!" Ryan exclaimed, half jumping in the air. "Mom, it' okay, it's Ash!"

"That's right," I said in my best game-show-host impersonation. "An you've just won the 'Make Dinner for Bruce Campbell' Sweepstakes!"

Jan stepped out from behind her son and became more animatec "Oh, my God, when do we get to make dinner?"

"Right *now*," I said, pushing my way into their cramped, cluttere bungalow.

The Gritton home was a loving one, but their interior had been dec orated by a gang of howler monkeys on crack.

"Nice place you have here," I said, allowing my eyes to slide past th piles of as-yet-undone laundry heaped in the kitchen. "Say, uh, do yo have a computer with a CD-ROM drive?"

"Sure do. In Ryan's room," Jan offered. "You're free to use it, while whip up dinner. Grilled cheese okay with you?"

"You read my mind, Jan," I said, following Ryan to his room, which in keeping with the general aesthetic, was a shithole.

"It's dial-up. I hope it's fast enough for you, Ash," Ryan said.

"Right now, I'd use an abacus if it would help," I said, turning o Ryan's Gateway 2000 computer, the same brand I had purchase years ago and threw in the trash because of piss-poor performance.

I logged on to my account and quickly deleted a wave of spam. Th CD-ROM in my pocket had gathered a dew of sweat from my body du ng flight, but it loaded just fine. Now, all I had to do was send the damning information to parties that might clear my name — the execs at Paramount, the Screen Actors Guild, trade magazines, my mother, and aint-it-cool-news.com, a fan website that thrives on inside information.

But just as I slid the compact disc into the Gateway's lame drive, the walkie-talkie I stole from Lanny Sticks squawked: "Uh, yeah, 212, we've sighted the suspect in a bungalow in Hollywood — please advise."

This intercepted broadcast confirmed my fears that the big hammer of the law was about to fall. I quickly gathered Jan and Ryan and sat them down on their Ikea living room couch.

"Okay guys, look — I came here under false pretenses. You see, there are dark forces arrayed against me, forces that want to sully my otherwise good reputation. I need you to stall while I use your computer to clear my name."

Ryan Gritton and his "only true friend."

"Are they punishing you because of *Jack of All Trades*?" Ryan asked. "Because that show sucked ass."

"It's not that," I explained, not wanting to debate the particulars of why a TV show succeeds or fails. "But if you don't help me get this information out, I'm going to prison. And if I go to prison, I won't judge any more costume contests at horror conventions, I won't be in any more failed TV shows, there won't be any more small roles in big movies, and there sure as hell won't be any more cult classics like *Maniac Cop*."

I had to stop myself because prison wasn't sounding so bad.

Ryan gave his mother a grim look. "Mom, break out the heavy metal," he instructed.

"Damn straight," she said with a nod. Then, to me: "You've got some e-mail to send, big guy."

Jan didn't have to tell me twice. I ran back to Ryan's room and began composing a heartfelt, clear-my-name/here's-my-proof letter. In the adjacent room, I could hear the muffled sounds of shotguns being breech-loaded, shell boxes being emptied and tossed on the floor, Tasers being charged.

My walkie-talkie squawked again: "Stand by, 39, waiting for enclosure signal...."

Shit, the feds are closing in. "Hey, guys, it's go time!"

Ryan ran down the hallway to the front room. He was packing a Desert Eagle in his belt and a Remington Wingmaster Magnum 12-gauge double-barreled shotgun in his arms. Jan was close behind with her Browning Citori Feather 12-gauge over/under shotgun, and a snub-nosed .38 pistol tucked into her jeans.

"Damn this dial-up!"

Above us, the *whop-whop-whop* sounds of a circling helicopter rattled the windows. My letter complete, I decided to send it in one mass e-mail to everyone I knew. I attached the incriminating files on the CD and hit Send.

There were several megabytes of information, and I knew from living in the dial-up hell of rural Oregon that the transfer was going to take time, something we had precious little of.

Then, without warning, federal agents swooped in from several directions — some on foot, some in souped-up SUVs — and surrounded the bungalow.

Inside the main room, Ryan and Jan were locked and loaded. The bright glare of spotlights poured through the checked curtains.

"They got us surrounded," Ryan said through gritted teeth. "Bastards."

The files were:

Trying to buy some time, I keyed the walkie-talkie and used my best NASA radio voice. "He's on the move, he's on the move! The perpetrator just took off on foot, heading north in the alley behind the bungalow!"

The airwaves immediately filled with chatter, and the helicopter swung its light away from the house. I cracked a self-assured smile, but before I could make a snide comment about how dumb they were and how smart I was, the chopper came back, hovering even closer to the house.

I glanced at the computer monitor:

"Damn this dial-up connection," I said, cursing telephone lines everywhere and slamming my fist on the keyboard.

"Hey, buster, I'm a single mom, okay?" Jan said defensively. "I can't afford that Ethernet shit, so screw you!"

"I'm sorry, Jan," I apologized. "I'm not mad at you, I'm mad at the world."

Then, my Sprint PCS rang.

"Hello?"

"Mr. Campbell, this is Agent Grunow, Secret Service. We shoul talk."

I switched on the handy speakerphone feature, and gestured fo Ryan and Jan to listen.

"I told you never to call me here," I said. "What do you want?"

"We need you to safely evacuate the occupants of the house, Grunow insisted.

"Over my dead body, pig!" Ryan shouted into the phone.

I shushed him, and checked the transfer.

I swore under my breath, but tried to keep cool and stall. "Have done something wrong, Agent Grunow? Am I charged with something?

"You are considered not only a fugitive, but you are, because of pric infractions, now a security threat to the United States of America."

Guantánamo Bay, here I come. "Yeah, well, you'll have to come an get us," I snarled, hanging up.

Ryan threw me a high five, and the three of us shared a moment c elated defiance, knowing we had taken on the Man. But my persona excitement was tempered by recollections of the F.B.I.'s well-know heavy-handed tactics. They had sharpshooters, and they knew how t use them.

"Turn the lights off — quick!" I warned, and we all dashed for diffe ent lights.

I bent down to click off Ryan's Lava Lamp and a federal bullet sha tered the globe, sending glass, water, and red paraffin everywhere.

"Take cover," I yelled, running back to the computer to check th upload.

74%

"That was my favorite lamp, assholes!" Ryan shouted, busting the glass out of a side window with the butt of his shotgun.

Boom! Boom! Boom! The fireworks began. Ryan pumped hot buckshot toward several of the bright spotlights, darkening one of them as a piercing scream filled the air — most likely from a S.W.A.T. team member.

Tear gas came next. Hissing canisters, spitting noxious plumes of yellow smoke crashed through three windows. The small dwelling didn't take long to fill up with the debilitating gas, so I grabbed a T-shirt off Ryan's pile of dirty laundry and shoved it over my mouth and nose. This was followed by a brief, internal debate as to whether a teenager's T-shirt stench was preferable to tear gas. Reluctantly, I stuck with the shirt.

Jan and Ryan began to hack uncontrollably, but never abandoned their posts, each flanking a different side of the bungalow and slinging lead into the haze.

I tried to open my stinging eyes long enough to see the upload. A quick glance to see "82 percent" was too much to bear, and I had to close them again.

Then, behind me, a dark figure burst through the window. It was like the end of a creepy horror film where you think everything is going to be okay, and then all of a sudden — *Boo!* — someone reaches out and scares the living crap out of you. In this case, it was Agent Grunow, my nemesis, and he was bent on bringing me into custody.

I was able to square off before he tackled me, but it didn't really matter — I couldn't see worth a damn. Grunow and I tumbled across dirty laundry, gum wrappers, and stray CDs until we hit the opposite wall. Neither of us could get the upper hand, but Grunow was able to get a clear look at the monitor. He assumed that my upload was something devious, and made stopping it his new number-one priority. He lunged for the mouse, but I grabbed his leg and twisted. Grunow crashed to the floor, and I put a knee in his back, hoping to stabilize him long enough to let the remaining 9 percent go through.

In the front room, all hell was breaking loose. The S.W.A.T. team had a highly armored battering ram, and proceeded to use it on a front door that was worth maybe three or four good hits.

But as far as Jan and Ryan were concerned, nobody was getting inside their home.

"Stay here, Ryan," Jan ordered, pulling back a portion of rug to reveal a crawl space. "I'll hit 'em from below."

"Okay," Ryan shouted above the din, reloading as fast as he could.

Grunow turned out to be one well-trained son of a bitch, because he had squirmed out from under me in less than four seconds and was now maneuvering

PRELIMINARY TACTICS

1. **Exaggerate probable cause.**
2. **Ignore due process.**
3. **Shoot all pets.**
4. **Shoot all spouses.**
5. **Set lots of stuff on fire.**
6. **Shoot all fires.**
7. **Play lulling sounds of woodland creatures being slaughtered.**
8. **Shoot the guy next to him.**
9. **Set all dead pets on fire.**
10. **Have a quick game of tag football with the ATF.**
11. **Repeat.**

Ruby Ridge

Waco

Gritton Household

to gain the advantage. As we wrestled, we had a perfect view of the power strip underneath the computer table. Grunow lunged for it. I tried to get there first, but the agent was exactly one second ahead of me. Before he could unplug the power strip, and my hopes of career salvation, I clamped a hand on top of Grunow's and froze his momentum.

Under the house, Jan crawled toward the front of her bungalow like a commando. From below, she soon had a clear shot at the rather broad side of a federal agent's butt — no Kevlar protection for that. She took aim, but decided against removing his cheek, and instead blew away several feet of dirt around his boots, sending him and the other battering ram operators scrambling for cover.

"Get gone if you know what's good for you!" Jan yelled after them with contempt.

For a layman, I was doing a damn good job holding my own against one of Uncle Sam's finest, but, hey, I wasn't trained in Quantico, so I didn't expect what came next, which was Agent Grunow's pointy elbow, lodging itself deep in my left temple. The impact stunned my brain long enough for him to finish his prime directive, and the power strip was effectively unplugged.

"No!" I screamed in horror, looking up at the monitor, expecting to find that the remaining 1 percent of the file had died somewhere in cyberspace, thereby ruining the transfer. But nothing was wrong, because the computer was actually plugged directly into a wall socket on the *opposite side of the table.*

Grunow looked at the monitor in amazement. He quickly shouted into his headset: "Cut the power, cut the —"

My fist prevented the agent from repeating the traitorous phrase. He was now a resident of dreamland.

The screen read: 99...100 percent — the file finished uploading, and

AOL cheerfully announced:

File Sent

And with that, the power to the bungalow was, in fact, cut — but no before the truth had echoed far and wide.

Immediately following the outage, the Feebs administered "Flash-Bangs," devices that deafen and disorient by emitting a huge booming noise accompanied by a blinding flash. Three or four of these got going at the same time, and none of us knew which direction was up.

A full-front assault began, and a mixture of F.B.I., local S.W.A.T., and Secret Service agents came through windows, doors, floors and attics. I was tackled by three guys at once. With my face shoved into the 1980s polyester carpet, I could hear the muffled cries of both Ryan and Jan as they were hauled away. The jig was up.

21

Aftermath

Internet - Consolidated News Online

CON News
Consolidated News Coverage ONLINE

General News

USA HOORAY — Actor's Rampage Halted

THE WALL STREET URINAL ONLINE — Viacom Stock Dizzy from Shake-Up at Paramound

detdot.com — Local Boy, Gone Bad

more...

"Slick" News

Peeplo.com — Confessions of a B-Movie Terrorist?

Weak Entertainment — And You Thought Sean Penn Was Bad!

more...

Tabloids

Stare — Campbell Says Aliens Made Him Do It (Shocking Photos)

LONDONLINE — Campbell's Love Child

more...

Hollywood Trade Papers

THE Variety REPORTER — Sticks a Hero: Campbell's Problems "Paramound"

HOLLYWOOD — Campbell Canning No "Love" Fest

more...

Recent News Articles for:

bruce campbell

USA Hooray
Actor's Rampage Halted

B-Movie actor Bruce Campbell was arrested yesterday for burglarizing a major film studio, impersonating a producer, annoying a U.S. Secret... [continued]

Weak Entertainment
And You Thought Sean Penn Was Bad!

"Punching photographers in the face was nothing compared to what this jerk did," said celebrated actor Jack Nicholson last week about the blight on society Bruce... [continued]

Stare
Campbell Says Aliens Made Him Do It

"Schmaliens," said Academy of Motion Picture Arts & Sciences spokesperson and full-time death penalty advocate Arthur McCloud when he heard of... [continued]

Variety Reporter
Campbell Canning No "Love" Fest

Even though he's been all over the news lately, 97% of Americans still have no idea who Bruce Campbell is. Truth be told, neither does the staff here at Variety... [continued]

len-
ect.
s-
r

FILM/TV

Campbell in Shambles?

Artie McCloud
Associate Press

The bizarre legal saga surrounding Bruce Campbell came to an end today as the actor, best known for his role as an 18-inch-tall action figure, was turned over to the custody of the California penal system. Federal prosecutor Gummo Wolverton, who had promised to make an example of Campbell to other out-of-work B movie actors, proclaimed that "justice had been served."

Campbell, upon his arrest for domestic terrorism and other charges last fall, immediately employed the services of celebrity lawyer Johnny Cochrane, who argued effectively that corporate giants can't discriminate between an "A" actor and a "B" actor. Cochrane felt that the issue "should play out on a big canvas."

Campbell was eventually found innocent of all state and local charges, including sabotage, and therefore not liable for the entire negative cost of *Let's Make Love!* as Paramound had alleged. The film in question, helmed by veteran Mike Nichols, was shut down three weeks after Campbell's departure.

Paramound Studios, in response to the news surrounding Campbell's sen-

*See **Campbell**, Page G4*

Campbell

Continued from Page G1

tencing, issued the following statement:

Bruce Campbell

"Paramound Studios and its affiliates are relieved to hear that the legal issues pertaining to Mr. Campbell have been resolved, but remain troubled that a once promising actor who had appeared in our company's *Congo* and *Escape from L.A.* could 'fall so far, so fast.'

"And, because of this remarkable incident, we're going to take a fresh look at actor Lanny Sticks. He's done some impressive work, both in front of and behind the camera, and this studio - which is proud of its long-term commitment to talent - owes him a big one. Thanks, Lanny."

Paramound also announced that it had decided not to renew its contract with up-and-coming executive Robert Stern because of "poor creative choices" and "reckless disregard for fiscal matters." As part of his severance package, Mr. Stern will retain a first look deal at Paramound, through his newly formed production company, Know-it-all Pictures.

The federal trial, which wrapped up today, left Campbell, a member of the dreaded "Terror Watch List," charged with three years for "threatening and endangering a federal official." Johnny Cochrane felt that the sentence, considered a slap on the wrist by some, to be "a fair and just verdict."

22

Bruce Man of Alcatraz

I'd been incarcerated before, dozens of times, in fact. I know what it's like to sweat under the hot lights of a lineup, or cry myself to sleep in a ten-by-ten cell. And unlike other men, I had actually planned great escapes and executed them, picked locks, and gone over the wall, laughing all the while. I even ripped off a prison laundry system, just to see the look on the warden's face. Granted, it was all while acting in films or TV shows, but the experience prepared me for doing time in the Chino Men's Facility in southern California.

It wasn't as bad as you might think. I got three squares a day, my own bed, and plenty of Latino-themed television. In return, all I had to do was empty the garbage once a day for two hours. Sure, you get the shit jobs at first, that's how the joint works, but with a little ingenuity and two cartons of Kool Extras, I worked my way up to cleaning executive offices.

Mostly, though, I just exercised, or read books in my three-man cell.

It took awhile, but I also earned a write-in degree in electrical engineering from the DeVry Institute.

One day, I had a visitor, which was unusual.

"Campbell — fresh shirt!" the jack called out.

I walked across the hardscrabble yard to the visitation room. There, waiting for me behind reinforced green glass, were Rob Stern, nemesis extraordinaire, and a lawyerly-type fellow.

"No offense, but of anyone on the entire planet I *wouldn't* want to see, it would be you," I said, taking my seat on a wobbly plastic chair.

"I can understand your disappointment," Rob agreed, "so let's get right down to business." He cleared his throat and wiped sweaty hands on his jeans. "Well, uh, as you know, I *left* Paramount...."

"Yeah, I read the release where they fired your ass. I wish I could say I was sorry."

"Oh, don't be, they gave me a first-look producing deal."

"Hey, I'm really impressed, but can you get to the point? I can only use free weights during certain hours."

"I just pitched a reality-based TV series, and Paramount bought thirteen on air. We'd like you to guest-star in an episode."

"What is it called?"

"*Celebrity Sing-Sing*," Rob said, barely able to contain his glee. "Each week, we do a bit on celebs that have either been in jail, or are currently serving. We've got Bob Downey, Jr., Heidi Fleiss, Glen

Campbell — it's a huge, ensemble cast."

"Thanks, but no thanks. I'll pass."

"Actually, Mr. Campbell, legally, you *can't*," Rob's previously silent partner said matter-of-factly.

"Okay, now who are *you*?" I asked, confused.

"I'm Eugene Glass, Paramount business affairs."

I rolled my eyes. "Look, you guys pulled the plug. I had a pay-or-play deal. I don't owe you anything —"

Eugene unfurled my signed *Let's Make Love!* contract. "In section three, paragraph nine, it implicitly states that in the event of a force majeure, which this production experienced, Paramount Studios has the right to recoup its pay-or-play investment by placing you, at their discretion, in a comparable piece."

"A guest shot on *Celebrity Sing-Sing* is comparable to costarring in a Mike Nichols film? How do you figure that, Clarence Darrow?"

"Paramount is prepared to vigorously defend its legal position," Eugene Glass said with a disturbing finality.

"Can I be the host instead?"

"That role has already been committed."

"To who, Pee-Wee Herman?" I asked bitterly.

"Lanny Sticks."

I exhaled and leaned back in my plastic chair, randomly studying the graffiti scrawled on the walls of the booth. Somehow, it was all fitting. "Let me talk to my people, Mr. Glass, and we'll get back to you."

Later that day, after listening to my cellmate, Buck, ruminate over whether Ten-G, in Block 3, was really interested in a long-term relationship or just shower sex, I suddenly had a revelation. It occurred to me that for the past several months, in the name of research for a movie, I had unwittingly attended nothing short of relationship boot camp. Having recently studied every aspect of men and women, from dating to divorce, I came out the other side with some valuable, *publishable* information.

I sharpened the tip of my No. 2 Fort Ticonderoga pencil on the concrete and pulled out a piece of scrap paper. I was going to get myself a job.

BARRY,

'SUP, SUCKA? B DAWG C HERE, CAN'T TALK LONG — HO CHECK SOON, KNOW WHA I'M SAYING? BEEN LONG TIME SINCE YOU BE MONKEY MOUTHIN' BOUT A RELATIONSHIP BOOK, AN' THE OFFER. WORD UP, FOO — I BEEN THINKIN' (PLENTY TIME FO THAT INNA JOYNT) AN' I THINK IT WOULD BE COO TO DO A BOOK AN SHIT 'BOUT MEN AND THEY BITCHES.

WRITE TO ME HERE:
B DAWG C
PRISONER #22987
C/O CHINO MENS CORRECTIONAL INSTITUTE
P.O. BOX 00-3344
CHINO, CA 91710

P.S. FYI, YOU WANT TO THROW DOWN, MAKE A REAL DEAL, FOO — TALK WITH MY ACE BOON COON, RANDY, HE BEEN SPENDIN' TIME IN THE LAW LIBRARY AN SHIT, SO, DONT FUCK ME OVER ON PAPER, DAWG, OR HE LL STICK YOU WITH HIS BANGER.

GOTTA BOUNCE,

B D C

P.P.S. THE WHITE SHIRTS IS ASS HOLES

23

Love Springs Eternal

I liken the *Let's Make Love!* experience to a forearm burn from a hot iron — it hurts like hell, and the scar takes forever to fade. Whenever I run into a member of the cast or crew at some function or on another film set, we shrug or laugh at the memory, but mostly we just change the subject.

I was on location in Hong Kong recently, strolling just outside the Central Market, and I noticed a DVD shop. The urge to buy a crappy Hong Kong kung fu movie in Hong Kong was too great, and I ducked inside. The cramped store was a shrine to older, crazier Jackie Chan films, the immortal Bruce Lee, and the new cool cat, Jet Li. But most surprising was a DVD I found in a bargain bin. Upon closer inspection, I recognized both Renée Zellweger and Richard Gere in various photos on the cover, but the film wasn't called *Let's Make Love!,* it was called *Love You to Death!* It sure as hell wasn't a romantic comedy, it was an over-the-top kung fu flick that had obviously cannibalized the action scenes from *Let's Make Love!*

At least it finally got released, I mused.

The *Love You to Death!* DVD makes for a great party favor at home, and an even better paperweight. It's also a fitting reminder that relationships in front of the camera aren't nearly as interesting as the ones in real life.

As for the "B-movie virus" I was accused of spreading, I've got news for you: the virus had already been active for years. What Hollywood considers A-list blockbusters are really just pumped-up, cheeseball, Saturday matinee serials: *Star Wars*, *Indiana Jones*, and *Pirates of the Caribbean* are all great examples of this.

B movies won a long time ago; the A movies just don't know it yet.

FADE OUT

Acknowledgments

This is undoubtedly the most boring part of every book, but acknowledgments are included for a reason. In my case, it's to admit that *Make Love the Bruce Campbell Way!* wasn't a one-man operation.

I write the words, but there are very talented people who join in during the process to make sure they are in the right order, are spelled correctly, and that they all add up to something in the end.

First and foremost, I want to give a fat-ass shout to Barry Neville. To call him my editor would be a mockery of his contribution. Through this sometimes bewildering process, Barry helped immensely to shape the fabric of the *Love* story and to establish, not only its tone, but its point-of-view, which is all-important when you're pulling this stuff out of your butt. FYI, for those of you who thought the book blew, I'll provide you with Barry's home phone number and you can bitch him out personally.

Backing up Barry's invaluable assistance is the ever-loopy Craig "Kif" Sanborn and his graphic design. I still have a dial-up internet connection in Oregon, so downloading preliminary images for the book was torture because it took forever, and I couldn't wait to see how he had spun the latest idea. I've known the little bastard long enough for him to start giving me lip. Good on ya, mate!

Mike Ditz has always been a quiet, steady source of cool ideas when it comes to photography. Mike shot the cover of the *Chins* book, and I knew he had to do the same for *Make Love*. He also shot gobs of reference photos used in those bizarre "morphed" images that appear throughout the book. I've known Mike for a hundred years, and I love the fact that we still work together. He's in Los Angeles — hire him.

Many thanks also to Melanie "Mel" Tooker. I not only stole her identity for the book without asking, I've taken advantage of her makeup talents for years. Thankfully, she's still willing to work around me.

Once the elements of a book start to come together, an author relies on the publishing house to finish the heavy lifting. Pete Wolverton, my editor and boss at St. Martin's Press, is one such laborer. Pete is a no-nonsense New Yorker with good insight into material and he keeps dizzy Oregonians like me on the right path. "Right away, sir!"

You can't have a successful book without sales, so I must belatedly recognize both Joe Rinaldi (PR) and Harriet Seltzer (author events queen) for their efforts on the tour and promotion for *Chins*, and for their hard work on *Bruce's Summer of Love Tour*. Getting an author to forty-five cities in three months — and letting people know how to find him — takes more effort than you might imagine.

Jodi Reamer is my literary agent. Having her around guarantees that deals will get made and important things will not be overlooked. Aside from actually reading the books she represents, Jodi is a big overall help behind the scenes. Thanks for the attention span!

My wife, Ida, and I just celebrated fourteen years of marital bliss.

She seems to think living with an actor is a good thing and I love her for . Rebecca and Andy are two of the grooviest kids a defacto gypsy dad ould ever have, and although we have difficulty recognizing each other om time to time, they are my favorite people to come home to. See ou at the swimmin' hole!

Joanne, my darling mother, started writing way before I ever did, just or the love of it, and I'm sure it had a positive influence on me. She's een an unwavering rock of support (except the time I broke the neigh-or's Christmas lights), and I love her dearly for it.

A general note to the real people portrayed in the book: I hope you're appy – you all come across way smarter than I do.

Finally, I dedicate this book to ny old man, Charles Newton Campbell, who passed away on November 3rd, 2004. Charlie was ne guy who inspired me to ecome an actor, and he put his noney where his mouth was as ne first investor of my first film, *Evil Dead*.

Everyone in the arts needs a atron and I will be eternally grate-ul to know that I had one in Charlie. Thanks, Chook.

Charles N. Campbell
1928-2004